THE MELODY OF SILENCE

CRESCENDO

LP TVORIK

TABLE OF CONTENTS

PREFACE

Three important notes:

(1) This book is part one of a four-part series. While I detest cliffhangers, I had no choice but to end this book (and this book only) on something of a low note. The next book will be released in August, so the wait will not be long. However, if you don't like to wait at all, you may want to shelve this one until the second is released. Books two through four all have their own happy endings. There are no more cliffhangers after this one.

(2) This book is part one of a four-part series. All four books are about the same couple, at different stages of their lives. While each book is self-contained and comes to its own conclusion, there are a number of plotlines and character arcs that span the entire series. If you get to the epilogue of book four and still feel bereft and annoyed by plotholes or stalled-out character development, I'll stand still while you eviscerate me for my shoddy writing. Until then, please bear with me. Some stories take a lifetime (or four books, as it were) to unfold.

(3) I do not consider it a spoiler to tell you that this series has a happily ever after, and that Alex and Nate end up together. They get married. They raise children. They grow old, happy and holding hands. So please don't get discouraged, and please don't lose hope. The title of this series alludes to the beauty of those moments in music that otherwise go unappreciated— the long pause before the bass drop or the triumphant, crashing finale; the relief in a resolving dissonant chord. So please bear with me as I drag you through the ugly discord and the painful silence. Please hang in there. The harmony is coming. I promise.

DISCLAIMER

This series contains triggering material, including—

– Child abuse

– Sexual Assault

– Depression

– Suicide

– Drug Abuse

– Violence

– Police Brutality

Oh, and of course the worst of all: cursing.

If mention of any of the above may cause you distress, I encourage you to put this down. If you're determined to persevere, I've put together a by-chapter trigger warning so you can at least determine which chapters to avoid. It can be found on my website (https://www.lptvorik.com).

CHAPTER ONE

NATE

On July 13th 1996, a miracle happened. I'm not sure how well I believe in God, god, or gods, but that day was a victory for faith no matter how you cut it. Love prevailed on that muggy summer afternoon. A ray of sunshine broke through the clouds and cast some hope into my miserable little existence.

In a fun twist, on July 13th 1996, I punched my aging female case worker in the face and called two kind, generous men 'disgusting faggots' and threatened to kill them in their sleep.

Let's back it up a bit, shall we? Quick history lesson— about six years prior to the day in question, Patrick Nguyen met Edward Parker at a dinner party. Patrick was a 26-year-old lawyer who had just passed the New York state bar. Edward was finishing his first year of medical school. The party was a birthday party, hosted by Veronica, a mutual friend who Patrick had met in law school and Edward met in his freshman year of college.

Ed and Pat hated each other instantaneously. Edward thought Patrick was arrogant. Patrick thought Edward's sarcasm was unnecessarily biting. They spent most of the party locked in fierce debate. They fought about U.S.-Soviet relations over hor d'oeuvres. They debated the ethics of Wall Street over cocktails. Shortly after sitting down to eat, Ed learned that Pat was raised Catholic which begat a furious debate regarding the validity of the sacrament.

Just before desert, Veronica leaned over and whispered to Pat. "Eddie's single," she murmured. "His boyfriend just moved to California."

After that, the tone of their conversation changed considerably.

In December of 1992, Ed and Pat went on their first official date.

In January of 1994, Ed moved into Pat's apartment in Greenwich Village.

In December 1994, on the anniversary of their first date, Pat asked Ed to marry him.

They had to go to Vermont to get a marriage license, but they held the ceremony at Pat's parents' farm in upstate New York. It was a raucous affair with an open bar, a bonfire, and a dance floor that didn't even begin to cool down until daybreak. Pat and Ed snuck off around midnight and loved for hours on a hilltop, miles away from the noise and light and joy of the party. They held each other and stared at the stars and knew with all certainty that what they had was forever.

Okay, now back to that fateful summer day in 1996, because I'm sure you're wondering what this happy couple has to do with a nascent homophobic shithead who punches women.

You see, Ed and Pat were happy together, but after a year or so of marriage they realized they were missing something. Or, rather, they were missing some*one*. They wanted a child. In the beginning, they wanted an infant. I guess that's normal. Nobody wants a kid who's *already* fucked up. You want a blank slate, that way you can twist things up in your own special way, right? Damaging a scarred up psyche is no fun at all.

They talked to a few agencies. Built up their hopes. Suffered devastation. Built up their hopes again. Suffered devastation again. A year later, a friend sat them down over drinks and talked to them about children in foster care. "There are kids out there who need a loving home," she said. "Kids who are a little older. Some have been hurt or neglected, but they're still children. Children who need the kind of love you guys have in spades. Think about it."

They thought about it, and I love Ed and Pat because they didn't have to think about it for long. The blank slate lost its appeal as they looked at the world with new eyes. They decided that, for them, parenthood would not be about the satisfaction of creating a perfect child or about churning out little carbon copies of themselves. Parenthood, they concluded, should be about one thing: love. Love for each other and love for a child who needed them.

On July 13th 1996, Pat and Ed adopted a five year old boy. He wasn't perfect. He didn't talk much, he struggled at school, and he was a little short and skinny for his age. He had cigarette burn pocks on his arms, a stiff pinky finger on his left hand from a broken bone that never healed right, and a jagged, silvery scar on his right cheek. He was terrified of the dark, suffered violent night terrors, and there was only one person on earth who he trusted enough to look in the eye. Neither Pat nor Ed were that person.

That little boy was eighty tons of baggage in a fifty-pound package, but Pat and Ed loved him immediately. They found room in their hearts for that messed up kid, because they saw in him what few others were able to. I don't know how, but they saw straight past the bruised up surface into his soul and they knew it would only take a nudge to push him into the light. Nothing but a little love and security, and that nervous, broken little boy would blossom into a bright and unstoppably infectious force for good.

I hated them for that. I hated my case worker for breaking the news, I hated Pat and Ed, and I hated whatever mocking deity had brought them into my life.

The problem, see, is that Ed and Pat had all that room for a sweet little five-year-old with a learning disability, floppy hair, and a gap between his two front teeth. What they *didn't* have room for was that five-year-old's pissed off older brother who, at the tender age of twelve, already had a file full of disciplinary issues and had mastered ugly things like homophobic slurs and a mean right hook.

Jake wailed. He wrapped his tiny arms around my leg and howled my name at the top of his lungs while I backed the two of us into a corner of the gaudy, colorful room and raised my fists, ready to brawl. Hatred and fear curdled in my blood as the adults loomed over me, greedy hands outstretched to snatch up the only good thing I had left in the world.

"Nathan, you need to calm down," my case worker said, holding her hands out in front of her as she approached us. Her voice was professional and calm, but her face was a stern mask and I saw fear in her eyes. Panic. *Weakness.* I bared my teeth.

"Get the fuck back," I growled. "They're not taking him!"

Ed and Pat stood by the desk. Pat had his arm around Ed's shoulders, and they looked deeply, painfully sad. More weakness, and I hated them even more for showing it.

"Nathan, you're scaring Jake," our case worker said. That gave me pause. I glanced down at my little brother's tear-streaked face. His eyes were bloodshot and puffy and a thick stream of snot coated his upper lip. He breathed in jagged hiccups. "This is happening, Nathan," she said, quieter this time. "You're making it much harder on Jake. This is a good thing. An amazing thing. He needs to know that. He needs to hear it from you."

I swallowed hard as bile rose in my throat and the inevitability of it sank in. She was right. Even if I fought her off, there were the two thieves to get past. And a whole building of social workers and security guards if we made it out the door. And I was twelve. I could barely keep him safe in foster care. How could I keep him safe if we went on the run?

For a moment, reason prevailed. I nodded jerkily. "Can we have a sec, Miss Meg?" I asked, and she nodded hesitantly, backing away. Ed and Pat followed her out the door, and she shut it behind them. The door to her tiny office had a giant window in the middle of it, and they were standing right outside. There wasn't much privacy, but at least we could talk.

"It's gonna be okay, Jakey," I said, sinking to my knees in front of him.

"I don't wanna go," he moaned, stepping into me and burying his face in my shirt. His tiny arms wrapped around me and squeezed, and his shoulders shook with gasping, hysterical sobs. "Please," he begged, his words punctuated by hiccups as he soaked my shirt with tears. "Please don't... don't... let... them... take... me."

"It's gonna be good, Jake," I said, rubbing his back. "You're gonna love it. You heard them. They're super rich, huh? I bet they'll get you a Nintendo, or maybe they already have one! They'll take you to movies in the theater. You'll get tons of presents for Christmas and your birthday, and I bet if you ask really nice they'll make you waffles for dinner."

Jake stilled, peering up at me, a frown wrinkling his brow. He looked skeptical and serious, and for a second I almost forgot where we were and laughed at him. Nothing got to Jake quite like waffles.

"For dinner?" he asked. "Tonight?"

"I mean you gotta ask, but they seem really nice and they really want you to like them. I bet you could get them to cave."

"I want blueberries in mine," he said, pulling away and wiping his nose with the back of his hand.

"Don't do that," I scolded out of habit. I reached for the tissues on Miss Meg's desk and snagged a handful. "You're gross," I grumbled, wiping the snot off his face. "Blow." I held the tissues over his nose and gagged dramatically as he hawked what had to be a gallon of snot into them. He giggled at my histrionics.

"What kind of waffles do *you* want?" Jake asked on a bracing sniffle, rubbing his eyes with his fists.

The question brought the nausea right back, and I felt cold sweat break out on my neck. "I'm not coming with you, Jakey. You know that."

"But I want you to."

"I know that. I..." *I want to, too.* "I gotta stay and look after Deb and Ian." It wasn't completely false. Deb was eleven, Ian was Jake's age, and our current foster parents were mean old drunks. They *did* need me.

"But you love me more than them," Jake said with a scowl.

"Well yeah," I shrugged. "But you got your two new dads, now. They're gonna love you and keep you safe, so I gotta stay with the others. Otherwise who's gonna keep them safe?"

Jake thought about it. I saw his little mind working behind his eyes and I saw the fierce courage and selflessness it took for him to nod. "You're right," he said, lifting his chin. "Will you come visit?"

"I dunno, buddy. I'll ask Miss Meg."

As if by cue, the door cracked open and my three mortal enemies re-entered the room. "It's time to go, Jake," the case worker said, but she was looking at me.

I nodded.

"Time to go with Pat and Ed," I said, standing and taking Jake's hand.

It almost went smoothly.

Almost.

Halfway across the tiny office, Jake planted his feet.

"No," he said, shaking his head vehemently. "I don't wanna go."

"You gotta, buddy," I cajoled. "C'mon."

"No!" he exclaimed. "I don't want waffles!"

My vision was blurring. I tried like hell not to cry, but it was a lost cause. "Please, just go," I said, tugging him toward his new parents.

"You don't love me!" Jake cried, glaring up at me with a fresh crop of tears in his puffy, red-rimmed eyes. "You don't want me!"

"Of course I do!" I snapped around my own tears.

"Then don't let them take me!" he argued. It was handy logic, and I guess it was good that Pat and Ed got to see their new son's latent intelligence. Learning disability aside, my brother was whip smart and, at five, was already a competent debater.

"You gotta go, Jakey," I said, kneeling and wrapping him in a hug. "You gotta be brave."

"No!" he screeched in my ear, deafening me. "Don't let them take me!"

Then the case worker was there. She tried to pick Jake up and he kicked out at her, arms latched around my neck. Sobbing.

"Don't let them take me!" he cried. "Don't let them, Nate! Don'tletthemdon'tletthemdon'tletthem—"

Something about his manic, garbled pleading got to me. It always had. Jakey in distress was like a trigger for the rage my dad handed down to me. Rage I normally kept wrapped up tight and buried deep inside where it couldn't hurt anyone. I guess I snapped a little. Jake kicked and I pulled and there I was, back in the corner of the office with my charge in my arms and the world bearing down on us.

"No!" I cried, tightening my grip on him as I cowered in the corner. It felt like a bad dream, where you need to run but your feet won't move fast enough. It felt like those living nightmares where you're trying so hard to be quiet that your own heartbeat thunders loud enough to give you away to the monsters. It felt like that ugly gurgle in your belly when someone calls you out on a lie you'd convinced even yourself was truth. "You can't take him!" I begged, shrinking away as the adults loomed so tall they blocked out the light. "Mom's gonna come back! She wants him! You can't take him! She's coming back!"

"Nathan, let go," came Miss Meg's patient voice. I was just a kid, and a skinny one at that, so it didn't take much effort for her to pull me away from the wall. Another case worker had responded to the racket and was prying Jake out of my arms as Meg held me back.

"Stop!" Jake sobbed, his fingers scrabbling at my shirt as he was pulled away. "Nate, make them stop! Please! Stop it! I don't want waffles! I DON'T WANT WAFFLES!"

Then he was gone, and so was my control. I lashed out, clipping Miss Meg in the chin with one furious, flying fist. She grunted and staggered back, and I tore loose from her grip and chased my brother and his captors out of the room.

"Give him back!" I yelled, my voice hoarse and thick with tears and hysteria. The second case worker was walking away with Jake, who was babbling incoherently, sobbing, hands outstretched over the man's back as he reached for me. Ed and Pat followed their new son, glancing back over their shoulders with tears in their eyes.

"Give him back, you disgusting faggots!" I screamed at their retreating backs as hands grabbed me, picking me up off the ground. I hated them, then, these men who had opened their home and their hearts, offering what I wanted for my brother more than anything else— love, safety, and happiness. I hated them with all of my soul. "You can't have my brother! You don't deserve my brother! I'll fucking kill you in your sleep!" I yelled, kicking and scrabbling and utterly unable to follow as a miracle carried the last of my family out of a life of pain, hunger, and darkness.

The hands carried me back into a room specially designed for stupid little kids having stupid mental breakdowns. The floor was a colorful patchwork rubber mat. Every toy in the room was soft and harmless. The chairs were of the beanbag variety. Inset on one wall was a smudged two-way mirror so that detachedly concerned adults could stand and watch and pity without the risk of contact.

Whoever was holding me dragged me into that room. I kicked and howled and clawed and bit. I called my sweet and kindly case worker a bitch. I elbowed the man holding me in the balls and slammed my forehead into his nose. When a third person entered the equation, stroking my face with calming hands to accompany her soothing words, I sank my teeth into her finger and bit until I tasted blood.

Eventually, they wrestled me to the floor and held me there until I stopped fighting and the furious stream of curses and threats faded to hiccupping sobs. Gradually, the hands moved away and I curled up on my side, pressing my face to the sticky rubber mat and clutching my stomach. My mouth watered as nausea rose in my throat and I made no effort to hold it back.

Bile, chicken nuggets, and orange drink surged up from my stomach as I heaved. The case workers were pissed at me. I could feel it. Even Miss Meg was mad, and somewhere deep down that made me sad because Miss Meg always seemed to have patience and there was something comforting in that. Even if it was her job, at least she was there. That day, though, she sighed and mumbled something about the janitor. Then her hand patted my back, but it was mechanical and grudging.

"Honestly, Nathan. You needed to be strong for Jake. What were you thinking?" she asked. Too mired in guilt and loss to speak, I shifted away from the malodorous puddle by my head and curled up tighter around the pain in my chest. I couldn't breathe past the constricting sensation that strangled my heart and twisted my stomach into knots.

On July 13th 1996, a miracle happened. A smart, sweet little boy found a happy, loving home. Two kind, generous men found a way to spread and multiply their love and compassion in an ugly, hateful world. It was a beautiful day. That afternoon, a thunderstorm rolled through, leaving the streets crisp and clean and the air ten degrees cooler and smelling of damp earth and wet pavement. There was a music festival in the city center, and the streets were raucous and colorful with celebration.

On July 13th 1996, fate smiled at the world. A drop of good splashed into the bucket and, for all intents and purposes, it was a wonderful day.

Except for me.

I had scarier days than July 13th 1996. I had harder days, longer days, lonelier days, and days that cast an obsidian shadow over the pain of losing my brother. But that was still the worst day of my life, because it was the last day I lived without *her*. My angel. My savior. My highest high. My haven. My everything good in the universe. From that point on, no matter how wretched the world was, at least I knew I shared it with her.

CHAPTER TWO

ALEX

I was twelve when I met the boy. Just twelve. Twelve on the dot.

It was my birthday, although it didn't really feel like one. You know when things just feel wrong? You can't put your finger on what it is, but you have this terrible, uneasy feeling in your stomach that won't let you sit still?

I had that feeling a lot back in those days. I suppose it might have been because we'd just moved to a new town. Daddy was a preacher, and the church plucked our family up out of our pleasant little southern hamlet and dropped us right into the belly of the big city midwest. It's a good thing they moved us in the summer. If we'd gone straight into the winter I'm pretty sure Momma and I would've died right then and there.

Even in the summer, though, things weren't good. I didn't have any friends, for one. That was a first for me, and I spent many long hours trying to goad Tommy into playing with me because I couldn't stand the silence. I suppose that was one positive. I'd been growing apart from my older brother before the move. When we were kids, we were thick as thieves, always playing outside and getting into trouble. When I got older, though, that changed. I suppose the best way to say it is that, when I was five and he was seven, Tommy and I were perfectly in sync. Then I kept maturing and Tommy didn't. Tommy never would.

That summer, though, we found each other again. Momma didn't seem to care much if we went outside, and she trusted me to look after Tommy. We explored the little patch of woods behind our house which, to us, seemed like a vast and magical land full of dangers and hidden beauties.

There was a creek cutting through the woods in which we splashed during the heat of the day, and a magic spot in that creek that we decided made the world stand still. It wasn't much. Just a spot where the flowing water had cut a particularly deep furrow through the earth. On one side, it had carved a cave

8

beneath the roots of a massive oak. On the other, the ground sloped up into a natural clearing. In the center of the creek, framed by the cave and the clearing, was a sandy island. In the center of the island was a boulder.

Just wide enough for me and Tommy to sit side by side, that boulder was our magical thinking spot. We'd sit there in silence and as long as our butts were planted on the granite nothing was bad. Momma wasn't sad, Daddy wasn't gone all the time, and we had friends again. The world was bright and hopeful, so long as we didn't leave the spot.

July 13th 1996 was my twelfth birthday. Like I said, it didn't really feel like one. If we were back home, there'd have been a party. Momma would have baked a big cake, Daddy would have filmed everything with his bulky old tape recorder. My friends would have come over and sang and beat the candy stuffing out of a colorful *piñata*.

There wasn't a party for my twelfth birthday. There was a cake, but Momma served it up on the plastic tray it came in, there weren't any candles, and my name was spelled wrong in the icing. There were a few presents— a bike from Daddy and a necklace from Momma. Cards from both sets of grandparents with crisp, twenty-dollar bills enclosed. Tommy called it a good haul, which made everyone laugh a little, so he called it a good haul four more times and before he could get the words out a fifth Daddy told him to be quit.

Tommy cried and Momma's face went dark and none of us ate much cake.

Tommy didn't give me his present until later that night. He came and knocked on my door after Momma tucked me in.

"Come in," I whispered and the door creaked open and Tommy's boyish face peeked into the moonlit room.

"Happy Birthday, Aly!" he said, tiptoeing noisily across the carpet. "I brought your present."

"Okay," I said hesitantly, sitting up in bed. "What is it?"

Tommy made a noise of exasperation and sat on the bed beside me. "Close your eyes and hold out your hand," he said, practically vibrating with excitement.

I obeyed, wondering what he'd come up with. The year before he'd given me a dead spider because he thought it would be funny. I hoped this year was better.

Something small, cold, and hard dropped into my hand and I opened my eyes, staring at my open palm.

"A rock?" I asked, looking up at my brother quizzically. He grinned, floppy hair falling into his eyes with his emphatic nod.

"From the spot!" he said.

Objectively, it was a pretty crappy gift. There were about a million and one rocks strewn about on our little island in the creek and, even as far as *those* rocks were concerned, this one was unremarkable. It was plain old gray with darker

9

gray spots. Ridged on one side and smooth on the other. Just a rock.

It was the best present anyone had ever given me, though, because I knew how Tommy's mind worked. He knew the peace we found in the spot. Even if things at home didn't bother him like they bothered me, he still felt it. He knew how much I needed it. This was his way of bringing that peace home. Of giving me a way to walk around with a little bit of it in my pocket.

"Thanks, Tommy," I said, leaning forward and wrapping him in a hug. I wanted to cry, but I knew if I did he'd think I was sad. "We'll have to get you one just like it."

He nodded sagely and stood. "We'll pick it out tomorrow," he said. "Night, Aly!"

He left the room as he'd entered it — noisily and thinking he was the picture of stealth.

I lay for a long time, watching the moon play over the speckled surface of my ceiling. The summer air was still so the tree branches outside my window were motionless, casting stark shadows on the wall. We'd been in the new house for over a month, but it still didn't feel like home. The bed was wrong no matter which wall I pushed it against, and the shadows cast by my furniture felt foreign and dangerous.

I palmed the rock and tried not to cry as loneliness gripped me. I wanted so badly to go home, but home was too far away. What wasn't too far, though? I squeezed the rock and smiled at the ceiling.

The spot.

I was normally a good girl, so sneaking out was a bit out of character. Call it my first foray into teenage rebellion. Call it the nexus linking what had been to what would come next. Call it the terminus of Aly and the inception of Alex. At the time, though, I probably just would've called it scary.

I waited until my parents stopped moving around and the house went quiet. Then I crawled out of bed and crept to my closet, shedding my jammies and pulling on shorts, sneakers, and a t-shirt. I tucked my hair into a ballcap and grabbed my adventuring backpack, full of rope and snacks and other odds and ends that I never actually ended up needing but which always felt good to have.

I slid my window open one hair-raising, butthole-clenching centimeter at a time. Then I popped my screen out, which was way easier than it should have been. If my parents knew they'd have had a conniption fit. Momma was always overprotective, I guess because of what happened to Tommy. She'd have died on the spot if she'd seen me crawling out the window and balancing on the ledge, reaching for the branches of the sycamore outside my window.

Back then, I wasn't afraid of heights. I hadn't learned to fear them, yet. That's the thing about fear. It doesn't come naturally. We aren't born afraid. We learn what hurts us through experience, and those are the things we fear. When I was twelve, heights didn't scare me at all. I hadn't learned, yet, that they could hurt me.

That lesson was coming.

With the wiry strength of an active child, I slipped my right hand and foot around the branch and pushed off the window sill with my left, transferring my weight onto the limb. It bounced and shifted but didn't break, and I shimmied confidently down to the stronger branches below. I dangled for a moment from the lowest branch, my toes scant inches off the ground. Then I dropped.

Freedom.

Normally I liked to walk in the woods, savoring the quiet sounds and the peaceful motion of the trees and the little animals that called them home. That night, I sprinted— headlong through the moonlit forest, backpack bouncing against my butt, shoes slapping the earth. Sweat beaded on my face and slid down my neck. My legs burned and my lungs ached. It felt so good, just to be free.

I slowed, though, as I approached my spot. Something felt wrong. The air was different— restless and tense. The sounds of the woods weren't quite right, either. The symphony was there, as always. Frogs croaking, leaves rustling, water trickling over rock. Harvest mice scrambling over the carpet of dead leaves on the forest floor. The sounds came together like music— my favorite song. But that night, some new sound joined it and it ruined the melody. Like a wrong note from the back of the orchestra. Quiet in itself, but amplified in its wrongness so that as I drew closer it was all I could hear.

Crying.

I slowed as I approached, peering at my moonlit haven from the privacy of the darkened woods. A boy was in my spot. On my rock. I didn't know at the time that he wasn't just *a* boy. He was *the* boy. *My* boy. I didn't see my future like I should have. I just saw an intruder.

I crouched in my hiding spot and watched him. He was sprawled on his back, his legs dangling over the edge of the rock. I liked to lay like that and watch the sky, but the boy had his hands over his face, digging the heels into his eyes. His body shook as he cried, but all I could hear was the occasional gasping breath. I knew all about crying quietly. I cried quietly all the time at home, but when I was alone I cried loud and reckless. Not the boy. He cried quietly, even in solitude.

He looked ragged. Not like me, in my shorts-just-for-adventures and my stained t-shirt that Momma insisted I throw away with the shorts but I kept because I liked the rainbow logo on the sleeve. I was dirt-stained and torn. The boy was frayed and worn. His jeans were three inches too short, with gaping holes in the knees. His t-shirt was two sizes too big. His arms, protruding from the massive sleeves of his shirt, were skinny. Too skinny.

He made me sad. I'd been sad a lot, before, but always sad for me. I was sad when we moved because I missed my friends. Sad when Momma got quiet because I missed her. Sad when Daddy was stressed because he didn't have time to read to me anymore.

The boy didn't make me sad for me, though. Just for him. I guess that's why I didn't turn tail and run. Nobody ought to be sad and alone.

"You're in my spot," I declared boldly, standing up from my hiding place.

The boy flew off the rock with a yelp, crouching in the sand with his fists held up like he was about to fight. His eyes were on fire, but I wasn't scared. Nothing about him scared me. I stepped out from the shadows.

"This is my spot," I said, pointing at the rock he had just vacated. "But you can use it if you want. It's a good spot. Especially if you're sad."

The boy hesitated, backing up a step. I took another step forward.

"Why are you here?" I asked.

He shook his head. "I just came here to think. I'll leave. I didn't know it was your spot."

"I told you, you can use it if you want. It's a good spot."

He frowned. "Yeah," he took another step back, but lowered his fists. "Yeah, it is."

"Do you come here a lot?"

"Yeah... I mean... sometimes. I didn't..." he shook his head. "I didn't know it was yours."

It was strange that it wasn't strange at all. Neither one of us questioned whether a creek in the woods with the moon overhead was a reasonable place for a twelve-year-old to go in order to contemplate life and cry as the need arose. Neither one of us questioned the other's presence. He didn't question my assertion that the spot was mine. I didn't question how he'd come by it in the first place. We both understood, I think. We understand each other, because whatever impulse drove me to my spot also drove him. Neither of us needed it explained.

"We can share it," I said, ignoring his nervous gaze as I toed my shoes off and, holding them in my hands, picked my way across the rocky creek bed. He'd moved as far to the edge of the tiny island as he could and stood there, hands clenched in fists at his sides, as I placed my shoes and backpack carefully by the rock and boosted myself up onto it.

"We don't have to share it," he said. "I'll find a new spot."

"That's silly," I declared, patting the rock. "There's room for both of us and I don't have any friends."

For some reason, that made him curious. "You don't have any friends?"

"No, I just moved here and school hasn't started."

He nodded in somber understanding and dropped to a seated position on the sand. I was inexplicably disappointed that he hadn't joined me on the rock. I was also inexplicably delighted that he wasn't turning away.

"I move a lot," he said with a shrug, grabbing a stick and drawing in the sand with it. "Do you?"

"No, this is my first time."

"It gets easier," he told me, looking up. His eyes locked on mine. Moonlight sparkled in them and I felt a strange warmth seep into my bones. It felt like going home. "The first couple days will suck, but you'll make friends fast, I bet. You seem nice."

"I'm nervous," I blurted. The words surprised me. I hadn't voiced them before. Momma needed me to be strong, and I knew Daddy wouldn't have time for my silly problems. As much as my honesty surprised me, though, it didn't seem to faze the boy.

"That's okay," he said, wrapping an arm around his belly as he drew in the sand with the other. I watched in silence as he doodled. He drew a circle and erased it. Drew a square and erased it. He looked up into the sky, squinting at the stars. Looked back at the sand and drew a star. Erased it. Drew a car. He stared at that one for a while, head cocked to the side. "It's normal to be nervous," he said thoughtfully, adding windows to the car. "I get nervous."

For some reason, that surprised me. "You do?"

"Yeah. I've had a bunch of new schools so I guess you'd think I was brave by now. I'm not, though. I don't think scared is something you can just choose not to be. You'll always be afraid. You just gotta find a way to be smarter than the fear."

"Smarter?"

"Yeah," he looked up and grinned at me. "That's what I…" He trailed off, staring at the sketched car in the sand. In a swift movement, he tossed the stick aside and smoothed a hand over the drawing. "My brother Jakey is scared of the dark," he said, sitting back on his hands and staring up at the sky. "He thought there were monsters everywhere. Under the bed, in the closet, outside the window, out in the… out in the hallway." He shook his head. "He keeps… he kept me up with his whining, so I tell…" he shook his head hard, as if to dislodge something. "I told him, every night, he's gotta smile while he's going to sleep."

"Smile?"

"Yeah," he flashed a grin at me, as if demonstrating his point. It kinda reminded me of one of Momma's smiles. His mouth was smiling but his eyes were sad and far away. "I made some stuff up about how monsters like fear so

13

you gotta fool them into thinking you're not afraid. If you smile they go away."

"That's dumb," I said. "You shoulda just told him monsters aren't real."

"Nah, he's too smart for that," the boy said.

His answer confused me, but I didn't press. "I can't really smile at everyone like a creepo on my first day of school, though," I said. "They'll think I'm crazy."

He smiled at me again, at that. This time it reached his eyes in a small way. Just a quick glimmer that might have been the moonlight.

"Yeah, that's true," he agreed, nodding. He sat forward, dusting his hands off and clasping them together, resting his chin on his fists in a mock display of thoughtfulness. "It still kinda works, though."

"It does?"

"Yeah, I mean… don't smile," he said, grinning at me. I caught the full force of it, in that moment. It was like the sun broke loose in the middle of the night. "But I guess, y'know… Jakey was scared of the monsters and he couldn't sleep because he was scared. But when he smiled he wasn't scared, so the monsters left him alone."

"Fake monsters."

"Real to him."

"Fake monsters," I repeated, firmly.

"Okay, okay. So you're scared of fake bullies."

"Bullies are real!"

"But you're pretty. They're not gonna be mean to you."

I felt my face heat at the unexpected compliment, but scowled. "Bullies are mean to everybody."

"At first, sure. But they'll leave you alone if they don't think it bothers you. They're like the monsters. They bully you so you'll be sad. It's the sadness they want. Not you. Jakey smiled and his monsters left him alone. You just gotta pretend you're happy and the bullies won't touch you."

"That won't work," I said, with absolute certainty.

"Have you tried it?"

Of course I hadn't. I'd never been bullied. I had been with the same kids since preschool. I was popular. I had at least twenty friends. Maybe more. If there were bullies at my school, I'd never been able to see them through my crowd of allies. Allies I'd left behind.

I sniffed back tears as my vision blurred. "No," I said forlornly, wiping a tear from my cheek.

"Why are you crying?" he asked, pushing himself to his feet. "I was trying to help. You're not supposed to cry."

"I don't have any friends," I said through my tears.

I buried my face in my hands, but I heard him approach and I felt him brush against me as he boosted himself up onto the rock. He nudged my shoulder with his. "Where are you going to school?" he asked.

"Sand Hill Junior High," I said.

"Well, then, you're wrong."

I lowered my hands and frowned at him. "Wrong about what?"

"About not having any friends!" he said brightly.

I shook my head, utterly lost.

"I go to Sand Hill, too," he explained. "At least for now. So you've got one friend."

"We're not friends," I snapped at him. Daddy never let me be friends with boys. I asked him, once, if my classmate Jeremy could come over after school and he put me in timeout. I didn't understand it, but there were a lot of things about Daddy that I didn't understand. The only thing I *did* know was that if he said something it was best to listen. "Don't tell anybody we're friends," I hissed into the darkness, suddenly very aware of the waywardness of my birthday adventure and the potential consequences thereof.

The boy's face went still at my words, and the smile dropped away. He swallowed and nodded. "Yeah," he said with a sigh, slipping off the rock and sitting back down in the sand. "Okay."

"Why do you want to be friends, anyway?" I asked, confused by the apparent sadness on his face. *He* hadn't just moved here. *He* probably already had friends. Why did *he* care?

He shrugged, reaching for a new stick and drawing zig zags in the dirt. "I don't," he muttered to the sand.

"But you said we were friends."

"Cuz I thought it'd make you feel better," he said, as if I was stupid for asking.

"Why do you even care?"

"Because you were sad."

"Why do you have to be my friend to make me feel better?"

"That's a stupid question!" he snapped at me, glaring.

Hurt, I clamped my mouth shut. I thought it was a pretty good question. He'd already made me feel better. We didn't have to be friends, especially not at *school*. It didn't make any sense to me. Maybe I *was* stupid.

"I just don't get it," I mumbled, flopping back on the rock and staring at the sky. The moon was directly overhead—a massive, glowing orb that hung in the sky and seemed liable, in that moment, to drop right onto me.

"What don't you get?" the boy sighed impatiently.

"Nevermind, it doesn't matter," I said to the sky. "My dad wouldn't let me be friends with you, anyway."

15

"Your dad?" His tone perked up.

"Yeah, my dad… he doesn't like me to be friends with boys."

"*That's* why you don't wanna be friends?" His voice was bright with hope and I sat up, gripping the edge of the rock. The gritty texture of the stone dug into my hands.

"Yeah," I said. "And I do wanna. I just can't."

"Sure you can!" he said cheerfully, bouncing to his feet and hopping up onto the rock next to me. "We'll just be secret friends!"

"Secret friends?"

"Yeah, like… we can meet here sometimes and talk about stuff. And if anybody's mean to you at school I'll beat 'em up. I just won't tell nobody why."

I laughed at that. He looked too skinny to beat anybody up. Skinny and tired, I noticed. I hadn't seen it from far away, but this close I saw the heavy shadows beneath his eyes and the gaunt angles of his face.

"Why are you laughing?" he asked, scowling at me.

"Do you beat up people very often?" I asked, by way of answer.

At that, his face darkened. It was odd. There were so many things about the boy that I didn't know. Heck, I didn't even know his name. But it was like he could speak to me without words. I knew my question made him sad, just as surely as I knew I'd hurt his feelings when I said we couldn't be friends. It was that same, strange sixth sense that told me it would make him feel better if I held his hand.

As skinny as he was, his hand dwarfed mine. The surface of his palm was rough, and his fingers felt strong and grown up as he linked them with mine and folded them over. We both stared at the connection. I was astonished at how unremarkable it was. I'd never held hands with a boy before. I thought it was supposed to be something special. I thought it was supposed to catapult me into feeling like a woman. Instead, it just felt the same as his smile. It felt like going home.

"What's your name?" I asked, still staring down at my skinny fingers, woven through his big ones.

"Nate," he said. "What's yours?"

"Alexandra," I said with a groan.

"You don't like your name?" he asked.

"Now *that's* a stupid question," I shot back. "Alexandra is my grandma's name. I hate it. It *sounds* like a grandma's name."

"Well, what do you *wanna* be called?" he asked.

I laughed. "What, I just get to choose?"

"It's *your* name," he said. "How 'bout Aly?"

I shuddered. "My family calls me that. Not my friends."

"Okayyy. Alex?"

I laughed and shook my head, rolling the names over in my head. "Isn't that a boy's name?" I asked.

"Not if it's your name. If it's yours it'll be a girl's name. Since you're a girl and all." Although I wasn't looking at him, I heard the grin in his voice.

"So… Alex? That's a good name?" I asked doubtfully.

"Do you like it?"

I shrugged. "Yeah."

"Then it's a good name. It's nice to meet you, Alex." He offered me his free hand to shake, and I stared at it, stifling a giggle. It seemed an absurd gesture, considering we were already holding hands. Then I looked up at his face and saw the humor in his eyes, and I laughed outright.

"It's nice to meet you too, Nate," I said, pulling my hand loose from his left and slipping it into his right, letting him pump it up and down dramatically.

"So we're friends now, Alex?" he asked, whispering conspiratorially.

"Secret friends," I whispered back.

Right then, in what was otherwise a glorious, memorable, flawless moment, my stomach bellowed out a massive, hungry growl. I hadn't eaten much of my birthday dinner, and I guess it was coming back to bite me.

Nate snickered, letting go of my hand, and I felt my face heat in embarrassment. I slid off the rock and fumbled with my backpack, pulling out a candy bar and hopping back up on the rock.

"I've never heard a girl's stomach make that sound before." Nate was still laughing, stretching out on his back as I tore open the candy bar and took a bite.

"I'm hungry," I said defensively, talking around my food in what Momma would have considered a gross display of unladylike behavior.

"So am I, but you don't hear my stomach roaring about it like that do you?" he teased, propping his hands behind his head and staring at the stars.

"If you're hungry I've got more."

Nate stilled my slide off the rock with a hand on my arm. "I'm good," he said, releasing me when I stopped moving. "I was just kidding."

"You can have a Snickers," I said, ignoring him. "I don't like the peanuts but they're my brother Tommy's favorite so I always bring them with me on adventures."

"I'm not hungry."

"You just said you were."

"Well, I'm not."

"Well," I said, slipping off the rock and rooting around in my backpack, "you can just save it for later, then."

Candy bar in hand, I boosted myself back up and dropped it on his stomach.

Then I reclined next to him, staring at the stars.

"Do you know the constellations?" I asked, pretending not to notice when he plucked the Snickers bar off his stomach and peeled the wrapper back, taking a large, hungry bite.

"Some of 'em," he said, his voice muffled as he chewed.

"That's gross, you shouldn't talk with your mouth full." I nudged him in the ribs and he nudged me right back.

"You were doing it earlier."

"Which ones do you know?" Better to change the subject before he knew he won the argument.

"Uhhh, the Big Dipper," he pointed up at the sky.

"The Big Dipper isn't up right now," I said, knocking his hand aside.

"Oh…" His voice trailed off as he took another bite, chewed, and swallowed. "I thought you were asking me cuz you didn't know. I was just gonna make some stuff up."

"Mm-mm," I said, shaking my head against the rock as I chewed on my last bite. "I know all of 'em."

"Okay, then, smartass. Show me one."

"Don't curse," I snapped, nudging him again in the ribs.

"Ouch, fine. Show me one… smartypants."

"That's Scorpius," I said, pointing at the J-shaped formation above us.

"What's it supposed to be?"

"A scorpion. Duh."

"I think you're making shit—" he broke off when I hissed at him, poised to poke him in the ribs again. "I think you're making *stuff* up," he corrected, stuffing the candy wrapper into his pocket and folding his hands behind his head once more. "All I see is a bunch of dots."

"Well they're not just dots. They're stars. They're *huge*. Bigger than the sun. They're just so far away they look tiny."

He made a thoughtful sound, and we sank into comfortable silence, staring at the stars. I don't know what Nate was thinking about, but I was thinking about how small the sky usually made me feel. Those tiny dots were so massive. Sometimes I felt like a star— so huge and important in my own portion of the world and so puny and insignificant to everyone and everything else.

Normally, it set me on edge, thinking about where I fit into everything. That night, it didn't. It seemed to me that the spot worked even better at night. The world not only stopped, it seemed to have faded away completely.

Then Nate sat up, breaking the spell. "Well, secret friend," he said without preamble. "It's been fun but I gotta go back to where I live."

"Oh," I mumbled, stifling my disappointment.

"I'll walk you home first, though."

"Why?"

He gaped at me in mock indignation. "Well I wouldn't be a good friend if I let you wander around in the woods by yourself, would I?"

"I wander around in the woods by myself all the time," I bragged.

"Sure, but that was before we were friends. C'mon, let's go."

He hopped off the rock and held out his hand and I took it, although I really didn't need his help getting down. He took off his shoes and we stepped across the creek together, still holding hands. We sat on the bank and tucked wet feet back into our shoes in comfortable silence.

"I'll take the lead," Nate said, pushing me behind him as I shrugged into my backpack and took a step toward the woods. I planted my feet, arms crossed over my chest, scowling.

"You don't even know where I live," I said crossly. "I'll take the lead."

"But it's dark," he countered, gesturing at the shadowy woods around us. "Aren't you like… scared or whatever?"

"Of the woods?" I asked. "I come here all the time. I'll take the lead."

He didn't say anything, so I jogged past him into the moonlit forest.

"Wait up!" he yelled after me, and I heard his footsteps pounding the dirt behind me.

When we reached the edge of the trees lining the expanse of perfectly manicured lawn that comprised my backyard, Nate grabbed my arm.

"Hold up," he hissed. We can't go through there. Let's go around."

I frowned, confused, and pulled my arm loose. "We can't go around. That's my house," I said, pointing at the white-paneled colonial I reluctantly called home.

"Are you serious?" he asked, his voice barely above a whisper.

"Yeah," I said. "What's the matter?"

He swallowed hard and shook his head. "I thought…"

"What?"

He took a deep breath and let it out, taking a step forward and bracing his hands on his hips as he studied my home. I stood back and took the moment to study him. His shoulder blades jutted out sharply from his back, and his graying t-shirt was spotted with tiny holes. I looked down at his feet and saw that the heel of his left shoe was reinforced with silver duct tape.

He's poor.

And he'd thought I was, too, since I'd shown up in my shabby adventure clothes. I'd never had a poor friend before, and I'd lived in nice houses like this my whole life. Daddy worked with poor people all the time, but I'd never really thought of the fact that they were real people. They'd always been a thing the adults talked to each other about in sad voices, or used as a tool to make us finish our dinner.

"It's okay," I said, stepping forward and linking my arm through his. "We're not *rich*. We don't have guard dogs or anything."

Nate just shook his head with a breath of disbelief and followed as I led the way, picking my route through dark corners of the yard. There were no fences in my neighborhood, and I didn't want any nosy neighbors to peek out and see two kids traipsing around in the middle of the night. I'd be grounded until my grandbabies died of old age.

"This is kinda cool," Nate whispered from behind me as we crawled behind a row of low shrubs. "I feel like a spy."

"I know, right?!" I whispered back, that fuzzy feeling of *home* curling into a warm ball in my chest. I'd always felt that way, sneaking about and exploring the outdoors. I felt like a warrior. A strong, stealthy warrior. I liked my dirty old cargo shorts for the same reason. They made me feel like someone else. Someone strong, and I was everything but strong in real life. It'd always felt silly, though, to pretend. Right now it didn't feel silly at all. Or pretend. Not with Nate's excitement so palpable and close and *real*.

We reached my sycamore tree without incident and stood below it, staring at each other. Dappled moonlight illuminated Nate's face and I smiled up at him. "I'm glad we're friends," I whispered.

He smiled back. A full smile that shone out at me from his eyes. "Me, too," he said.

"Can I have a boost?" I asked, reaching my hands up and standing on my tip toes to show that I needed help reaching the branch above me. I didn't, really. I could jump up and grab the branch myself. I'd done it loads of times. I guess I just liked the thought of him helping me. "That window up there is my bedroom. I have to climb."

Nate looked from me to the window, lines creasing his forehead. "There's no other way?" he asked, frowning at me.

"It's fine. I do it all the time." Not true, but he didn't need to know that. "Just give me a boost."

Sighing, he stepped forward and sank to a knee, looping his fingers together for me to step in. I stepped into his makeshift foothold and grabbed the branch, using it to steady myself as he stood, boosting me up so that all I had to do was sling a leg over the branch. I straddled it and leaned down so I could whisper to him.

"Will you be at the spot tomorrow?" I asked.

He hesitated, then nodded. "Same time?" he asked.

"Same time," I affirmed.

Without looking back, I scrambled up the branches and launched myself at the window, smiling when Nate hissed out an anxious breath as I gracefully latched onto the ledge and crawled through the opening. I poked my head and chest out, waving down at him. He waved back and, for a moment, hesitated, staring up at the window. I couldn't see his expression in the dim light, but it felt like he was smiling. Although perhaps it just felt that way because of how hard *I* was smiling.

"Good night, Nate," I whispered to myself as he turned and snuck away, retracing our steps back to the safety of the woods.

Within ten minutes I was back in my pretty pink nighty and safe under the covers of my bed. The bed felt better, and the shadows of the furniture weren't so strange. I smiled at the ceiling and crossed my hands behind my head. It was a good birthday. My whole family was home for dinner. Tommy gave me an awesome present. I went for a moonlit adventure in the woods.

Best of all — better than all of it — I had a friend.

CHAPTER THREE

NATE

Five Years Later

"Nate?"

I jerked awake, even before small fingers closed over my arm, shaking gently. I'd never been a heavy sleeper, even before things turned really sour. Something always hit me — that shift in the air that came before the hands or the voice or the alarm, jolting me to consciousness, wide awake with a pounding heart and sweating palms.

What was it like to wake up slow and sluggish? Was that really even a thing?

"'Sup?" I mumbled, sitting up and prying Trish's tiny hand off my wrist. The bedroom I shared with Paul and Ronnie was never really dark. The windows didn't have blinds and the streetlight outside cast a haunting orange glow and ominous shadows over the room. I glanced at the other two beds and saw quiet lumps beneath covers. The boys were still asleep. Good.

"Can I stay with you tonight?" Trish pleaded, her eyes wide and shiny in the eerie light. She clutched her tattered safety blanket in her hands, her lips trembling, and my heart cracked open. She was only six and had only lived with us for three months, but she was a smart kid and she knew how things worked. She knew the sounds of her foster parents getting rip-roaring drunk. She knew that those sounds most often preceded trouble. She knew what all my other foster siblings had learned throughout the years — that the safest place to be when there was trouble was with me.

Or, more specifically, behind me.

It wasn't that I was so great in a fight. Especially not back when I was little. Even now, at sixteen and finally filling out, there wasn't much I could do against a hulking monster like our foster father. Nah, it wasn't that I could kick ass. My strength lay in my unique and unparalleled ability to piss people off. Something

22

about my face just made folks angry, and I took a perverse pride in that. Anger at me was better than anger at the littler kids and it was *far* preferable to the desire that glittered in my foster father's otherwise-dull eyes when he looked at the girls.

"Fine," I said, reaching out and tucking my hand beneath Trish's arms, swinging her up onto the bed so fast it made her giggle. "You gotta be quiet, though."

"'Kay," she whispered, kicking her way beneath the covers and snuggling into the pillow. Trish broke my heart a little bit every time I looked at her. She wasn't like the rest of us. She hadn't ended up here because of shitty parents and bad behavior. She was here because her parents had no other relatives and were too dumb to plan a safety net for their daughter in case they did something stupid like die in a fiery car wreck. Trish didn't have an ounce of fight in her. Even Paul, the youngest, had a little fire and steel, born of abuse and neglect. Trish was just sweet. She cried when she hurt and smiled when she was happy. It killed me to see because I knew it wouldn't last.

"Did you shut your door behind you?" I asked, slipping out from beneath the blankets and stretching out on top of them, shoving a hand beneath my head.

"Mmhm," she mumbled. Trish was a smart kid. She knew the drill.

"Stuffed your pillow under your blanket so it looks like you're still there?"

"Uh-huh." She was asleep by the second half of her answer. She didn't get enough sleep. Didn't get enough food, either. I hadn't done a very good job of bringing snacks home, lately. Not after getting caught red-handed with a backpack full of shoplifted groceries. I guess it was on me. I should've stuck to small hauls like I had in the beginning but I'd grown more arrogant with each success and stepped up my payout without stepping up my game. It pissed me off a little, though, that nobody asked why the reprobate was stealing stupid healthy shit like protein bars and dried fruit. My probation officer just dragged me over the coals and handed me back to my foster parents for the real punishment.

Whatever. If six years in 'the system' had taught me anything it was that adults didn't care about the truth or doing the right thing. They cared about one thing: the bottom line. My case worker did her job and cashed her check and went home to her real kids. My PO did *his* job and cashed *his* check and bought a new motorcycle. Tim and Marsha, my foster parents, let the lot of us sleep under their roof, cashed their check, and then drank, injected, huffed, sniffed, and smoked their way to oblivion. Really, who can blame any of them? Life sucks. All anybody's ever after is a way to forget about reality. Raise your kids, ride your motorcycle, get high as a kite— whatever it takes to fabricate a little good— to carve out a portion of the world that doesn't completely fucking suck.

I was guilty of it, too. Every night I could, I slipped off into the woods to the one part of my life that wasn't garbage.

As if reading my thoughts, my watch alarm beeped, and I turned it off. That was my cue— my cue to abandon the kids who needed me, climb out the window, and flee to the good. What did that say about me? I was no better than any of the adults, chasing happiness at the expense of those who needed me.

If Trish hadn't woken me up I'd be halfway gone. Tim and Marsha had been quiet when I went to sleep, and they weren't too loud now. I wouldn't have heard their noisy stumble off to bed five minutes ago or the gag-inducing sounds of clumsy, drunken lovemaking. The sounds were disgusting, but they didn't just make me nauseous. They sent chills of dread running up my spine and raised every hair on my body.

Something uglier than usual happened to Tim when he drunk-fucked his hag of a wife. Stoned fucking was okay. Blazed fucking was okay. Those sessions didn't usually last too long and they always ended with both parties in a coma-like sleep that lasted until well after the sun rose.

Drunk fucking, though? I guess when Tim was drunk, Marsha didn't quite sate him. The idiot probably didn't realize the problem was his own pickled pecker and not Marsha's dried up old cunt. The reasons don't matter, though. What matters is that when Tim got drunk and fucked his wife he always did the same thing. He waited until she went to sleep and then he climbed out of bed and turned into a predator.

My stomach clenched at the sound of creaking floorboards as Tim leveraged his hulking frame out of bed. What if I'd left? What if Trish hadn't woken me up?

Trish didn't twitch as I slipped off the bed, but Ronnie did. At twelve, Ronnie was every bit the perpetually pissed off little shithead I had been at his age. Maybe even worse.

"Where are you going?" he whispered, sitting up and rubbing his eyes.

"Tim's up." That was all I needed to say. Ronnie was too worldly for his age. He knew what it meant. His eyes skipped to Trish, asleep in my bed. Then they widened.

"Deb!" he whispered, anxiously.

"She's at Rob's." I didn't have to worry much about Deb anymore. She was fifteen and spent more nights with an endless string of boyfriends than she did at 'home.'

"Keep them inside," I said, jerking my chin at Trish and our youngest sibling, Paul.

Ronnie nodded silently. Once, a long time ago, he had challenged my methods of dealing with Tim. Just once he'd interfered, and Tim had beat him so bad he pissed blood for a week. After that he let me do my thing. I could take a beating better than any of them. That was my job. My purpose. Ronnie understood that, now, and he'd take care of the kids until they learned it for themselves.

Cold sweat broke out on the back of my neck as I pulled the door open and slipped out into the hallway. It was stupid, what I was about to do, but I knew it would work. Tim's perverse lust for his young female charges only came out of the woodwork in certain conditions. His rage, on the other hand, was a living thing that owned him every minute of every day. All it would take was a gentle nudge and he'd forget Trish. He'd forget why he'd gone looking for her and he wouldn't have the brain power to wonder at the timing of my interference.

I forced my hands to stay steady as I pulled the door shut behind me and turned to Tim, who was fumbling with the girls' doorknob. "What are you doing?" I asked, crossing my arms over my chest as Tim spun around, glaring at me.

"None of your business, boy. Get back to bed," he growled, stalking forward. Tim was a good three inches taller than my lanky 5'11" and he worked part time at the shipping yard and part time laying bricks. He didn't know the word 'exercise' and he smoked and drank and did every drug under the sun, but the man was undeniably strong. Muscles strengthened by years of manual labor were coated in a thick layer of fat, as well, which lent him bulk. The sight of him, towering before me, made my throat go dry with fear.

"Not tired," I said, trying to convince both of us that I didn't give a shit about his meaty fists or the dark rage spreading over his face at my recalcitrance. "What are you doin' trying to go in the girls' room? You pervin' again?"

Tim hated that. The only thing he hated more than me existing was me pointing out his flaws. He took a few lumbering steps forward and I fought the urge to flee and stood my ground.

"What did you say to me, you little shit?" Tim growled, snatching the front of my shirt in one meaty hand and pulling me close. His breath smelled like sour milk and beer and I swallowed the urge to vomit.

"I asked if you were pervin' on the girls," I spat at him. "You know you ain't s'posed to touch 'em. What if I told the case worker?"

"The case worker wouldn't believe you, boy," Tim hissed in my face. That was probably true. Miss Meg might have cared, but I hadn't seen her since the day they took Jakey. I guess punching a woman in the face is a good way to lose her support. Or maybe they just save the kindly, maternal-figure case workers for the nice kids like Jake, and once it was just me she didn't want to waste her effort.

Whatever the reason, the next time CPS picked me up for an appointment I was introduced to my new case worker: Mrs. Jones. Mrs. Jones was a skeletally thin, pinch-lipped older lady whose cold, dead eyes always seemed to look through me.

She hated me almost as much as Tim, I think.

25

"I bet they would," I goaded Tim. "And I bet Marsha wouldn't be too happy, neither."

"You shut your mouth," Tim snapped, jerking me up by the neck of my shirt so that my toes barely touched the ground. He was good and angry, now, and I knew just what to do to send him over the edge.

My balled-up fist caught Tim in the stomach, bouncing off the fleshy surface without doing much harm. My knee, however, struck gold. His fingers dropped away from my shirt and I staggered back as he bent over, gasping and clutching his junk.

"You little *shit*," he breathed, and I backed up to the wall of the narrow hallway. I could've fled, but if I ran he might not chase me. He might turn his rage on Paul or Ronnie. He might find Trish in my bed and twist it into something it wasn't. He'd tell my prune-faced case worker that *I* was the pervert and she'd call the cops. Nobody would listen to me. I'd go to juvie and the kids would be alone.

Terrifying possibilities sprang up in my head, as they always did, battling back the urge to run. I only had two real options: fight back or to take it lying down. Either way would distract him, but I'd long since come to crave the fiery satisfaction of landing a punch. I'd fight.

I'd always fight.

Recovering, Tim pushed himself upright and staggered forward, grabbing me by the neck before I could duck and flinging me to the floor. I landed hard, dull pain radiating up my shoulder, and only barely managed to roll away in time to avoid being crushed by Tim's weight as he knelt over me. As it was, he pinned me to the ground with a forearm against my neck, the fist of his other hand pounding repeatedly into my stomach. Even drunk, Tim knew better than to hit me in the face. It was only in the blindest rage that he'd leave a mark where it could be seen at school.

I, however, had no such quibbles. I scrabbled at his face with my fingers, digging my thumbs into his eyes, and he yelled out, lashing out on instinct and cuffing me in the side of the head so hard my ears rang. I bucked against his weight, catching him in the stomach with a knee, and he roared with anger, staggering to his feet.

Even when I fought back, it never did much good and it always ended the same way. Like this. I was still reeling from the blow to the head and gasping for air when Tim's bare foot caught me in the ribs and all I could do was curl around the nauseating pain.

"Stupid little shit," Tim hissed as he kicked, again and again. Peripherally, I realized he was stepping over me and didn't even have time to brace myself before he kicked me in the back. "Stupid, retarded little bastard. You think you can take

26

me, boy? Really?"

"Tim?" Marsha's voice filtered in from the master bedroom and Tim froze. Marsha was a useless bitch, and I hated her almost as much as I hated Tim. She didn't like it when he beat us, though. Our presence in their home kept her in decent drug money, and she worried that the flow would stop coming if we got taken away.

"Be right there," Tim called back, crouching down and shoving at my shoulder until I rolled onto my back. "You're fucking lucky, kid," he hissed. "When are you going to learn your lesson?"

Then he stood and left, staggering drunkenly down the hall, having completely forgotten his original mission. And the man thought that *I* was stupid. I almost laughed, but caught myself because laughing would hurt like hell.

I lay on the dirty carpet of the hallway for a long time, mustering the willpower to climb to my feet. I lifted my arm and glanced at the glowing dial of my watch. It was way too late to go see Alex, and that was all I really wanted. I wanted to see her face and hear her voice. I wanted to lay on our rock and stare up at the sky and talk about how she was gonna go there, someday. I wanted to close my eyes and imagine a universe where I could go with her.

Alex didn't know jack shit about my life. True to our original agreement, we hadn't exchanged more than passing glances at school. We did meet at the spot nearly every night, though and she had quickly become my favorite person on earth. Our spot was in the darkness of the woods in the middle of the night, but Alex, to me, was sunshine.

Also true to our agreement, I beat the shit out of Jimmy Campbell for spreading a rumor in our freshman year that she was putting out. I didn't tell her why, though. She was mad as hell at me for getting in trouble, and didn't speak to me for three days, but I just let her think I was pissy and violent. Her being mad didn't hurt me much. Definitely less than it'd hurt her to know the truth.

Alex was a fantasy for me, and I couldn't bear the thought of letting darkness touch her. Not darkness like Jimmy Campbell and his stupid rumors and especially not the darkness of my reality.

Biting back a groan, I used one hand to push myself up and pressed the other to my ribs. The world swam dizzily around me as I clawed my way up the doorjamb and let myself back into the bedroom.

All the kids were up. Paul and Trish were sitting on my bed, clinging to each other. Orange light glistened off the tears on Trish's cheeks, and Paul's eyes were shiny with them. Ronnie was standing in the middle of the floor and I could tell from his hooded, guilty expression that he was halfway through the motions of coming out to check on me.

"You know to stay inside," I hissed at him, not at all surprised when he met my anger with a fierce look of his own.

"I heard Tim go back to bed," he snapped back. "I'm not stupid."

"Next time, stay the fuck in bed," I ground out, trying not to limp as I crossed the room and settled on the edge of my stiff mattress. "Trish, do you wanna sleep with Paul?" The two children had developed a bond during Trish's short few months with us. I think it made her feel better to be the older sibling. Paul was only four, and I guess taking care of him made her feel stronger, and that was a feeling I understood well.

Trish whispered her answer, staring guiltily at the floor. "Can I stay with you?"

"Sure, hon," I sighed. "You okay, Paulie?"

Paul nodded and swallowed his tears, clambering off the bed and climbing into his own. I stretched out on my back, swallowing a groan as bruised ribs protested the movement. Trish stretched out beneath the covers, her hand wrapped around the fabric of my shirt. I guess living, breathing safety blankets are better than the inanimate variety. Ronnie slunk to his bed and sat on the edge but didn't lay down.

"What's the matter?" I asked, turning my head to look at him. His hands curled around the sheets with a white-knuckled grip and he was worrying furiously at his bottom lip.

"Nothing," he spat.

"C'mon, kid," I muttered. "Tell me what's wrong."

"Are we supposed to just let him kill you?" Ronnie asked, finally, glaring at me from across the room.

"He's not gonna kill me," I sighed, closing my eyes. "He's not that stupid." Tim and I had a tentative agreement. Mutually assured destruction. He let me stay and kept the beatings just this side of deadly and, in return, I didn't tell a soul what was happening under his roof. It wasn't great, but it worked. If I snitched Tim might get in trouble, but it wouldn't solve anything. They'd break us up and farm us out to different houses that would probably be just as bad. Maybe worse. And worst of all, I might move school districts. I might lose Alex.

"I hate this," Ronnie mumbled, laying down.

"Well, I'm not a huge fan of it either," I shot back, but I kept my tone light. Ronnie didn't need any more stress in his life. He was volatile enough as it was.

"I wanna beat him up," Ronnie said to the semi darkness. I smiled.

"Well, when I leave you can try. 'Till then, you gotta wait and let me deal with it my way. You know the rules."

"I know," Ronnie sighed, and he drifted into silence. Trish and Paul fell back to sleep, and the rhythmic pattern of their breath caused the tense air in the room to settle. After a while, my eyelids started to droop as well and I was half asleep when Ronnie finally spoke again. "When are you gonna leave?" he whispered. It wasn't a challenge. It was a plea. A desperate bid for comfort.

"No time soon, buddy," I mumbled. "By the time I leave you'll be twice my size and you'll be able to beat him up in your sleep."

"Are you sure?"

"I'm sure."

"Whatever… night, Nate."

"Night, Ronnie."

.. .. ..

Alex was pissed.

I could feel it the second I walked into third-period civics, the one class I had with her. I hated civics, but I lemme tell you I *loved* that class. It was my one chance to linger in the presence of the strange girl who inhabited my best friend during the day. As I passed, I let my eyes trail over her for one glorious moment.

Her hair was in a perfectly-coiffed bun, hair-sprayed into compliance. Gold studs glittered at me from her ears, and her lips were painted a delicate shade of pink. Her shirt was a flowy white thing that dipped just low enough to showcase a delicate gold cross, sitting against her skin just above that perfect valley that I longed to explore. The skirt she wore was knee-length and modest, but it had a mind of its own, molding itself against her thighs like it was *trying* to fuck with me. Her feet were crossed at the ankle, tucked primly beneath her chair.

This girl was beautiful, but she wasn't *my* Alex. My Alex wore baggy shorts and worn out t-shirts. She was dirt-smudged and had delicate scratches on her arms and legs where the branches and brambles snagged at her while she ran through the woods. My Alex never wore that cross because she had it in her head God was a manmade construct and the church was a tool used to manipulate the masses. *My* Alex had a mosquito bite the size of Mt. Vesuvius on her forehead that I knew she wanted to scratch at but wouldn't because she'd covered it up with make-up and nobody else could see it.

I winked at her as I passed her front row seat. It wasn't in compliance with our deal, but I liked to piss her off sometimes, and I needed a little touch of heaven that morning.

Her lips tightened and a touch of flame flared up in her sweet blue eyes. Definitely pissed, and my transgression wasn't helping. Good. The pink flush creeping up her neck warmed me up from the inside out. This was my Alex. Fierce and fiery and stubborn as hell. The world could keep the quiet, gentle little churchgoer with the fancy clothes, the preacher daddy, and the 4.0 GPA. Angry Alex in ragged old clothes, raging against the machine, tearing into me for being an idiot? That girl was all mine and I loved her more with every pitiful beat of my fucked-up heart.

Fighting the urge to press a hand to my aching ribs, I hid a smile and rolled my eyes as I strode past her, dropping my bookbag by my desk in the back of the room and sinking into the chair. My eyes were heavy, and I didn't exactly have an A-plus-student reputation to uphold, so I put my head down on the desk and zonked out.

I awoke with the sudden wisp of a breeze, just before the flat of a ruler cracked against my desk. Startled, I jerked upright, barely maintaining the presence of mind to hide a wince as my body protested the sudden movement. Our civics teacher, Mr. Quinn, stood above me, a smug look on his face and a ruler in one hand. The rest of the students were laughing.

"Would you like to join the rest of the class, Mr. Reynolds, or shall we wait for you to finish your beauty rest?"

God, I hated that fucking name. I inherited three things from my father: a handful of scars, a hair-trigger temper, and that shitty fucking surname.

I hated Mr. Quinn, too. I hated this fucking school. I cast a catch-all glare around the room and the majority of our giggling audience fell silent and turned back to the front of the classroom or made hasty conversation with each other. Mr. Quinn didn't seemed phased, though. "Well?" he asked.

"I'm awake," I snapped at him.

"Alright!" he said brightly, turning on his heel and marching back to the front of the classroom. "Now that Mr. Reynolds has decided to grace us with his presence, everyone pull out your textbooks and turn to page 427. Miss Winger, do you mind recalling what we discussed last class?"

Alex answered quickly, the dulcet tones of her voice tinged with panic. She hated — *hated* — being called on in class. It made her break into a nervous sweat, and although she was eight rows in front of me, I imagined I could see the sheen on the back of her neck. That made me irrationally angry at Mr. Quinn or calling on her… and irrationally aroused.

"We talked about the checks provided by the executive branch to the legislative branch's function," she said.

"Excellent. Mr. Reynolds, can you give us an example of one of these checks?"

Oh, hell. I hadn't been paying any attention at all. Alex's hair was too distracting. It was pulled up too tight and I knew it hurt her head to wear it like that. She kept reaching up and tugging gently at the hair at the nape of her neck and I knew she'd have a headache later. That knowledge didn't stop me from enjoying the way the sun came through the window and brought out the reddish streaks in her brown curls.

"Mr. Reynolds?"

"Fuck if I know," I shot at Mr. Quinn, and Alex spun around in her seat, shooting me a death glare. She hated it when I acted out in class. She had it in her head I might actually graduate if I stopped being such a shithead. Alex can be a little delusional.

"Language," Mr. Quinn said sternly, his face impassive. "The question was very simple. What is an example of a check the executive branch can use against the legislative branch?"

He said it was a simple question, but I was drawing a blank. Silence fell in the classroom, and I felt heat creep up my neck as my classmates started to snicker. I cut them down with a look and went back to panicking.

"I said I don't know," I shot at Mr. Quinn. "Ask somebody else."

"I'm asking you. We can sit here all day, or you can answer the question."

Alex's face softened and she mouthed something at me. It was so subtle, I doubt anybody else picked up on it, although it helped her cause that all eyes were on me. I saw her upper teeth scrape against her lower lip and her mouth pucker slightly around a silent 'o' sound. Something-o? She mouthed it again, and the answer came to me with a rush of relief.

"Veto," I mumbled.

"You'll have to speak up," Mr. Quinn said, smiling at his own douchebaggery.

"Veto," I stated again, louder.

"Well done. See, that wasn't so bad, was it?"

I'll show you what's bad, you fucking asshole.

"No, sir."

Thank you, I mouthed at Alex, but she just shook her head in disappointment and turned back around. I'd rather Tim kick my ass a thousand times than have her look at me like that. Anger was fine. Anger was *great*. Disappointment, though? It stung like salt in a wound I didn't even know I had. Maybe it'd be worth it to at least *try* to pay attention in class. Just for her.

CHAPTER FOUR

ALEX

An exasperated sigh tore me away from my textbook as my best friend Gemma sat down across from me. *Alexandra's* best friend Gemma. Alex's best friend sat ten tables behind me, inhaling artery-clogging cafeteria pizza and probably talking with his mouth full.

"Why are you always studying?" Gemma groaned, dumping her bag beneath the table and sitting down, unzipping her lunch box. "Ugh. Plain carrots. Yum."

She pulled a plastic container of sliced carrots out of her bag and popped it open as I shut my book and pulled out my own lunch.

"You know why," I said, unfolding the top of my paper bag and pulling out the bagel I'd packed for myself. Cream cheese and cucumbers. My favorite. Tom's favorite was bologna and cheese, and my dad's favorite was roast beef on rye. I knew because I packed all three lunches every morning while Momma sat on the back porch with a mug of rapidly-cooling coffee in her hands, staring blankly at the sliver of night fading into the western horizon.

"I don't understand why you're so stubborn about it," Gemma said, munching on a carrot as she rifled through the rest of her lunch for something fun. She always searched and always came up empty. Her mom was crazy about healthy food. On her birthday Gemma got a carob chip cookie but that was as out-there as it got. I tried to pack extra Oreos for her. "Just go to the stupid college your dad wants. It's the same education and you won't have to worry so much about scholarships."

"No it's not," I snapped, taking a bite of my bagel and using the time it took to chew to calm myself down. I shouldn't have snapped. Snapping was a very *Alex* thing to do, and here at school I had to be nice, soft-spoken *Aly*. Polite, mild-mannered *Miss Winger*. It was what everyone expected. Even Gemma. "It's not the same. It's the difference between science classes taught by scientists and science classes taught by folks who think humans were majicked into existence by a big man in the sky."

"You gotta talk to your dad, girl," Gemma said, shaking her head. "He's gonna find out eventually that his baby girl is an atheist. Might as well tell him now while he's still legally obligated to love you."

"Mm-mm," I said, mouth full of bagel. I chewed and swallowed, taking a sip of water. "I'm just gonna ride it out to the end. Kick school's butt and get a whole bunch of scholarships and it won't even matter that he won't help me pay for it. I'll be able to make it on my own."

"Ugh, well you still talk like a church girl," Gemma snarked. "Do you have chips or something? I'll trade you for these... homemade fig bars?" She held up a waxpaper sandwich bag containing a thick slab of something gooey and brown. It could've been a brownie but we both know it wasn't. Gemma's mom didn't believe in dairy products, so decent brownies were off the table. Gemma came from a family of crazy hippies. I came from a family of crazy Christians. We made a good pair.

"Hey, Aly! Hi Gem!"

The words made me grin, and I scooted over on the bench to make more room for my brother. Tom climbed into the seat beside me, setting his lunch on the table before him.

"Did you wash your hands?" I asked as he started digging through the paper bag.

"Yeah, Aly," he muttered, blushing furiously. My brother might be developmentally disabled, but he was a still very much a guy and quick to embarrassment and exasperation at my mother hen routine.

"How's your day going?" I asked, and alarm bells went off in my head when he bent his head over the bag, clearly avoiding my gaze.

"Fine," he said, pulling out the bologna and cheese I'd made for him that morning.

"Is everything okay?" I asked, leaning back and scanning him for any sign of injury or distress. Most people liked Tom, and for good reason. He was the friendliest guy I'd ever known, and quick with a compliment or a cheerful hello. But there were some guys who still gave him trouble if they caught him alone. Insecure jerks who only felt good when they were making other people feel bad.

"It's fine," he mumbled.

"You're a terrible liar," I said fondly, pressing a hand to his back, leaning close and speaking softly. "Will you tell me later?"

He nodded, eyes flicking up to Gemma who was, bless her, effectively pretending not to hear our conversation. Gemma's a good friend.

"Well my day's going crappy," I said, infusing some levity into my voice as I sat back. "Mr. Quinn keeps calling on me in civics class."

"Yeah, cuz you know the answer," Gemma said, rolling her eyes. "Your sister is a smartass, Tom."

Tom laughed at the curse word and I glared at Gemma without much heat.

"She's the smartest smartass," Tom agreed, his voice jovial and proud. Sometimes life is a slog. Sometimes it hurts and feels pointless and too painful to endure. Sometimes, though, it's not so bad.

.. .. ..

"We're home!" I yelled, hooking my keys on the ring and toeing off my shoes while Tom shut the door behind us.

Our house was as pristine as ever. Momma kept it that way. I think that was her way of keeping herself together. She couldn't control my dad and she couldn't control the world, but she could control the house and the dust. She could control where we put our shoes and which rooms we were allowed to eat in. "Momma?"

"In here." Her voice wound through the stale, conditioned air and Tom and I followed it to the living room. She sat in her chair, eyes glued to the television. I glanced at the screen and saw some sitcom re-run. The sound of a laugh track crackled out of the speakers, but if you just looked at Momma you'd think she was watching a documentary about the making of a number two pencil. Her gaze was far away, and no part of her looked happy or entertained.

"How was school?" she asked as we sat on the couch, not looking away from the screen.

"Good!" I said, brightly, like I always did. I had it in my head if I was cheerful enough some of my happy would seep into her. All I ever got was a pinched smile, but that didn't stop me from trying. I felt like if I stopped I'd sink right down into the gray that had swallowed her up.

"Good," Tom echoed, but he didn't sound so bright. He watched Momma's face, always searching for something that he never found. His mother, probably. The woman who had disappeared, leaving us alone with a husk that looked just like her, trapped in the life that had chased her away.

"Why don't you have some snacks and do your homework," Momma said, turning her attention back to the TV. "Dinner will be ready at five."

Tommy opened his mouth to argue but I stood, tugging him to his feet behind me and dragging him from the room.

I set Tommy up at the desk in my room with an activity book and a box of colored pencils before pulling my textbooks out of my bag and hopping up onto my bed. It was Thursday, but I didn't have much homework. Twenty math problems, five pages of civics textbook, and a chapter of <u>Ethan Frome</u> for English. If Tommy stayed busy, I could finish it by dinner time.

I tried to stifle my excitement at the thought of getting out to the spot early. It'd probably be another long, lonely night, I reminded myself. Lately, Nate had been showing up less and less frequently. He was a good friend — my best friend — so I didn't think he was blowing me off for a stupid reason. I wasn't angry that he wasn't showing up. I was angry he wouldn't tell me why. Every time I asked, he got weird and evasive, changing the subject to something about me, like I was some dummy who wouldn't notice what he was doing.

Math was my best subject, and I flew through the problem set with ease. The familiar rhythm of the work pulled me away from the world and I felt myself relax into the patterns.

"So what happened at school today?" I asked after a while, flipping my pencil over and erasing a minus sign I'd erroneously carried.

"Nothing," Tom said after a long pause, scribbling furiously at the notebook and pointedly not looking at me.

"C'mon, Tom," I said, tapping my pencil on the paper and looking up at him. "Don't lie to me."

"It was just Freddy," he grumbled, shoving a hand up into his hair.

"Don't pull on your hair," I said sternly, trying to hide the acid that burned in my veins at his words. That jerk Freddy was always messing with Tom and it made me want to scream. I'd confronted him once but he just laughed at me and said I didn't have any proof and, sadly, it was the truth. He and his friends always managed to corner Tom when he was alone. No witnesses. "What did he do?"

"Nothing."

"C'mon, Tommy. I can't fix it if you don't tell me what happened."

"You don't need to fix it," he said flatly, eyes studiously fixed on coloring.

It's a common emotional affliction for people to feel like they just don't have the answers. That was never my problem. My problem was that I had all the answers, but nobody would listen to me. Momma wouldn't talk to me about what was making her so empty. Tommy wouldn't talk to me about his bullies. Nate wouldn't talk to me about whatever kept him away from me, night after night.

I knew I could have fixed it all, if they would only give the chance. But instead I just had to wonder and worry and come up with theories and ways to test them, and then come up with new theories when the old ones were disproven by some hint they didn't even mean to give me.

It was exhausting.

I resolved to check in on Tommy between classes for the next week or so. If he didn't want to tell me what was going on I'd just have to find out myself.

We worked in silence until dinner, and I was just finishing up my English reading when Momma's hollow voice summoned us downstairs.

Dinner was quiet. Daddy said a prayer like always. I hated his prayers. He talked a lot about God and Jesus and how we should all be thankful, but he never really went into much depth on what we should be thankful *for*.

As I always did, I tacked my own silent, shoddy prayer onto the end of Daddy's. Gemma thought I was an atheist, but I didn't believe in *nothing*. I believed something was listening when I closed my eyes and poured my heart out into the void. I just didn't think it was a wizard man in the sky.

Thank you for saving Tommy's life. Thank you for Momma who loves me and Daddy who helps people. Thank you for making me smart enough to want the stars. Thank you for giving me the spot. Thank you for the food and the roof and for letting me laugh. I'll find a way to pay it all back someday, I promise.

I kept Tommy entertained with funny faces as we slowly worked our way through dry chicken breast, unseasoned green beans, and boxed mashed potatoes. Nobody said anything about the meal not being very good. Not even Daddy. We all knew better.

After dinner, Tommy went to enjoy his hour of Playstation time, Daddy went to his study to work on his next sermon, and Momma and I did the dishes.

"Hey, Momma?" I asked, bussing the last of the plates to the counter by the sink and pulling open the dishwasher.

"Yes?" she asked absently, listlessly spooning leftovers into little plastic containers.

I hesitated, flipping the sink on and rinsing the dishes, hoping that I could mask the depth of my question by asking it on top of the everyday task. "Are you okay?"

"What?" Her tone had a bite to it, and she stopped working. I glanced at her over my shoulder.

"I'm just wondering if you're okay," I said, turning back to the sink and running another plate under the faucet. Streaks of mashed potato, chicken skin, and watery bits of green bean slid off the plate and down the drain and I wished life was so easy to clean up. "You seem kinda sad and—"

"I'm fine, Alexandra," she snapped, cutting me off. Tears bit at the area behind my eyes and we didn't talk at all, after that. Momma shoved the leftovers in the refrigerator and left me to finish tidying up. I put the dirty dishes in the dishwasher, washed the big pots by hand, and wiped down the counter. I was just finishing up when Momma came back in. She stared at me for a moment, something powerfully sad shining out at me from her hollow, tired eyes. The fingers of one thin, graceful hand worried at a button on her crisp white blouse.

"I shouldn't have snapped at you," she said, tears brimming in her eyes.

I didn't really understand why she was crying. She snapped at us often enough. It wasn't a big deal. Usually it was justified. Me and Tommy could get pretty raucous.

"It's fine, Momma," I said, drying my hands on a towel. "No big deal."

"It is a big deal," she argued feebly, stepping forward so that she stood right in front of me. I was already a couple inches taller than her, but I felt small when she pressed her soft palm to my cheek, peering up into my eyes.

"You're a sweet girl, Aly," she said. "My sweet, smart, beautiful girl..." she trailed off, choking on tears and I didn't know what to do.

"Momma, are you okay?" I asked, every muscle but my mouth frozen.

"I'm okay, sweetie," she said. Her arms went around me, one hand cradling the back of my head, gently pushing my face into her shoulder. I returned the hug, on the verge of tears myself. I felt relieved. I guess I thought I'd brought her back. That it was that easy.

I should've known better.

.. .. ..

I got to the spot just after ten. Of course, it was abandoned. Nothing but the me, the stars, and the swirling mist that hung over the water.

Over the years, the spot had accumulated a healthy pile of comfort objects. There was a cooler buried in the mud beneath the cave. Two lawn chairs were hidden amongst a pile of vines in the roots of the oak tree. Two years ago, Nate and I had hung a swing from one of the branches, and the next day when I took Tommy out there, I'd acted like I was as surprised to see it as he was. He thought it was magic. I dunno. I guess it kinda was.

Nate knew my brother and I came here during the day, but Tommy didn't even know Nate existed. Sometimes I wanted to tell him, but I didn't. Tommy wasn't much good at keeping secrets. He always got excited and gave up the ghost, like with Momma's Christmas present the year before and the dent we actually put in Daddy's car when we dropped his bike on it.

I was starting to wonder if Nate had the same problem. He'd grown increasingly less careful about our pact of secrecy over the last year or so. In a way, I understood. I felt the same pull. We were closer to each other than to anyone, and it was strange to see him at school and pretend I didn't know him.

It had to stay the way it was, though. To be honest, I was afraid to let Nate meet Aly. I knew he liked Alex. Sometimes I thought maybe he loved her as much as she loved him. But what if he hated Aly? What if he hated the make-up and the constant studying and the fierce need to be liked by everyone? Aly was as much a part of me as Alex, and if he came to hate one it was only a matter of time before he came to hate the other.

I couldn't take that risk. Not with my best friend. Especially not when I just as nervous that *I* wouldn't like *him*. He was a jerk at school. Kind of a scary jerk. What if he sucked into his group of friends and I ended up some serial truant with a shoplifting record and a cigarette addiction? No college would accept me! Not even the ones where Daddy wanted me to go.

I didn't bother to put my shoes back on after crossing the stream. I left them in the sand and climbed up onto the rock, stretching out on my back.

I'd grown since discovering the spot. Back then I could lay on my back with only my feet dangling over the end. Now my whole lower leg hung down against the front end. Now, when Nate was with me, we had to lay pressed against each other to avoid rolling off opposite sides. I didn't mind the change.

The moon was full so there weren't many stars up. I lay, staring at the washed out sky, and worried. About Tom's bully, who he said I didn't have to worry about but of course I did, because what was *Tom* going to do about a bully like freakin' Freddy Whitehouse? About Momma, who logic told me wouldn't just wake up tomorrow cured of her sadness. About Nate, who kept getting himself into trouble and who wouldn't tell me what was—

"Hey, Al."

I jolted upright with a startled gasp, pressing a hand to my heart, and he laughed, crossing the stream in one leap and sending up a spray of water that misted my bare legs.

"Hey!" I grumbled, laying back. "Be careful."

"Sorry," he said, but I knew he was smiling. I could hear it in his voice. Just like I heard the disappointment as he splashed over to the cave and opened the cooler. "What the hell, Alex?" he said, his tone bereft as the lid thudded shut. "No food?"

"Well, you haven't been showing up," I grumbled, trying not to sound as guilty as I felt. "I'm not just gonna lug food back and forth for no reason."

In reality, I had wanted to make a point. I wanted him to know that I was angry. The plan had felt better in theory than in execution, though. There was something about the way his stomach growled as he crossed the stream and climbed back up onto the rock beside me. Or maybe it was how quickly he sank into remorse.

"I know, Al, I'm sorry," he mumbled, lowering himself down beside me, the warmth of his body pressed against mine from shoulder to knee. His foot knocked into mine gently. "I swear I tried to come. Don't be mad."

He'd have known even if I hadn't made a point with the empty cooler. Nate always knew when I was mad. Mad, sad, happy, nervous… he always had a finger on the pulse of my emotions. The only one he couldn't seem to detect was the warm, fluttering excitement that ghosted through my veins every time we touched. Every time our eyes met. Every time he laughed at something I said.

Sometimes I thought maybe he saw it, and sometimes, when the moonlight was just right, I thought I saw the same *want* in his eyes when he looked at me.

Most of the time, though, we existed in this perpetual state of comfort. Comfortable touching. Comfortable conversation. Comfortable, constant bickering. Back then, with my body waking up and my mind stretching out to test the boundaries of my universe, I didn't want to feel comfortable and safe.

I wanted to feel alive.

"I'm not mad," I muttered, and I knew he knew I was lying.

"Yeah you are. I'm sorry I couldn't come, Al. Something came up where I live."

"What came up?" I asked, turning my head and studying his profile in the moonlight. His jaw clenched as he blinked up at the sky and I knew he felt my scrutiny.

"Just some stuff, Al. Nothing serious. I just couldn't leave, that's all."

"Is something the matter? I can help, you know. I'm really smart."

"I know you are," he said on a quiet laugh, rolling his head on the rock to flash me a grin. "I swear it's nothing."

I sighed but didn't press him further. If I did, we'd end up fighting, and the last thing I wanted to do was spend what little time I had with him in a fight. Letting my foot swing, I knocked it against his in a slow rhythm as we stared up at the few stars bright enough to pierce through the light of the moon.

"Any constellations tonight?"

"Uhh," I squinted up at the sky, studying the little flecks of light. "You can kinda see Draco."

"The dragon?" Nate asked, shifting close to me as I pointed, like that would somehow help him see what I was seeing. He smelled like equal parts cheap soap, fresh sweat, and the clean, heady scent of the forest that lingered on both of us after we spent the night in the fresh air.

"Yeah, that's his head, see?" I traced the four stars before shifting my finger to the dragon's belly. "And that one, sorta nestled in there, is Ursa Minor."

"The bear," he said skeptically, angling his head on the rock so that it touched mine.

"Or the little dipper," I said.

"That I can kinda see," he said brightly. "I see a dipper. Not a bear. *Definitely* not the dragon."

"That's cuz you've got no imagination," I said, trying to breathe through my mouth because the scent of him turned my insides to jelly and my brain into peanut butter.

"Maybe," he said with a shrug. He was silent for a long time, and I listened to the crickets chirp and the frogs croak—a sphere of natural music that contracted around us a little more with each passing second. "Hey, thanks for your help with that question, today. Mr. Quinn is a dick."

"You shouldn't sleep in his class," I said, pulling away and propping myself up on an elbow. He grimaced at the sky as I poked him in the shoulder. "You're smart, Nate. You need to shape up and stop being such a jerk. Actually study."

He laughed at that, the sound cut short as he shifted uncomfortably on the rock, wiggling his shoulders against the surface and wrapping an arm around his middle. When he finally spoke he sounded thoughtful, his voice uncharacteristically serious. "If I get my ass in gear," he said, "we could hang out at school."

My turn to laugh.

Our school was heavily stratified. There were the athletic guys who played football and basketball and the athletic girls who played soccer and field hockey. There were the pimply-faced nerds who played Dungeons&Dragons in the library during the lunch hour and the girls who wore short skirts and platform heels. There was me and my cluster of oddballs who kept to ourselves and followed the rules and didn't bother anybody or impress anybody. Then, finally, there were the kids who didn't really belong in school. Kids who looked a little older than they were, who wore ragged clothes and smoked in the parking lot and cursed at teachers. And their ringleader wanted to be *my* friend? In real life?

Ha.

"That's funny," I said, flopping onto my back and poking his ribs with my elbow. He hissed and pulled away like I'd actually hurt him. "Can you imagine what your friends would think if you started hanging out with the goody-goody preacher's daughter?"

"That I'm a lucky sonofabitch," he muttered angrily. Then, before I could work up the courage to ask what he meant by that, he sighed and shook his head. "Forget I asked. How's your mom doing?"

"Still sad," I shrugged, thinking of our strange breakthrough. I didn't want to jinx the progress by talking about it. "Let's talk about something fun. We're bumming each other out tonight."

"Okay," he said thoughtfully. "Best case worst case?"

My spirits lifted, and I nodded. *Best case worst case* was my favorite of the games we'd made up.

"I'll start" I said, squinting at the stars. "Best case scenario, Mr. Quinn gets fired for stealing school supplies and both of us actually survive eleventh grade civics class."

Nate laughed at that, the sound dripping over my nerves like honey. "Worst

40

case," he said, "his replacement is a crotchety old wind bag who keeps us after the bell."

"Best case, the crotchety old windbag and I form an unlikely bond and she mentors me and helps me with my college applications."

"Worst case, she convinces you to abandon your passion for science and study politics."

"Best case, I become a high level politician, get a security clearance and learn that aliens are real."

"Worst case, your first day on the job you piss the aliens off and they attack. Everyone's dead. Way to go, Madam President."

I laughed, humming thoughtfully as I tried to think of a way to spin the story. Nate was better at playing the best case side than me. He could make anything sound good. Then again, maybe I was just biased. "Best case," I said hesitantly. "I survive the apocalypse and finally have some peace and quiet."

"Worst case..." Nate trailed off, folding his hands behind his head. I shifted, resting my own head on his arm. Just because there wasn't much space on the rock. Not because I liked the way it felt. Definitely not. "Worst case," he said again, his tone brightening. "The quiet drives you crazy and you start talking to inanimate objects."

"Best case, my best friend's name is Melanie. She's a deflated basketball, mounted on a broomstick and she's a good listener."

He barked out a laugh again, the sound clipped, dying quickly as if he'd startled himself, and I had to fight not to press a hand to the warm feeling that settled into my belly. "Worst case, Melanie is an alien imposter. She's been using your crazed ramblings to learn about the human race."

"Uh, you lose. That's a best case," I said, laughing. "I got to meet an alien."

Nate laughed again, and we fell into silence.

"I'm sorry I didn't bring food," I said finally, exorcising the guilt that had been gnawing on me since he arrived. "I'll bring some tomorrow."

"It's okay, Alex," he said on a sigh, reaching across his body to poke me in the ribs. "I don't come here for the food."

CHAPTER FIVE

NATE

I woke just before the sound of the bell pierced through the hard, cold air of the classroom. Blinking away sleep, I peeled my cheek off the surface of my desk and, yawning, slipped out of my chair.

If I had to rank sleeping locations, the spot would be number one and Mrs. Parker's English class would be a close number two. Unlike Mr. Quinn, she never startled me awake for the sake of the class's entertainment. Unlike Trish and Ronnie and Paul and Deb, she never shook me awake to fend off a nightmare. Hell, she never woke me up at all. It was like she didn't even know I was there.

Slinging my mostly-empty bag over my shoulder, I trudged past her desk, giddy with excitement. Lunchtime. *Food.*

"Nathan, why don't you stay back a minute."

I bit back a groan, drawing to a halt by her desk. The rest of the students filed past me and I turned a glare at my teacher. "It's lunchtime," I growled warningly.

"I understand that, but the food can wait." She said it sweetly, completely unphased by my very clear, very real anger.

No, it damn well couldn't. If I missed stupid lunch I wouldn't see another square meal for twenty four hours. Why was that so hard to understand? Honestly, sometimes it felt like everyone I knew was conspiring to starve me to death.

Still, Mrs. Parker was the least awful teacher I had. I didn't want to piss her off.

"Fine," I bit out, slumping into a chair at the front of the classroom. She'd see it as attitude and disrespect, but mostly I just wanted to sit before my stupid knees gave out. God, I was fucking hungry. Maybe I could lift a couple power bars from the gas station down the street on my way home. The owner had only installed one camera and it pointed at the register, not the aisles.

Mrs. Parker didn't say anything about my disrespectful posture. She just stared at me, cocking her head to the side and narrowing her eyes like she was studying some kind of fascinating, otherworldly specimen. *Study away, lady. Whatever gets me out of here faster.*

"Stay here," she said sternly, pinning me to the chair with a glance as she stood from her desk. "I'll be back in two minutes. If you're gone when I get back I *will* come find you, so don't even think about leaving."

She left, and I contemplated dipping out. She'd be pissed but I could probably cut the lunch line and stuff some food in my face before she found me. That sounded like a lot of work, though. That plan involved some running or, at the very least, brisk walking. Too much effort.

Mrs. Parker returned less than two minutes later with a Styrofoam tray, which she set on the desk in front of me before returning to her seat.

"Lunch detention with Mr. Gideon down the hall has the meals delivered," she explained, nodding her head toward the tray. "We'll eat together while we talk, okay? That way we don't have to rush."

Suspicion crept up my spine, but the smell of the food wrapped around my head and made me stupid. It was all I could do to fumble the plastic spork free from its filmy wrapper, spilling the toilet-paper napkin and salt and pepper packets onto the desk, and use that instead of digging into the meal with my bare hands like the animal she probably thought I was.

"So, Nathan," Mrs. Parker said, pulling a paper bag from a drawer in her desk and meticulously arranging her own lunch in front of her. Sandwich in the middle. Plastic container of wilting apple slices to the left. Glass bottle of heavily-sweetened coffee drink to the right. "Why do you suppose I want to talk to you, today?"

I froze, mouth full of peas and instant mashed potatoes. Buying myself time, I chewed slowly and swallowed. Maybe if I was just honest she'd be impressed with my integrity and leave me alone.

"'Cuz I've been sleeping in class," I said with a shrug, like it didn't matter to me at all and it shouldn't matter to her either.

Mrs. Parker took a small bite of her sandwich and shook her head as she swallowed. "Nathan, the school year is almost over and you've been sleeping in my classroom since last August. If that was the problem we'd have had this discussion a long time ago. Any other theories?"

I shrugged. "Grades?"

She sighed, pulling a piece of paper out of a notebook on her desk and folding it open. I scraped the last of my mashed potatoes and peas off the plate, shoving them in my mouth, and started in on the shitty chicken tenders— little nuggets of salty, homogenized bliss.

"Yes, let's talk about grades," Mrs. Parker said, running a finger down the paper and studying me at intervals over the top of her glasses as she read. "You have a D minus in Mr. Quinn's civics class and an F in gym, which…" she trailed off, shooting me a quizzical look. "I didn't even know it was *possible* to fail gym." The look on her face almost made me laugh, and I decided I didn't completely hate Mrs. Parker. "You're wrapping up the year with a D plus in Spanish, and I know for a fact Ms. Martinez will do everything in her power not to give any student less than a C."

"Just a shitty student, I guess," I mumbled. This wasn't a new conversation. I'd had it with every teacher. Every guidance counselor. Every case worker. They'd threaten to hold me back like that meant something to me. I'd roll my eyes. Round and round we go.

My second-grade teacher had been a do-gooder like Mrs. Parker. One of those concerned, motherly types who decided she could tell the difference between a rough-housing bruise and a this-kid's-getting-smacked-around bruise. She was the first and the last teacher I'd trusted. My little confessional with Miss Lovett, and her subsequent conference with my folks, had earned me a month and a half of peace, followed by the mother of all beatings the day after summer vacation started.

Teachers are great. They have the power to change lives. There's just not much a single person, no matter how noble, could have done with a life as janky as mine. It was easier for all of us, especially me, to avoid the whole charade altogether.

"See, that's what I want to talk about, though," Mrs. Parker said, shoving the paper back in her notebook and picking up her sandwich again. I was out of food. All that was left was the little carton of chocolate milk and I slowly pulled open the top and took a sip, savoring it. *Heaven. Nirvana. Valhalla?*

"Listen, Mrs. Parker," I said, setting the milk down and shifting forward in my seat, bracing my elbows on the desk. "I've already got a guidance counselor. And a case worker. *And* a court-appointed therapist. *And* a parole officer. I don't need another font of wisdom spewing inspirational bullshit at me. I'm not gonna get my ass in gear because I don't give a shit about graduating and I don't give a shit about my bright future. I'm just here until they let me drop out. You seem like an okay lady, so I don't wanna be an asshole, but can you please bother someone else with your wannabe altruism?"

Mrs. Parker was a middle aged lady who was about as prim and unremarkable as they come. She had plain brown hair that she dumped so much hair spray in it didn't seem to move at all, even though she wore it down. Her shoes were ugly, blocky monstrosities, her clothes were a never-ending series of ugly old sweaters, and she brought her supplies to school every day in a tattered old canvas tote bag.

Mrs. Parker was as vanilla as they come, so it surprised me when she didn't balk at my tone or show any sign of hurt at my attitude. She just smiled and nodded, taking another bite of her sandwich.

"You're missing the point here, Nathan," she said, pulling out her gradebook and flipping through it with one hand. When she found the page she was looking for, she traced a nail down it, speaking without looking up. "I just want you to explain to me why the kid who can't even pass gym is ending the year with an A in my class and a B plus in Mr. Gideon's trig class. That's all."

Fuck

"Dunno," I said with a forced shrug, crumpling my empty milk carton in a fist and dropping it on the tray. "Maybe I've been cheating."

"Cheating takes work," Mrs. Parker said, shooting me a dubious look, and I caught myself almost laughing again. "So does intentionally failing an exam. I think you just took the easiest route here, and the easiest route was to pass."

"I don't see your point," I said, trying to keep the panic from my voice. I couldn't afford for people to be taking an *actual* interest in me. Mandated interest was fine, because it didn't take much to shrug off the attention. *Actual* interest? That meant scrutiny. Scrutiny I couldn't afford.

"The point is that I think you're an intelligent young man," Mrs. Parker said, closing her grade book. "I wanted to talk to you about signing up for AP Lit next year, and Mr. Gideon wants to recommend we shunt you into the calculus route now that your math requirement is satisfied, rather than let you use the free period for an elective."

"No," I shot at her, shaking my head hard before she'd even finished speaking. "That's fucking dumb."

"Listen, Nathan, I know you don't want to go to college." She held up a finger to stall my fierce argument that *fuck college,* I didn't even care about graduating high school. "And I know you plan on dropping out. But the fact remains you are stuck with us until the end of next year. Since you *have* to come here all day for at least another year, why not get something out of it?"

"It's just harder work," I argued, frowning at her. "What exactly do I get out of that?"

"Well, frankly, I think you'll enjoy my advanced placement class," she said. "You clearly like to read, and the books we'll tackle will be more nuanced than the ones we read this year. Plus, I'm the teacher," a smile quirked her lips, "so you can continue to be disrespectful and sleep in the back while I lecture. Provided, of course, that you also continue to do the readings and complete the essays.

"As for pre-calc, Mr. Nunez will most likely require you to stay awake. However, I want you to try, just for a second, to think about your future. Eventually you're going to escape whatever it is that's holding you back. I know you can't see it now, but someday you're going to want to have a life and a job.

45

This school's pre-calculus class is a community college credit, which means one less prerequisite if you ever decide you want to pursue an associate or a technical degree. Think of it as an opportunity to get for free what you may have to pay for down the road."

Poor Mrs. Parker didn't even know the strongest case she could've made for her argument. It had dawned on me as she spoke, rising like a chorus in the back of my mind so that I didn't really hear a word she said. I knew for a fact Alex was signed up for both of those classes next semester. I'd be guaranteed at least two blocks with her. I wouldn't be able to talk to her because of our deal, but I could still be with her. In real life.

Best of all, maybe being classmates could lead to something more. Maybe if she saw me in a class doing something other than sleep and fail to answer easy questions she'd give me more than a disappointed passing glance. Maybe she'd let us bring our clandestine friendship into the light.

"Fine," I grumbled, trying to hide my sudden enthusiasm for this stupid, stupid plan.

Mrs. Parker's face brightened as she balled up her empty sandwich bag and tossed it into the bin beside her desk. "Excellent! I'll talk to your guidance counselor this afternoon."

"Can I go, now?" I asked, fighting to keep my own face from showing her just how much she'd improved my day. My week. My life? Hell, maybe I was wrong about the limited reach of one person's kindness.

"In a minute," she said, pulling out her tote bag and unloading a stack of books onto the desk. "Take those with you."

I frowned at the books. "I thought we were done reading for the semester"

"We are. Those are for the summer."

"Like homework?"

"Try not to be so defensive, Nathan. They're just books. You can throw them all away if you like, although I recommend you don't. I think you'll enjoy them."

Good thing my backpack was empty, or I wouldn't have had room. I crammed the mini library inside and zipped the bag up, slinging it over a shoulder.

"Thanks for lunch," I grumbled. "Can I leave now?"

"Of course," she said at my already-retreating back. "Have a nice day, Nathan!"

I didn't answer her. Partly because I'm a rude piece of shit, but mostly because I didn't want her to hear the shit-eating grin that broke out on my stupid face the second I turned away.

.. .. ..

As always, Alex beat me to the spot. When I pushed into the clearing she was sitting on the rock, drumming her heels and chewing her lip, deep in thought. She nodded at me absently as I leapt over the creek to the island, then again to the cave beneath the oak. The cooler was stocked. A couple sandwiches, a small bag of chips, and a roll of Oreos. My girl treated me pretty good when she wasn't pissed off.

"What's on your mind?" I asked around a mouthful of ham-and-cheese delicacy, hopping up on the rock beside her.

Alex shrugged listlessly and I slung a friendly arm around her shoulder, pulling her against my side and rocking sideways until she bit out a laugh and pushed me away. Her hands struck old bruises and I damn near choked on my sandwich as I let her go.

"Okay, okay," I said, shoving her gently away. "Seriously, though, what's wrong?"

"Just home stuff," she said, shrugging and lying back. I finished chewing on my sandwich and brushed crumbs off my hands, spinning myself around on the rock so that I sat facing her.

"What home stuff?" I prodded. Alex always put up a fight and she always buckled with a little insistence. She carried the weight of her family's problems around with her all day, and it wore her down. I hated to see it, and nothing made me feel stronger than the quiet moments out here in the woods when she'd crack and confide in me.

"Just my mom…" she trailed off, shaking her head as she stared at the stars. "And Tommy."

"What's going on with Tom?" I asked, suddenly worried. As far as I was concerned, her parents could go fuck themselves. They sounded like shitty people to me and I only cared about their stupid problems insofar as they affected Alex. Tom, though, was a good dude. He got to me the same way Trish did. He laughed when he was happy and cried when he was sad and didn't understand the bad shit in the world.

For some reason, people like Tom and Trish seemed to bring out the predator in people. Their good was like gasoline to the flame of evil in stupid assholes like Tim and that little twat Freddy Whitehouse.

I saw by the hard set of Alex's jaw that my mental tangent was right on point. "It's that jerk, Freddy," she said through her teeth, her fists clenching at her sides. That made me a little conflicted. I hated to think of Tom being bullied, but pissed off warrior Alex had me shifting uncomfortably on the rock, praying my dumbass dick would settle down before it made things awkward.

"Have you tried talking to a teacher or something?" I asked, already plotting my own solution.

"They don't listen," Alex said. "His dad's on the school board. Everyone thinks he's perfect and Tom's not exactly a reliable witness."

"So what's your plan?" I asked, trying to hide a grin. I favored quick, bloody justice. Alex was more of a dish-served-cold kinda girl.

"I'm gonna follow Tom around between classes," she said, sitting up with fire in her eyes. "I'm gonna catch Freddy in the act and film it. That way I have proof. I think I might even pull Gemma into it and have *her* film while I confront him. That way if he hits me we'll have him bullying a disabled kid and punching a girl."

Freddy Whitehouse would punch my girl over my cold, dead body. Even the thought had my skin prickling with adrenaline and I hopped off the rock, suddenly desperate to blow off some steam.

"Hide and seek?" I asked, nodding at the woods. "The moon's out so the light is good for it..."

Is hide and seek kind of a juvenile game for two half-grown young adults to be playing? Sure. Is it fun as hell when your playground is the forest at night and your opponent can climb trees and burrow herself into nature's little caves and cubbyholes? Fuck yes, it is.

"Sure," Alex said, slipping off the rock. "I'll hide."

"Since you're having a bad day you get an extra head start," I said, smirking arrogantly at her. "I'll count to 100. You gotta stay in the boundaries, though. Don't go wandering off like last time. That's cheating."

"Are you gonna start counting or what?" She was bouncing on the balls of her feet, excitement bright on her face in the dim light of the waning moon. I grinned and hopped onto the rock, closing my eyes.

"100...99...98…" I heard a splash as she hopped the stream and the sound of rustling leaves as she scampered into the forest. "97...96...95…" I didn't bother memorizing the direction she'd run. She'd find a way to double back and wind up on the complete opposite side of our preset hide-and-seek arena. "94...93...92…" now what in the hell was I gonna do about that stupid fucking asshole Freddy?

.. .. ..

The moon hung high in the sky, casting sharp beams through the branches overhead and painting the forest floor in swathes of silver-blue. The air was damp and warm, with just a knife's edge of cool to warn of the changing season. That mild air felt thick as chowder as I gasped for air, legs churning, feet kicking up clumps of half-rotted leaves.

Alex squealed as she raced through the woods with me hot on her heels. I'd found her hiding place within ten minutes, but our rule was that if she managed to slip away and make it back to the rock without me tagging her, she'd still win.

"You're too slow!" I yelled between puffs of air, my lungs burning as I leaped over a fallen log in pursuit.

Alex didn't answer. She just huffed out a breathless giggle, lowered her head, and pumped her arms, bounding gracefully down the gently sloping hill toward the creak.

She wasn't too slow. She was definitely gonna win. I was built for throwing punches, not sprinting through the woods. My girl, on the other hand, was like a fucking gazelle— all long, slim legs and graceful power.

She tripped and went sprawling just before she reached the creek, and my heart jammed itself up into my throat.

"Al!"

I needn't have worried. She tucked herself into a ball as she fell, rolled a couple times through the leaves, and sprang back to her feet. She cleared the creek in one flying leap. By the time I reached the island, she was picking debris out of her hair, grinning like a maniac.

"You're... a fucking... cheater..." I gasped, bending over and bracing my hands on my knees as I fought to catch my breath.

"How am I a cheater?" she asked, glaring at me in mock indignation.

"You started running before I spotted you," I said, stepping closer and brushing a clump of dirt off her shoulder.

"No, I didn't."

"Yes, you did."

"We made eye contact!"

"You gotta wait 'til I say I see you."

"That's not the rule."

It wasn't. She was right, I was wrong, and I knew it. I just loved the string of steel that wove its way into her voice when she was pissed off. I loved the little spark of anger in her eye. I loved all of it. I loved *her*.

"Whatever. Are you okay? That was a hell of a fall." I stepped back, scanning her for signs of injury. I didn't see much except a small scrape on her right knee and a liberal coat of dirt on her right arm. Pretty standard for Alex.

She grimaced, pulling her foot up onto the rock and peering at the scrape on her knee. "I'm okay," she said, lowering her leg and stretching back out on the rock. "I think your poor bruised ego probably hurts more than my knee. Y'know... because you *lost*."

I made a vague noise of disagreement and hopped over to the buried cooler, pulling out the roll of Oreos and bringing them back to the island.

Alex pulled a cookie out of the package when I held it out, pulling it apart and biting into the creme-covered side while she handed me the plain one. I shoved it in my mouth, chewing thoughtfully.

"So," I said once my mouth was no longer full of cookie. "I talked to Mrs. Parker, today."

"The English teacher?" Alex asked, reaching into the package for another cookie.

"Yeah," I said, accepting the creme-covered half she handed to me. I didn't eat it, though. I'd wait another round and put two good ones together to make a double-stuffed. "She wanted to talk about my schedule next year."

"Do you have to retake her class or something?"

It was a reasonable question. She had every reason to believe I was an idiot, failing every class I took. Reasonable as it was, though, it stung a little and I took unreasonable pride in being able, just this once, to defy her expectations.

"Nope." I accepted the shitty half of the Oreo and tossed it in my mouth. "She wants to put me in AP Lit next year," I said around the cookie, "and Mr. Gideon is recommending me for pre-calc."

"What?" Alex shot upright, turning to look down at me with pride and confusion in her eyes. The pride had my ego inflating like a balloon. The confusion popped it. "I thought... how... what?"

"You're in those classes, right?" I asked, shaking off the pang of wounded pride and sitting up to rattle the Oreo package at her. She pulled one out and absently split it, handing me the good half. She didn't eat hers, though. She just held it in her hand and stared at me.

"Yeah?"

"So we'll have at least two classes together."

"Are you gonna stay awake?" she asked suspiciously, narrowing her eyes at me.

"Probably not," I said honestly, smushing my two cookie halves together and taking a bite, trying not to roll my eyes in pleasure. There wasn't a whole lot of joy in my life back then, but I'd have classified that moment as bordering on perfect. I had food, I had Alex, and I had value. Demonstrable, brag-worthy value. I was going to be an advanced placement student. A smart kid. The kind of guy she might smile at in the hallway. "I'm gonna do the homework, though. Maybe put a little effort into it."

"That's great!" Alex cried, reaching out and shoving my shoulder. Not exactly the celebratory gesture I'd prefer, but she did seem genuinely happy. Not disappointed in me for once, and that felt really fucking good.

"So, I was thinking," I said carefully, leaning back on a hand and studying her face, searching for the real answer because I knew Alex was too nice to let me down hard on purpose. "Since we're gonna be in the same classes, and since I don't really know how to try in school, maybe..." I swallowed hard, trying to work moisture into my suddenly-dry mouth. "Maybe we could study together?"

I saw the answer in the shutters that dropped over her eyes before they tore away from mine and focused intently on her hands. "We're just so different," she whispered, breaking her half of the cookie in half again and staring at the pieces. "I don't think you'd like me much in real life."

"Is that really what you're afraid of?" I asked, trying to keep the hurt from my voice. "How could you possibly think that, Al? You're my best friend."

"And you're mine!" she said, glaring up at me. "But… here. You're my best friend *here* and I'm not this person at school. I'm boring. I follow the rules. I wear skirts, Nate. *Skirts.*"

She said the word with so much disgusted incredulity, I laughed. "Yeah, I noticed that," I said. "I think they look… nice."

Nice? Really asshole? Nice?!

Al seemed as amused by my lack of verbal finesse as I was horrified by it.

"Gee, thanks," she said, but she offered me a weak grin and tossed a piece of Oreo into her mouth, chewing thoughtfully. "I'm serious, though. You know I wanna be friends with you in real life…"

No, I don't.

"… I just… I guess I don't want you to decide you don't like who I am during the day. Cuz then you won't like the night version, either."

"That's dumb." The words just spilled out of my mouth on their own, rude and unwieldy. Alex glared at me, and I guess I deserved it. I shrugged, trying to soften my tone. "It is though, Al. You're the coolest person I know. I love hanging out with you. And you're not two separate people. You just show different parts of yourself, depending on who you're with. I've always known you toe the line during the day. That doesn't make me like you less, it just makes me love it that much more that I get to be the person who sees you cut loose."

Shut the hell up, moron. I was getting perilously close to a dangerous degree of honesty so I clapped my mouth shut and watched her face as she puzzled over my words, praying she wouldn't read too far or accurately between the lines.

"Can I think about it?" she asked, and I wanted to say no. Alex was the queen of introspection. She'd go way too deep into her own head and wind up coming up with some theory that was as self-deprecating as it was outlandish. Or maybe she'd just muster up the courage to tell me the truth— that her reluctance had nothing to do with what I'd come to think of her and everything to do with how she already thought of me.

You're a fucking loser. An advanced placement delinquent. You think derivatives and Beowulf are gonna change that?

"Sure," I said reluctantly. "Get back to me."

CHAPTER SIX

ALEX

"Girl, you look like shit," Gemma muttered as I slid into my desk beside her in first period French.

Nate's proposition had kept me up well into the night, even after I returned home and slipped into bed. I'd stared at the ceiling for hours, trying to wrap my head around what he'd said and what the future might look like if we were more open about our friendship.

He'd made very clear that he wasn't at all ashamed of me. I wasn't going to waste time convincing myself that was a lie. I was good at reading people, even ones I didn't know very well and *Nate* I knew plenty well. He wasn't lying. He had no anxiety about the thought of his friends and the world at large knowing he was friends with me.

Unfortunately, liberation from that insecurity left me with the cold, hard knowledge that I was, in a sense, ashamed of him. Not of who he truly was, of course. With me he was sweet, smart, and funny. He was by far the greatest guy I knew.

It was the facade he presented to the world that had me worried. He was a jerk in real life. He cursed at teachers and slept in class and had everyone in the school so scared of him and his legendary rage that the crowded hallways parted like the Red Sea when he walked down them.

I, on the other hand, took pride in staying off the grid. My teachers liked me. My classmates either liked me or didn't think much of me at all. High school was just a stepping stone to somewhere better and I had to stay the course if I wanted to get where I was going.

How could I stay the course if everyone in school knew I was cavorting with the guy who threw punches with no more incentive than a wrong look? People would ask questions. Teachers would pay more attention to me and question

52

my work. Rumor would fly and, eventually, the unthinkable might happen… someone might carry it to my father.

Why did he have to be so insistent? What was so wrong with what we had? Sure, sometimes funny stuff happened at school and all I wanted was to find him in the crowd and share the joke. Sometimes I had a bad day and I didn't want to wait until the dead of night to talk to him about it. But those were little things— not worth risking discovery, and the loss of the much bigger, more important thing we had in the safety of the woods at night.

"Uh… hello?" Gemma craned across the aisle between our desks and waved her hand in front of my face. "Are you okay?"

"Yeah," I said, pushing her hand away and leaning over to pull my books out of my bag, setting them on my desk. "Yeah, I'm good."

I wasn't, though. I was distracted. I didn't absorb even a second of the French lecture, and I missed three entrances during concert band to the point where the conductor called me out, specifically.

"Do you need someone to help you count the rests, Ms. Winger?" he snapped, after drawing the whole band to a halt and glaring at me where I sat amidst the flute section.

"No, sir," I mumbled, trying to fight the red hot flush that crept into my cheeks as everyone turned to look at me.

I forced myself to stay tuned for the rest of band, but I drifted back into deliberation through lunch. Gemma eventually gave up talking to me.

"I dunno what's gotten into you," she huffed, pulling out a textbook and slapping it on the desk. "But if you don't want to talk about it I'll just leave you to your daydreaming."

Honestly, I *did* want to talk to her. She was smart and no-nonsense and she'd probably have some wisdom to offer. That's the problem with secret friendships, I guess. They exist in a vacuum, so when things go wrong there's no external force to bring back the equilibrium. The conflict just spins farther and farther out of control.

I was walking back to class after lunch, still lost in my head, when an office runner found me, holding a slip of blue paper in her hand.

"You need to go to the nurse's office," she said, winded from her sprint down the hallway. Did she know the term 'runner' was just a word? She didn't actually have to run.

"Thanks," I said, taking the paper as a sour ball of dread settled in my stomach. I only ever got called to the nurse's office when Tom had an incident. Everyone on the staff knew I was the only one who could calm him down during an episode.

Suddenly I was grateful to the runner for taking her job seriously. I spun, backpack smacking me in the back as I sprinted to the nurse's office to calm my hysterical brother.

Except Tommy wasn't hysterical. He sat calmly on the exam table, holding an ice pack to his face. When he saw me his face lit up and he lifted his free hand to wave.

"Hi, Aly!"

"Tom, what happened?" I asked, breathless, ignoring the adults scattered through the room.

"Nothing," Tom mumbled, his natural brightness dimming somewhat as he slumped, looking at the floor.

"Where is he?" I growled. "Where is that *jerk*, Freddy? None of you believed me when—"

"Miss Winger, please calm down." The vice principal was in the room. That couldn't be good. "Mr. Whitehouse's mother just picked him up and is taking him to the emergency room."

Oh, God. This was my nightmare. Tom was gentle as a lamb, but he was a big guy and he was a human being. There was always a chance he'd lash out if he was backed into a corner. I told him not to fight, though. I *told* him that'd make things worse.

"Tom," I whispered, stepping close and taking his hands, looking for torn up knuckles or some other sign that he'd been in a fight. I found nothing. "What happened?"

"It's okay, Aly!" Tom said cheerfully, tossing the ice pack aside and pulling me into his arms in a too-tight hug. I couldn't breathe, but I wrapped my arms around him and squeezed right back, relieved that he wasn't badly hurt and bore no evidence of having hurt anyone himself.

"What happened?" I asked, turning to face the adults in the room. Tom's in-school therapist stood by the door, the vice principal sat in a chair nearby, and the nurse lingered by her little cabinet of supplies.

"Well, Ms. Winger, that's what we'd like to know," the vice principal said, frowning at me. "Your brother doesn't seem to want to talk. Nor do Mr. Whitehouse or any of his friends. We were hoping you could convince Tommy, here, to tell us what happened."

There were very few things that fueled my ire to such an extent as to overwhelm my fierce need to stay under the radar.

My brother was one of those things.

"I'll tell you what happened," I said. "I came to you five times this year, telling you Freddy was picking on Tom. You didn't do anything to stop it. If my brother doesn't want to talk about what happened, I'm not gonna manipulate him. Now, can I please call our mom to come pick us up?"

"The school day is barely halfway complete, Miss Winger," the administrator said, giving me a stern look.

"You dragged me out of class for this, didn't you? Tommy's not going back to class today and neither am I. Let me call my mom. If you don't I'll make sure to tell her all about my repeated attempts to get your help with this *and* about your refusal to let me call her after my brother was *beat up* on your watch."

My mom wouldn't care about either, but these people didn't know that and didn't need to. All three adults exchanged a look before the vice principal sighed and shrugged.

"You can use my phone, hon," the nurse said, shooting me a small smile as she nodded toward the phone mounted to the wall by her cabinet.

Momma didn't work, so she was at the school to get us within twenty minutes. Tom and I had passed the time in silence. He just grinned and held the stupid ice pack to his face, and I sat on the edge of my chair, knee bouncing up and down in anticipation. I didn't really care about my mom arriving, I just wanted to get Tommy away from these jerk adults and figure out what had happened. Once I had all the facts I could work through how to deal with the violence and how to defend him if stupid Freddy Whitehouse decided to retaliate.

"What happened?" Momma asked the vice principal as she signed the requisite paperwork, offering a pale look of concern in my brother's direction.

"We don't know, ma'am. Tom's therapist found him and another student in a hallway during the lunch hour. There was clearly a fight and Mr. Whitehouse is on the way to the ER with his mother. I hope you understand, this is a matter of serious concern, and there will be a full investigation.

"I hope so," Momma said absently, turning to leave the office and nodding her head to indicate Tom and I should follow her. I hoped the vice principal would see her behavior as some kind of icy power play and not what it really was — disinterest. I wondered if she'd even registered the accusation against Tom.

"What happened, Tom?" she asked once we were safely on the road.

"Nothing," Tom said, smiling out the window.

Momma just sighed and kept driving and I wanted to scream. *You can't just ask once! You have to persist! He wants to trust you! He'll tell you everything if you just press him a little!*

I spent the rest of the day trying to goad the truth out of my brother. I plied him with food, I took him out to the spot, I promised him a new Lego set. Nothing worked. He just smiled, the bright effect offset by the crust of blood beneath his nose and the bruises working their way up the bridge and swelling by his eyes.

"It's okay, Aly," he kept saying, like that was somehow supposed to make me

55

feel better. "Freddy won't bother me anymore."

What the hell did you do to him? I wanted to scream, but Tom had enough accusation and distrust in his life. He didn't need it from me, too.

Daddy showed as little interest in Tom's appearance as Momma.

"What happened, Tom? Did you get in a fight?" he asked brusquely across the dinner table.

Tom just shook his head, grinning.

"You know what the Bible says, son. Violence gets you nowhere. It's what bullies want, is to rile you up. In the long term, it's better to turn the other cheek."

"What, so he's supposed to just let himself get beat up?" I asked in spite of myself, scowling at my father.

He glared right back, and I felt my courage whither under the powerful wash of disappointment emanating from him. My father never had to get angry. He just got disappointed, and it always felt like the whole universe agreed with him. Like god herself thought you had failed.

"Don't argue with me, Alexandra," he ordered, and I shut my mouth and lowered my gaze to my plate. "Tom, you know better than to fight."

"I didn't fight," Tom said, frowning.

"The school said there will be an investigation," Momma offered, setting her silverware down and taking a sip of wine. Glass number three if I wasn't mistaken. "The boy he beat up is the son of a school board member. Freddy Whitehouse."

"I didn't beat anyone up," Tom said, turning his frown to me, tears in his eyes.

"Jack and Millie Whitehouse are in my congregation," Daddy said with a nod, ignoring my brother. "I'll talk to them on Sunday. See if we can resolve this quietly."

Tom's face was growing blotchy with frustration, his fork *tap tap tapping* in a staccato rhythm against his plate. I excused us from the dinner table and dragged him up to my room to color while I tried and failed to concentrate on my homework until bedtime.

I'd all but forgotten the stress of Nate's proposition by the time the house went quiet that night. I scrambled out of bed as soon as my father's weight shifted the floorboards on his walk to bed. Hastily, desperate to talk to my friend, I pulled on my dirty old shorts and ragged t-shirt, slipping my feet into sneakers and pulling my hair into a messy ponytail.

It was a rarity that Nate beat me to the spot, but there he was when I arrived, sprawled on the rock and staring at the sky. I leapt over the stream as he sat up, leaning back on his hands.

"'Sup, Al?!" he said, grinning brightly. The moon was waning, and every night it was harder to see him and easier to see the stars above.

"I had a crazy day," I breathed, winded from my jog through the woods. I slipped up onto the rock beside him, flopping onto my back and gathering the scattered stars together into my mind, soaking up the steady peace they always offered.

"Wanna talk about it?" It wasn't a question so much as a prompt. Unlike my mother—unlike *me*, I realize in retrospect—Nate was good about pressing until he got an answer. He seemed to understand that the truth was just below the surface, begging to be set free.

That night, the truth was already bubbling over. I didn't even fight it.

"Tommy got in a fight!" I said without preamble, throwing my arms out to my sides as I stared at the sky, finally letting my bottled-up stress and disbelief erupt. "Stupid Freddy Whitehouse cornered him and Tommy beat him so bad he had to go to the ER!" My heartbeat thundered in time with my frantic words. I'd always understood that I would be Tom's caretaker once my parents got too old. It was a burden I was happy to carry, but times like now the worry rose up like floodwaters.

There was a long pause, during which I took deep, steadying breaths to try to calm myself down. I'd always taken a tentative comfort in Tom's gentle nature. He'd gotten so big in his teens, it started to scare me. Such a big guy with so little common sense and emotional maturity was a scary thing. I lived in fear of the day he snapped and hurt someone just because he didn't know better. Now that day had come. How well could I care for him if violence became part of his pathology? Would I have to put him in a home?

"I don't think he'd do that, Al," Nate said, the words low and calming. They washed like a warm breeze over my frazzled nerves, and my body reacted on its own. My breath calmed, my heart slowed, and the tremor of panic that gripped my muscles eased. My mind, however, knew better than my stupid body.

"You don't know that. You don't even know *him*," I moaned, rubbing my hands over my face. "He's a big guy, Nate, and Freddy's been tormenting him for years."

"Tom wouldn't hurt a fly," Nate said, again so slow and easy even my soul went the way of my body, soothed by the gentle caress of his voice.

"You don't know that," I said, but my own voice was limpid and drained—not even an ounce of fight. I wanted to believe he was right. So badly.

"Sure I do." He sat up straight, clasping his hands in his lap as he leaned forward, studying the creek. "Me and Tom go way back, Alex. We took shop together freshman year. We're friends."

I lowered my hands from my face. Tom had taken shop for half a year in a well-intentioned but ill-fated attempt to see if he would handle hands-on learning better than classroom skills. He'd never mentioned Nate to me, which didn't surprise me. He didn't tell me about all his friends. What surprised me was that *Nate* hadn't told me. He knew Tom was my brother.

"Why didn't you tell me?" I asked, sitting up so I could read him better in the darkness.

He shrugged one shoulder, glancing at me before looking back at the water. When he spoke, there was a tinge of guilt in his voice. "I knew if I told you, you'd ask me not to talk to him," he said. "I know that's fucked up, I just..." he trailed off, shaking his head. "I like Tom. He's a good guy. He needs friends who can look out for him. I figured it'd be easier to keep it secret than to convince you it was okay."

I opened my mouth to tell him that was stupid, but clapped it right back shut, because it wasn't stupid. He was dead on. I would have pushed back on it. Hard.

"So you're secret friends with my brother," I stated flatly, trying not to be annoyed. "How many secret friends have you got?"

His lips quirked up in a smile I could barely make out in the darkness. "Just the two of you."

Most of Nate's secrets were packed down so deep you'd need a map and a shovel to excavate them. The core of him, back then, was a suppurating, burning mass of secrets and pain, buried so deep between bravado and responsibility and stubborn strength you'd never even know it was there.

Sometimes, though, a little snippet of truth found its way to the crust. I'd tap the surface and just enough honesty would slip out to convince me I'd unearthed it all. That I knew exactly who he was.

I chewed my lip, studying the side of his face as puzzle pieces slowly fell into place.

"Hey, Nate?"

"Yeah?"

"Did Tom beat up Freddy?"

"No."

"Who did?"

He set his jaw and didn't answer, but he also didn't pull away when I reached out and tugged his hand into my lap. I brushed my thumb over the raw skin on his knuckles and leaned into him, resting my head on his shoulder.

"You shouldn't have done that," I said. "Freddy will tell his dad, eventually."

"I know," he sighed. "I'll tell the vice principal what happened, tomorrow. I just wanted a chance to talk to you, first. Once they find out they'll suspend me, and once they suspend me, my... I won't be coming around here for a few nights. I didn't want you sitting out here all pissed off without being here to defend myself."

My heart clenched in my chest. "Why the hell did you do it?" I asked.

"I told you, I like Tom," he said, tipping his head so it rested on mine. It was a platonic gesture. We'd sat like this a thousand times. For some reason, though, it felt different that night. The warm, comfortable energy that always wove itself around us had come alive. Fueled by the little drop of truth, it sparked and danced in the air, prickling my skin wherever we touched.

"That's it?" I asked, pulling away and looking up at him. Who needed the stars when I had his eyes glinting at me like that in the darkness? "You're gonna get in so much trouble," I said with a groan, thumping my forehead against his shoulder before pulling back and glaring at him.

"It's not a big deal, Alex," he said. "I get in fights all the time, you know that. Only difference is that this time I got to fight for you. Freddy and his little minions aren't gonna fuck with Tom anymore, and I don't have to worry about you getting your little ass handed to you in a quest for justice."

God, he made me so mad.

I scowled up at him, watching the hard lines of his face ease into a cocky grin. He knew he was pissing me off and he loved it.

"I would have been fine," I growled through gritted teeth, nevermind that I was still holding his hand, cradling it in my lap like it was mine to hold and protect and cherish. And why was that so crazy? I could love him and want to hit him at the same time, couldn't I?

"You would've gotten yourself into trouble," he said, and I saw the same fierce mixture of love and annoyance in his eyes that coursed through my veins.

"You're a chauvinist," I sneered up at him, leaning closer and injecting as much vitriol into the words as I could muster.

"I wouldn't have to be if you weren't such an idiot," he hissed back, bending to meet my fury until we found ourselves nose to nose in the darkness.

That energy — so familiar and yet so foreign in its intensity — crackled in the scant centimeters of air between us. I felt more than saw Nate's free hand shift, rising up to hover just beside my face. Each tiny hair on my body rose, as if pulled by a magnet toward his touch. His eyes were locked on mine, the whites glistening in the dim light, and his unspoken question roared with the rush of blood in my ears.

He gave me a choice, in that moment. In those long, tense seconds I stood before a fork in the road. Down one path lay a stable, happy life— contentment and a long to-do list full of check marks. College, *check*. Career, *check*. White wedding, *check*. Babies, *check*. PTA meetings, soccer practice, grandbabies, world travel, *check check check check*. Dappled sunshine played on the packed dirt of that path and birds chirped cheerfully in the trees that lined its long, straight length.

Then there was the second path— dark and narrow, winding its way through dense foliage that captured the moonlight, holding it hostage before it had a chance to hit the ground. Lightning and thunder cracked over the second path, and the ground was treacherous and muddy. It was beautiful and wild and dangerous. It sang to me— a sad and powerful song that skipped straight past my ears and braided itself with my spine, sending shocks of pure, electric passion straight to the core of me. I couldn't see the future down that path, but as I stared at the darkness my list of goals and to-dos fluttered to the ground beside me, forgotten.

I had a choice. He gave me a choice. So I suppose everything that came after was, in a sense, my fault. I could have gone down that first path. I could have lived the rest of my life in the light, with the reins grasped tight in my hands and both feet planted firmly on solid ground. I could have been content.

Instead, I closed my eyes, pulled in a breath that smelled like soap, sweat, and comfort, and surrendered myself to the darkness. At the time I could not even have fathomed what that darkness contained. I could not have foreseen the agony I would encounter on that path, nor could I comprehend the sheer magnitude of the passion and devotion that would carry me to its end.

It was momentous. It was pivotal. My whole life came to a screeching halt in that split second when his hand came to rest against the side of my face and his lips brushed over mine.

My first kiss.

Even knowing what came next— even knowing what wrenching, treacherous existence that kiss begat— I would do it again. A thousand times over, I would go back to that moment and let him kiss me— let him drag me down the dark and winding path.

See, the first path might be sunny and simple. The first path might make sense. But the second path? That's where *he* is and that's where he'll always be— strong and sure in the chaos, unflinching, matching every evil with ferocious good and every pain with steady comfort. I'd weather every storm, endure every agony, and live every moment of my life in darkness just for the warmth of his hand in mine and the feel of him standing beside me.

I guess that's love.

CHAPTER SEVEN

NATE

Maybe it was just my imagination— bewildered delight leaking into my physical senses— but she tasted sweet.

She smelled the same as she always did. Sweat and dirt overlayed on the crisp remnants of the perfume she wore during the day. Her skin had the same perfect, silky texture that it always had when we touched, but it felt warmer. More electric.

I wanted to consume her. I wanted to gather up every ounce of what she was and claim it as my own until the end of time. I wanted to pull her so close there wasn't a breath of air between us. I wanted to leave my mark on her so everyone would know— *she's mine.*

But this was *Alex.* Strong Alex. Sweet Alex. Fierce Alex. *Innocent* Alex.

So, instead, I cupped the soft, warm curve of her cheek in my palm and hovered a hair's breadth away. The last thing I wanted was for the moment to end before it began, but I had to give her the chance. I had to give her a choice. So I waited with baited breath, and when she surrendered I felt it down to my toes. She didn't move a muscle, but the air between us shifted, from a tense, crackling energy to a magnetic pull.

Even so, I was slow. I was gentle. I was everything that, in truth and reality and every place but her arms, I am not. I brushed her lips with mine and she sucked in a breath. I felt her shock and I wondered if she shared my disbelief— not that it was happening but that it had taken this goddamn long. Because, now that we were here, I found it hard to imagine a world in which we'd ever been elsewhere.

Her brisk inhalation seemed to draw me in, and I deepened the kiss, letting my hand slip from her cheek up into her hair, pulling her closer. When her lips parted again, I let my tongue stray into her mouth. A polite intrusion, compared to what I truly wanted. An anxious, skittish part of me waited for the daytime version of my girl to show up. I was ready for her to push me away and say it went too far.

Instead, she met me halfway and explored right back. She was a little inept and a little awkward, and somehow so much better than every girl I'd ever kissed before. Because she tasted sweet. Because her fumbling foray into frenching made me smile in a way that seemed to come from the center of my chest. Her tongue didn't know what the hell it was doing, but it was the same tongue that lashed at me when I was an idiot and rattled off the constellations in the perfect stillness of the night.

I should have stopped it when we both pulled back for air. It was her first kiss. I knew because if some other guy had kissed her she'd have told me and I'd have spent the rest of my life holding back the urge to beat him to a bloody pulp. No, this was her first. *I* was her first, and because of that I should have let it rest. I should have let it sit and simmer and soak in that I'd stolen that aspect of her innocence. I should have held her hand while I walked her home and hugged her goodbye and told her thank you.

I should have been a gentleman.

But I was neither gentle nor a man. I was a mean, ill-mannered kid. A boy, who finally had his hands and his mouth on the girl he had loved for as long as he could remember.

I was not a gentleman.

When we pulled away to breathe, I didn't move off the rock and give her distance. I pulled my right hand from her hair, my left hand from her grip, and slipped both beneath her, twisting as I lifted, pulling her in my lap.

My ribs twinged from Tim's fists, my hands hurt from Freddy's stupid face, and my head ached from hunger, but I shut out the little annoyances. I was hungry and sore every day of my life. *This* was new. *This* was special. *This* deserved my undivided attention.

You know that phrase '*like putty in my hands?*' I feel sorry for the guy who coined it because he was missing out. Alex wasn't putty. She wasn't some inanimate object for me to shape and mold. She was a living, breathing creature who conformed to me of her own free will. She fit against me so naturally it didn't matter that she didn't know what she was doing and I couldn't think my way around my need for her. She just fit— against my body and into my life— perfectly.

Her arms went around my neck, her chest pressing against mine as she pulled herself to me, raising her face. She didn't speak but she begged for more with those pink lips— swollen and parted in anticipation— and her sweet blue eyes which fluttered closed— entirely trusting.

I kissed her again, sealing my mouth over hers as if, through that contact alone, I could pull every ounce of good out of her body and into mine. I kept my left hand on the small of her back, holding her against me, but I let the right roam. I brushed my fingertips over her cheek once more, plowed my hand through the tangled mess of her hair, and followed the length of her spine through her shirt. Daytime Alex probably would have slapped me when I squeezed her ass, but this one just giggled against my mouth and shifted in my lap.

Her hands were busy, too, although they stayed safely away from the one part of me that most needed her attention. It felt like she was trying to touch every inch of me that she could reach. Her fingers combed through my hair, raked down my back, and clung to my waist with the same desperation I felt as I explored every inch of her mouth, drinking in the sweet, perfect taste of her.

Everything about that kiss was familiar. It doesn't make much sense, because it was her first kiss and my first time kissing anyone I really cared about. It should've been earth shattering and novel, but it felt more like a release of tension. Like we were magnets, held apart for lifetimes, and in that moment we finally snapped back together like the universe intended.

Even when Alex stopped the kiss, we didn't part. Neither of us wanted to. She sat there in my lap, her arms once more linked around my neck, her face scant inches from mine. I held her, my hands plastered against the small of her back. I don't know when they found their way beneath the hem of her shirt, but there they were, skin on skin, and she didn't seem to mind.

Our eyes locked in the darkness, and Alex cocked her head slightly and licked her lips.

"Thanks," she whispered, like I'd done her some kind of favor.

I cleared my throat. "Anything for you," I told her, hoping she'd think I was making some kind of joke. I wasn't quite ready for her to know the truth— that I truly would do anything for her. Die, kill, lie, kiss, steal, fight... leave. Whatever she needed, I was hers. But we were kids, and the intensity of what I felt would probably freak her out, so I just smirked like everything was a joke. "It was a burden, though. Next time, try to ask a little less of me, okay?"

Alex scowled, smacking me in the back of the head and immediately erasing the effect by dropping a gentle kiss on my cheek. "You're a jerk," she murmured.

"You're a pain in the ass," I returned. "Now get off me before my legs fall asleep. I gotta walk you home so I can get back."

"I've told you a billion times, you don't have to walk me home," Alex said, sliding off me and standing with her hands on her hips. I followed, thanking whatever gods might be listening that it was dark enough she couldn't see how ready my body was to finish our little escapade. Walking was... let's say difficult.

"And I've told *you* a billion times, I don't give a shit," I said, following her across the creek and onto the game trail we both knew by heart. We'd walked it so many times it was beaten down to the point that we could walk abreast. As I drew even with her, Alex reached out and took my hand. We'd held hands before, but that night it felt heavier. Like we were signing our names at the bottom of a contract we'd drawn up when we kissed. I clasped her hand in mine and swore to myself I'd never let go.

We walked in silence for a while, enjoying the still night air. You don't know this if you haven't spent much time in the woods, but it's quieter on darker nights. It's not that there isn't movement. You still have crickets chirping and frogs croaking and owls rustling the branches overhead. It's just a little more subdued. Like the dark is a blanket, resting over everything, smothering it.

"So," Alex said, as we drew near to the edge of the treeline. I could see the lights of her neighborhood through the trees and, as it always did, my stomach began to churn at the thought of parting with her. I never really knew when I'd see her again. It could be less than a day. It could be a week. Everything depended on the place I lived, and that was chaos— by definition unpredictable.

"So...?" I implored. She'd trailed off, her footsteps slowing, drawing us to a halt at the woodline.

"So we should probably talk about what just happened," she said, turning to face me but keeping hold of my hand.

"Should we?" I asked. "I thought you enjoyed it."

"I did," she said quickly.

"Me too. You wanna do it again sometime?"

"Well yeah." She nodded, but still looked uneasy.

"So what's the problem?" The anxiety on her face took a pin to my inflated heart, and I felt it begin to collapse.

"What about our deal?" she asked. She was facing me, but she turned her head and stared at her house, worry etching deep lines in her forehead.

"Hey," I whispered, taking her chin in my free hand and turning her face toward me. There were tears in her eyes, and I hated that I'd caused them. "You worried about your dad?"

Alex nodded, still not looking me in the eye. "It's not you," she said hoarsely, and I appreciated the lie. "I don't want you to think it's you. He'll just... he'll be so disappointed and he'll find a way to keep us apart."

"So we'll keep our deal," I said with a shrug. It didn't matter. It shouldn't matter. I wouldn't let it matter. "The only difference is I'm not your secret friend, anymore."

Alex just frowned.

"I'm your secret *boy*friend."

I smiled when her face split into a grin and she threw herself forward, wrapping her arms around my neck and kissing me again. I locked my hands behind her back and held her against me as she stood on her tiptoes to deepen it. That kiss was short but it was just as powerful as the first. It set off the same crazy fireworks at the base of my spine. Would every kiss with her be like this?

We were both breathless when I pulled away from her with a frustrated groan.

"You're a fast learner," I croaked. "But we gotta save some progress for next time."

Alex grinned and pulled away without a word, leading the way through the maze of her neighborhood's shared backyard. When we reached the tree beside her house I hefted her up onto the lowest branch, watching with clenched, sweaty fists as she clambered up to her window and slipped inside.

After her window slid shut, I turned and made my way back across the yard to the sanctity of the trees. I followed the same worn-down path back to the spot and then past it to my neighborhood. I clambered through my own window, stripped off my shoes and jeans, and slid beneath the covers. It was the same pattern I always followed. Nothing was different. And yet, somehow, everything had changed.

.. ..

I'd always hated summer break. For most kids I guess summer meant a magical three months of adventure and freedom. Pool parties and Disney trips and camp. Sleeping late, cartoons, and lazy days eating popsicles. That kind of crap.

For me, though, summer always just meant more stress. Work instead of school. More overlap where the kids and I were at home with our foster parents. High temperatures and higher tempers. Worst of all: no school lunches.

The summer before my senior year, though, wasn't so bad.

I did what I told Alex and went to the vice principal the day after we kissed. I told him it was me who beat up Freddy Whitehouse. I told them a version of the truth, wherein I stumbled upon Freddy and his buddies giving Tom a hard time. I just left out of the part where I'd been following the kid around all day waiting for an excuse to confront him.

They brought Tom in and he vouched for my story, but it didn't make much of a difference. I was suspended for a week. Freddy somehow escaped with three days of detention. Not that it bothered me, much. Suspension just meant more time to myself. Plus, Freddy might have escaped punishment from the school but he didn't escape justice. His face was a puffed-up mess and I knew he and his buddies would leave Tom alone as long as I was around.

My foster dad kicked my ass when he found out, but I didn't mind that, either. Nothing got to me, that week. I had the taste of Alex on my lips and her scent on my skin no matter how many times I showered or brushed my teeth. I was invincible.

After my suspension was over there were only two weeks left in school and I drifted through those in a happy haze. Although my deal with Alex remained intact, the energy between us shifted. She no longer averted her gaze when she saw me. Our eyes would lock across the room and her skin would flush pink, her lips would pinch together, and I knew without asking that the shadow of my kiss followed her around the way hers followed me.

When the school year ended I went to work with a kind of fervor. Years before, as soon as it was legal, I'd secured a job at an auto shop within walking distance of my foster parents' house. In the beginning it was just stupid shitwork the older guys didn't wanna do. I cleaned bathrooms and swept floors and crap like that. After a while, though, some of the mechanics took me under their wing. They let me tag along and help on the simpler jobs. By the time I turned sixteen I was doing the simpler jobs on my own and helping out with more complicated work. By the time I turned seventeen I was doing complicated jobs by myself.

The shop's owner, Red Mattis, was a pudgy older guy who chain smoked Marlboro Reds and sported a shiny bald patch that was perpetually smeared with engine grease. He was gruff and brusque, but he was a good guy. He worked on the floor with the rest of us and had a strict code of honor that built a loyal customer base. Red treated his workers well and would never lie to a customer or charge them for something they didn't need.

He didn't pay me a mechanic's salary, because I wasn't a mechanic. He did, however, offer to pay for a technical degree after I graduated high school and to keep me on in the interim. He gave me as many hours as he could and often showed up at work with plastic containers of leftovers he claimed he would never eat. He got mad when I got suspended and studied my black eyes and busted knuckles like they left a bad taste in his mouth. Idiot that I was, it was a few years down the road before I finally recognized the concern for what it was.

Red was a good guy, but his charity grated on me and I'd never seriously considered his offer to pay for school and keep a job for me after high school. I'd never seriously considered *anything* after high school. All I knew was that I wanted out of the life I was living. So I worked my job and saved my pennies and didn't bother to ask myself what I'd do when I finally turned eighteen and escaped. I knew I wanted to keep looking after my foster siblings but I never asked myself how I'd do it. I knew I wanted to follow Alex but I never wondered if she'd really appreciate a homeless, jobless loser following her around the green lawns and storied brick buildings of her college campus.

That night we kissed, though, it was like a veil lifted. All of a sudden I saw my future and, let me tell you, that shit was bleak.

So I decided to try. It was too late to scrape together the grades to graduate on time, but I resolved to at least obtain the requisite knowledge to pass the GED. I picked up extra hours at Red's shop to make money enough for an apartment. I spent every free minute devouring the books Mrs. Parker had given me. I pulled my boss aside and told him I was interested in that technical degree.

The summer before my senior year was a chaos of tension and hope. Every day meant long hours on my back or hunched over an engine block, covered in grease and dreaming of something better. Every evening meant finding enough food for the kids and piecing together a semblance of normalcy for them before they grew too old to realize it was fabricated. Every sunset meant lying in my bed in tense wakefulness while I waited for our legal guardians to stumble off to bed.

Every night meant bliss. Sheer, unadulterated heaven. I spent many long hours stretched out on the rock with the weight of Alex's head on my shoulder, following her finger to the stars and listening to her voice as she talked about dark matter and quarks and the Big Bang Theory. I chased her through the woods playing stupid little kid games, listening to her giggle, and I tasted the sweat on her skin when I finally caught her.

We pushed the boundaries of Alex's comfort zone that summer and I remember every anniversary like it was yesterday.

On May 10th 2001, the last day of school, I groped her boobs through her shirt.

On May 21st it was raining, so we huddled in the cave beneath the tree and made out for the duration of the time we both had to spare. No constellations, no games in the woods, no distractions. Just her and me and the sound of the raindrops hitting the water of the creek. Alex was straddling my lap and I remember the silky smoothness of her skin and the hard tone of her muscles as I ran my hands up her thighs. I remember her shuddering in pleasure and shifting on my lap. I remember slipping my hands past the hem of her shorts and cupping her bare ass, pulling her tighter against me.

On June 10th she reached between us and, cautious and hesitant and experimental, finally gave a little through-the-pants attention to the part of me that had gone too long neglected.

On June 23rd we spread a blanket out on the sand so we could admire the sky and each other at the same time without tumbling off the rock. She tried to show me a star cluster she'd read about earlier that day. I said she was making shit up. She told me I was being deliberately obtuse. I rolled over and kissed her until she forgot why she was angry. She gripped my shirt and pulled me closer. I snuck a hand to her shorts and released the button. She didn't stop me.

I moved slowly, sliding my fingers down, feeling the smooth surface of her stomach give way to a small thatch of soft, curly hair. Alex released her grip on my shirt and her hands found their way to my sides, fingers digging into my ribs.

"You okay?" I murmured breathlessly, pulling back to look down at her. She swallowed hard, eyes locked on mine, and nodded.

With a groan of relief, I bent to kiss her, letting my fingers continue to explore. I thought I might've died and gone to heaven when I slid one finger deeper and Alex gasped, arching against me. I wish I could say I brought her to a swift and epic orgasm, but I was still young and selfish and hadn't yet discovered how to coax bliss out of her with just my fingers. Not to say I didn't figure it out quickly, but June 23rd isn't that anniversary.

On July 5th we lay on the rock and listened to late-night fireworks, no doubt set off by drunken patriots. We listened to sirens sing through the night, no doubt carrying drunken patriots minus a few blown-off digits.

"It's Independence Day," Alex said, rolling to her side so that her chest was pressed against my ribs, throwing a leg over mine to hold herself up. She rested a possessive hand on my stomach, and I could feel the heat of each finger through my shirt.

"Technically it's the fifth," I said around the thick lump of arousal in my throat. "It's past midnight."

"Do you have to be a jerk all the time?" Alex asked, resting her head on my chest. Her hair tickled my chin and filled my nose with the heady scent of her.

"Yeah, I do," I answered, trailing my fingertips over her upper arm. "It's kinda my gimmick."

Alex sighed dramatically. "Can we just pretend it's still Independence Day?" she implored.

"Sure, why?"

"'Cuz I wanna feel free." The wistfulness in her tone leveled me. She lived in a prison, just like me. Sometimes I forgot that, because her prison looked so different from the one I knew. I knew her parents didn't hit her. Her father didn't molest her. There was food at her table three times a day and snacks in her cabinet if she got hungry between. I suppose because of those basic luxuries I often slipped into the assumption that her life was sunshine and roses.

It wasn't, though. Food and safety aren't the only things a person needs to survive. Alex didn't have love. Not from her parents. Perhaps, once upon a time, things had been good, but her father cared more for his parish than his family and her mom was tailspinning. And despite their shoddy parenting, neither of them seemed to want to let her live. She was trapped in a cage with apathetic guards who should have had the decency to either love her or let her go but did neither.

"Alright, you got it," I said, squeezing her with my arm. "It's still Independence Day. What are you gonna do with your freedom?"

I felt the hesitation in every line in her body. She was nervous, and nervous Alex usually meant good things for me. *Please, please, please be ready,* I thought, trying to keep my breathing steady. Every night since we'd first kissed I left the house with a condom in my pocket. Just in case.

"I kinda wanna get naked," Alex said, her voice tinny and stifled by the humid summer air. Her head was still tucked up under my chin so I couldn't see her face and she couldn't see mine. Good thing, too, because all of a sudden I was grinning like a maniac.

"Okay," I said hesitantly. "That's it, just get naked?"

Soaring hope.

"Yeah!" Alex popped up on an elbow, smiling down at me with excitement all over her features. "It's hot. I wanna get naked and play in the creek."

Crashing disappointment.

"Well don't let me stop you," I said, shoving her off me playfully. "Get to it."

"I'm not gonna do it alone," she said, planting her hands on her hips. When she did that it was a sure sign I was about to lose an argument.

"What, so I gotta do it too?"

"Uh huh!"

"And in return I get to look at you, right? I don't wanna do some bullshit where we keep our backs turned. That's no fun."

In answer, Alex reached down to the hem of her shirt and ripped it off with a flourish, tossing it onto the rock. I swear, my jaw hit the sand. She was wearing a plain white bra and dirty old cargo shorts, her hair in a messy ponytail. Moonlight didn't gleam off her skin, it just seemed to settle there, making her glow.

"Now you," Alex said, gesturing at me as if unaware that she'd just stopped my world from spinning.

"Uh…" I cleared my throat. "Not yet. I'm not wearing a bra you know, so you gotta… it wouldn't be fair if you were still wearing that."

Her eyes held mine as she reached behind her and unclasped the bra and, with a small motion, tossed it onto the rock with her shirt. "Better?" she asked, placing her hands back on her hips. She was still a little nervous. I could tell by the set of her jaw and the way her throat worked as she swallowed. If you didn't know her like I did, though, you'd think she'd done this a thousand times.

Unable to conjure my voice, I tugged my shirt over my head, praying like hell it was too dark for her to make out the smattering of fading, yellowish bruises that decorated my rib cage. Fortunately, they seemed to escape Alex's notice. She nodded, a small smile tugging up the corners of her lips as her fingers unclasped the button of her shorts. With a single, smooth motion she shimmied them down her legs and kicked them off to the side.

Throat dry, dick straining, I fumbled with my belt and shoved my jeans down, kicking them over by her shorts.

There we stood, staring. I stared at plain white underwear and she stared at faded blue boxers, both of which probably came in a value pack from the dollar store. We were so ordinary. Just two kids in the heart of America, standing in a creek beneath a pale moon, wearing store-brand underwear and a gleam of sweat from the humid summer air. Just two kids falling deeply, madly, irresponsibly in love.

What a cliché.

"Count of three?" Alex asked, and I heard a quaver in her voice and I guess I'm a sick son of a bitch, because the fact that she was nervous turned me on all the more.

"Sure," I managed. "One…"

"Two…" Alex whispered.

"Three," we said together.

That was it. My eyes ate every inch of her perfect body. The soft mounds of her breasts and the smooth curve of her hips. The small patch of hair between her legs and ten small toes with perfectly painted nails curling in the sand.

Fireworks went off overhead and for a moment she stood in spectacular relief, blue and white light flashing on her skin. Then we were plunged back into darkness. I'll hold that moment in my mind until the universe collapses. July 4th by Alex's standard, July 5th by mine. Independence Day: the first time I saw my girl naked.

July 13th was Alex's seventeenth birthday. I didn't have a lot of money and I was a miser with what I did have, but I shelled out $50 bucks for her. I asked Red what I should get my girlfriend for her birthday and he told me chicks love jewelry. I went to a jewelry store but the sight of me made the clerk grow pale and I guess that makes sense. The only way I was walking out of that place with any merchandise was if I stole it.

It made me a little sick to get my perfect girl a gift from Wal-Mart, but it was all I could afford. I stalked the case for ten minutes, trying to find something suitable but everything seemed dumb. What would *my* Alex do with a fake diamond bracelet? What would she do with some gaudy gold earrings? Nothing looked right. Not for her.

I was starting to lose hope when I found the small card on a turntable sitting by the display case. In retrospect, I think the brand was for kids. There were little earrings shaped like dolphins and necklace sets with Best/Friend written on two halves of a heart.

At the bottom of the turntable, though, I found a card with the two tiny silver studs shaped like stars. I picked it off the rack, staring at the stars glinting at me and the price sticker on the corner of the card. $35. That much money for two stupid little earrings meant they had to be at least half decent, right?

So I bought the earrings, a package of Oreos, and some tissue paper and tape to wrap up my shitty attempt at a birthday gift. The bill came out to $48.63, so I tossed a Snickers into the mix for my walk home.

We didn't break down any physical barriers that night. Alex squealed like a little girl when she saw the earrings and made me put them in for her right there. We each ate a row of Oreos and then lay on the rock in a sugar coma.

"Thanks for the earrings," Alex said eventually, rolling onto her back. It was hot as hell outside, but I felt cold from the loss of her head against my chest.

"I'll get you something fancier next year," I said, vowing to follow up on the promise. I'd set aside a whole separate account just for Alex. I'd get her whatever the hell she wanted.

"I don't like fancy, you know that," she said. "They're perfect. Stop being stubborn and just say 'you're welcome.'"

"You're welcome," I grumbled. My arm was quickly falling asleep under the weight of her head but I didn't dare shift. I needed her touch like I needed air.

"Hey Nate?"

"Yeah?"

She hesitated, suddenly tense with nervous energy, and I tried not to get too excited. What would it be this time? I'd been doing some research and I was pretty sure I could get her to come if she'd let me try. Now *that'd* be a good birthday gift. Screw earrings.

"Would it weird you out if…" she trailed off, gnawing on her lip.

I did cartwheels in my mind, bursting with anticipation. "If what?"

Alex huffed out a breath of frustration and rolled onto her side once more, burying her face in my chest. Her voice was muffled in my shirt, but her words still stopped my heart in its tracks. "Would it weird you out if I told you I think I might love you?"

The fireworks going off inside me put Independence Day to shame. I smiled and pressed a kiss to the top of her head. "That depends," I said, and I know I'm an ass for the way I strung it out. "Would it weird you out if I told you I *know* I love you?"

On July 13th, Alex's birthday and the anniversary of the best and worst day of my life, we finally admitted that we loved each other.

On July 26th, two weeks later, the moon was new and the plunging darkness was apropos, I suppose. That night, for the first time ever, without explanation or warning, Alex failed to show up at the spot.

71

CHAPTER EIGHT
ALEX

July 26th started out like every other day. I guess that's how a lot of great tragedies get started, isn't it? With an otherwise ordinary day?

I woke with my alarm at 7 o'clock. As I had every morning for the last two weeks, I stretched and smiled at the sunlight slanting across the ceiling and clutched my hands over my heart like the lovestruck teenager that I was.

He loves me. And I loved him. So much it hurt. Being around him made my heart feel like it was going to beat right out of my chest and parting from him made my stomach turn over in my gut.

I carried his love with me like a pendant as I climbed out of bed and trudged to the bathroom I shared with Tommy. My brother was away for the whole month of July. Daddy sent him to some camp every summer, ostensibly to expand his horizons and make friends, but I knew the real reason. Parting with that money was easier for my parents than facing him every day. I think they hated what he was. They saw it as some kind of punishment, or maybe as a reflection of their own failure. I never understood it. All I ever saw when I looked at Tom was my brother.

After I showered I pulled on my work clothes— conservative khaki pants and a black polo shirt with the ice-cream shop's logo on the breast pocket— I pulled my hair up into a bun and put my earrings in. I had a whole jewelry-box full of diamonds and pearls and studs, but those cheapo star earrings were the only thing I ever wore. The first time I wore them I was worried my parents would ask where I got them, but they didn't notice.

Momma wasn't up yet when I made my way into the kitchen, but Daddy was sitting at the table, sipping coffee and reading some book on theology that had little sticky notes and tabs hanging off the pages. He had a pencil behind his ear, and I thought for the thousandth time how crazy it was that his god had to make things so complicated for him. I wish I could go back and tell him the Truth is simple. Maybe it would have saved him some energy.

"Morning, Daddy!" I said brightly, kissing his cheek and helping myself to a cup of coffee.

"Morning, sugar," he said absently, without looking up.

"Where's Momma?"

"Still asleep, last I checked," he said, taking a sip of coffee and peering at me over the rim. "Why?"

"Just wondering."

In truth, I was worried. I hadn't seen much of my mother all summer. She seemed to sleep until after I left for work and go to bed just after dinner. When she was around she was listless and pale, thin and gaunt. She got up every day and did her hair and dressed in pearls and a crisp white shirt. Then she mopped spotless floors, dusted dust-less shelves, and sat in front of her TV. It sounds so ordinary when I say it, but in reality it struck me as sinister

"Hey, Daddy?"

My father sighed and set his book down, folding his hands in front of him and giving me his grudging attention. "What, Alexandra?"

I hesitated, grasping my coffee cup in my hands and staring at the oily surface of the liquid. "Is Momma okay?"

I looked up to see my father frown, grip tightening on the handle of his own mug.

"Of course she is. Why do you ask?"

I shrugged. "She just seems… do you think she's depressed?"

My father shook his head. "Your mother's just a quiet woman, Aly. She's always been this way."

I didn't remember it that way. Back before we moved, she had all kinds of life. She told us stories and chased us around the yard. She was still fastidious back then, but not obsessive. She didn't turn pale at shoes inside or a glass without a coaster. And she smiled. I remembered her smiling where it actually reached her eyes.

"Can you talk to her?" I asked, unable to shake the feeling that something was wrong and I wasn't doing enough to fix it.

My father sighed again, picking up his book. "You ask me that as if I haven't already. She's my wife, sugar. I talk to her every day."

"Can you ask her, though? Specifically, I mean? Can you ask her if she's depressed?"

"I'll talk to her this evening."

It was grudging and he clearly just wanted to end the conversation, but I still felt as if a weight had been lifted from my shoulders. My father was an adult—

trained in helping people through their troubles. I'd passed responsibility off to him and I was happy to see it go.

.. .. ..

"Dish, Aly," Gemma said, bracing her hands on her hips and fixing me with a piercing stare.

"Dish what?" I asked innocently, plucking my bright-green work apron off its hook and slipping the loop over my head.

"You know what. You realize you haven't stopped smiling for weeks, right? It's starting to creep me out."

Gemma was the one person on earth who knew about Nate. I didn't want to tell anybody, but after that first kiss I'd gone home and stared at my bedroom ceiling and I had to tell *someone* before all the gooey happiness built up inside me and burst out my chest like the eponymous creature in the Alien franchise.

She still didn't know who he was, though. All she knew was that I had a secret boyfriend who I ran off with every night. She hassled me endlessly for his identity, but I think she enjoyed the game more than she'd enjoy actually knowing. Just like I enjoyed hanging onto new tidbits until both of us were half mad—me with the need to spill and her with the need to know.

"We said 'I love you,'" I blurted, tying my apron behind my back and heading to the front door to unlock it, flipping on the neon OPEN sign in the window. When I turned around, Gemma was gaping at me from behind the register, frozen with one hand on the till and the other in the air as if to halt the conversation.

"You *what*?!" she exclaimed, eyes wide.

"It's not a big deal," I lied, slipping back behind the counter and taking up my place behind the second register.

"The hell it isn't!" my friend yelled, reaching out and shoving me in the shoulder. "Aly that's crazy. You've only known this guy like a month."

"Well..." I trailed off, wondering how much information I should offer.

"Well what?"

"I've actually known him for a long time."

"Like three months?"

"Like... five years."

Gemma made a dramatic noise of frustration and grasped her register between her hands, gently thumping her forehead against it. "Aly you're going to kill me. Who the hell is this guy? Do I know him?"

"You know I'm not gonna tell you," I said, rolling my eyes.

"Will you at least tell me what he looks like?"

74

"No!"

"You're the worst! You gotta give me something. Is he hot at least?"

I was about to tell her to shut up when that stupid smile split my face again and my heart decided to talk instead of my brain. "Yeah, he's hot," I mumbled, staring pointedly at the window-front of the store as heat crept up my neck.

"Good," Gemma said. "Since you won't tell me who he is I'll just guess every time I see a guy and if I guess right you gotta tell me."

"Fine," I agreed.

"Scout's honor," Gemma said.

"We're not scouts."

"Pinky swear?"

I reached out with my pinky extended and Gemma linked her finger with mine. I wasn't worried about the sanctity of the swear. Gemma wouldn't guess Nate if he walked in right then and kissed me full on the lips. That's how little sense he and I made.

Our conversation petered out as the morning turned to afternoon and the sun heated up the streets outside, driving more folks into the crisp air of the ice cream parlor. I spent the day filling cups and cones, my customer service smile wide and genuine.

All day, Gemma guessed, and she stayed true to her promise to guess every time she saw a guy. Every time.

She guessed if it was the frat bro with the salmon-colored shirt and the shades on the back of his head.

She guessed if it was the 90-year-old grandfather with the walker and the pants up around his armpits.

She guessed if it was the middle-aged balding guy with four rambunctious kids and a frazzled-looking wife.

She guessed if it was any of the four football players who went to our school and who were all, we both knew, dating cheerleaders.

Then, just at the end of the lunch rush, the bell above the door dinged and in walked Nate. My stomach plunged, my heart leapt, and my brain short-circuited.

He looked like he was coming straight from work. Although his hands were scrubbed clean, his arms and shirt were covered in smears of engine oil and his hair, peeking out from beneath a backwards baseball cap, was damp with sweat.

He wasn't alone, either. To his right stood a kid who looked to be in his early teens, wearing a too-big basketball jersey, a cheap crew cut, and a scowl. His tough-guy demeanor was offset slightly by the smattering of freckles across his nose and the wary look in his eye as he glanced around the crowded ice cream shop.

Clinging to Nate's left hand was a little girl who couldn't have been older than ten. She was as cute as she was dirty, with brown ringlets pulled back in a disastrous ponytail, wide brown eyes, and smears of dirt and some sticky, blueish mystery substance on her face and hands.

The last kid looked like he was about five. Nate had him hoisted up on a hip and the little boy clung to his shirtsleeve as he looked around the shop with the same wariness as the other boy.

A restrained smile tugged at the corner of Nate's mouth as he and his entourage made their way to my register.

"Good afternoon and welcome to Cream of the Crop!" I said brightly, clinging to the counter so my hands wouldn't shake. "What can I get for you?"

"Just one flavor, guys," Nate said, setting the little boy on the ground, and all three kids scrambled to the display case, faces and palms pressed to the glass as they stared with wide eyes at the array of flavors.

While they browsed, Nate and I just stood and stared at each other. We had so little experience interacting during the day. Even at school, we never had to speak. I was overwhelmed. How do you look at a guy who's had his hands on every part of your body— who carries your heart with him everywhere he goes— and pretend you don't know him?

"Anything for you?" I asked, trying to inject some customer-service cheer back into my voice.

"You have coffee, right?" he asked, and I nodded. "Just a small. And one-scoop cones for the kids."

"I want chocolate," the older boy said, sidling up next to Nate and glaring at me.

"Ronnie," Nate growled. "C'mon, man. We talked about this"

Ronnie grimaced and clenched his fists. "I'd like chocolate, *please*," he said snottily before slinking off and slouching into a booth.

"How 'bout you, Paul?" Nate asked, glancing down at the youngest boy, who had returned and was clinging to his pant leg. When the boy spoke, it was so quiet I couldn't make it out.

"Cookie dough for this one," Nate said to me. "Trish?"

"I want strawberry, please!" the little girl said brightly, clinging to the edge of the counter and pulling herself up onto her tiptoes. She grinned at me, displaying a gap in her teeth. "We're celebrating!"

God, she was cute.

"Oh yeah?" I asked, bending closer. "Is it your birthday?"

"No," the girl said, frowning and shaking her head like I was an idiot for suggesting it. "That's silly, my birthday's in December. My mommy said it's like Jesus."

76

"Oh, then what are you celebrating?" I asked, pulling away to scoop their ice cream but watching the girl so she'd know I was still listening.

"I dunno!" she said cheerily, following me and pressing her face to the glass, watching me serve up the largest one-scoop cones I could manage. "Nate makes the rules and he says we're celebrating, so we're celebrating."

"That makes sense," I said, trying not to smile too wide as I handed the cones over. I had a feeling I knew exactly what they were celebrating. Last night had been particularly... engaging. I tugged the collar of my shirt to make sure it covered the bruised red mark on my collarbone.

Nate crouched and placed the ice cream in the younger kids' hands, nodding his head toward the table where the other boy already sat. "How much?" he asked, digging his wallet out as he rose to his feet.

I tallied it up on the register. "$6.15," I said, trying not to grimace in sympathy as his jaw clenched and he pulled the bills out, handing them over.

I counted out his change and poured a small coffee from the carafe behind the counter, handing it over. Every time our fingers brushed I felt like I'd been electrocuted.

I was worried my reaction had been apparent, but Gemma didn't even look at me as Nate walked away. She did stare at his table, though, with a mournful look in her eye.

"It's so sad, isn't it?" she asked as soon as Nate had slid into the booth, safely out of earshot.

"What's sad?" I asked, trying not to fidget with my apron or show any sign of investment in the conversation.

"Those kids," Gemma said, turning and leaning her hip against the counter. "You know they're in the system."

"Yeah, I know," I said. Nate never talked about home, but it wasn't a secret he was in foster care. Our school's gossip machine wasn't *that* inefficient. "They seem okay, though. They look like they're being taken care of, at least."

Gemma made a noise in her throat, and when she spoke again it was in a conspiratorial whisper. "My mom says the foster parents are hardcore druggies," she whispered.

Her words hit me like cold water. "What?" I asked, unable to keep the horror from my voice.

Gemma nodded, raising her eyebrows. "Apparently they've got the same dealer. My mom just uses him for pot and shrooms, obviously, but her guy deals harder stuff, too. Apparently they're into heroin and crack and stuff, too. That's why they foster kids. For the money."

I just stared at the table. I have to admit it didn't feel good having to learn my soulmate's tragic backstory through the grapevine. I was so sick of him blowing me off every time I asked him questions. That night I'd press him until he told me the truth.

"Still," Gemma said, popping off the counter and raising her voice back to a normal level. "You're right, they do look like they're okay. Especially Nate. Mean streak aside, that boy turned out just fine. I don't suppose *he's* your secret lover, is he?"

She laughed as she said it and I forced a laugh of my own. Unfortunately, my friend wasn't that easy to fool. She immediately clapped her mouth shut, staring at me with wide eyes.

"Aly," she gasped, before slapping her hand over her mouth to hide an incredulous smile.

"What?" I asked, feigning confusion. I'm a terrible liar, though. I blush bright red, my hands shake, and I can't for the life of me make eye contact with the person I'm lying to.

"Aly, look at me," Gemma demanded. I glanced over at her before turning back to my till. My friend barked out a shocked laugh. "Aly Winger, are you fucking kidding me?" she hissed, but was interrupted when a fresh crop of customers flooded through the door.

I suppose it was naive to hope she'd forget. As soon as the customers cleared away, cones in hand, Gemma took my shoulders in her hands, grinning into my face.

"Aly, tell me the truth," she whispered, eyes locked on mine. "Is Nathan Reynolds your secret lover?"

"Stop calling it that," I said, wrinkling my nose in disgust.

"Answer the question!" Gemma demanded, even though we both knew there was no point in denying it.

I pinched my lips shut and glared at her in answer.

"Holy shit," she breathed, letting me go and turning so that we stood shoulder to shoulder. She crossed her arms over her chest and cocked her head, studying Nate's table. "*He* told you he loves you?" she asked quizzically.

"He does love me," I snapped, offended by her tone.

"Sure, sure," she flapped a hand. "Who wouldn't? I'm just saying, I've seen him around school. He doesn't seem like a lovey-dovey type to me."

"Do I seem like a secret tryst type to you?" I asked.

"That's fair." For a second she was silent, head cocked as she observed the guy I loved and his dirt-smeared charges. Then she jerked around, eyes wide, a wide grin on her face. "You have to tell me *everything*!"

.. .. ..

78

Despite Gemma's revelation, the day continued to proceed as normal. After work we walked to the coffee shop down the street. We sat on the patio like we always did, sipping iced lattes and talking. I dominated the conversation that day, catching Gemma up on the sprawling saga that constituted my relationship with Nate.

After coffee I walked to the library and picked up two new books about string theory. At the time I was fascinated with a scientific explanation for the origin of the universe. If my dad had found those books it would've started a fight, so I only checked out two at a time and kept them hidden between my mattress and box spring.

My house was a mile from the library, and I walked home by the same route as always. I greeted neighbors and smiled at kids running through sprinklers in verdant green lawns. It wasn't yet evening and the sun beat down on my head, but I didn't mind the heat. Sweat trickled down my back and my pants clung uncomfortably to my legs, but I was impervious.

Nothing could bring me down. Nate loved me. I didn't have to lie to Gemma anymore. I'd talked to my father about Momma. I was smart and happy and carefree and everything was fine. I was immune to the universe's cruelty.

The house was silent when I pushed the front door open, as usual. Momma had taken to watching the TV on mute.

"I'm home!" I yelled, kicking off my work sneakers and lining them up by the door. I dropped my bag as well, breathing a sigh of relief as the cold, conditioned air hit the sweat on the back of my neck, cooling me instantly. "Momma?"

She didn't respond, so I padded to the kitchen and opened the refrigerator, staring at the contents. I pulled an apple out of the drawer, polishing it on my shirt before taking a large bite. It was crisp and perfect, and to this day the taste of apples makes my stomach heave.

Momma wasn't in the living room, so I slouched into her chair and flipped the TV on. She was probably out getting groceries or something, and between my parents and Tom I never got to pick the channel.

I lazed away the afternoon, half-dozing to a documentary about the space race. When five o'clock rolled around and Momma still hadn't returned from the grocery store, I decided to give her a call.

I used the kitchen phone to dial the Nokia daddy bought her for Christmas. Just as it rang through the headset, I heard a chime from upstairs.

"Momma?" I called, hanging up the phone and jogging up the stairs. "Are you home?"

She didn't answer. Nor did she respond when I rapped three times on her bedroom door. Cautiously, I jiggled the handle and found it unlocked.

"Momma?" I pushed the door open, bracing myself for a lecture on privacy as I stepped into my parents' bedroom.

The master suite of our home had a west-facing window, with the door set into the southern wall. The walk-in closet and bathroom were set against the northern wall. On July 26th, evening sunlight pierced through the gauzy curtains on the window, casting a bright red glow over beige carpet and my parents' perfectly-made king-size bed.

The closet door was shut, but the bathroom door was open. In retrospect, I think part of her actually wanted someone to walk in before it was done. Otherwise I suppose she'd have shut both doors and locked them behind her.

My feet pulled me toward the bathroom, even while my heart clung to the doorframe, screaming at my body to stop. At first all I could see was her head, tipped back against the rim of the tub. She'd done up her hair. That's crazy, right? She had it piled on top of her head just so, hair sprayed into perfection. She was even wearing make-up and jewelry.

All dressed up with nowhere left to go.

As my feet carried me into the bathroom, my mind clung to little details, frantically distracting itself from the horrifying truth of the big picture. I noticed that she was wearing a dress— not her usual white button up and slacks. I'd never seen the dress before. It was black and sleeveless, the skirt floating peacefully in the pink-tinged water around her legs. I noticed that she'd removed her wedding ring, and it sat on the edge of the tub, next to a bloodied razor and an empty glass of wine. I noticed that she was wearing the necklace Tom and I got her for Christmas when I was just ten. It was a heart-shaped locket that had both our pictures glued sloppily to the inside.

I stood there, staring down at her motionless form, and noticed little details. Then, all at once, those details came together and my world fell apart.

"Momma," I said, staring at her pale face. Beneath the painted-on blush of her cheeks, her face was worse than pale. It was gray, the skin waxen, lips and eyelids tinged blue. Her eyes were half-closed, rolled back in her head so what sliver I could see was just blank white and lifeless. "Momma!" I yelled uselessly, fists clenched at my sides.

Of course, she didn't respond, and instinct took over for me. I didn't even think as I bent, plunging my hands into bloody water and grabbing the front of my mother's dress. I just screamed for her, over and over again. Her body was completely stiff, which made it easier to leverage her up over the edge of the tub. I looked it up later and learned that rigor mortis doesn't set in until at least four hours after a person dies. I didn't know that at the time. I didn't know my efforts were more than four hours too late.

"Momma, wake up!" I cried, heaving with all my might and dragging her waterlogged form onto the bathroom floor. Her skull cracked against the tile as I set her down, and bloodstained water poured over the edge of the tub and dripped off her body, staining the grout between the tiles.

I'd taken a CPR class in middle school, but for some reason the details wouldn't come to me. All I could remember was chest compressions and rescue breaths. I couldn't remember the ratio. I couldn't remember if they'd taught us what to do with all the blood. I couldn't remember how fast to do the compressions, or where I was supposed to put my hands, or how to call 911 when I was busy breathing for her and pumping her heart.

I rose up over my mother's body and clasped my fists over the center of her chest, dropping my body weight into compressions and holding my own breath. When my lungs began to burn for air I sucked in a huge breath and bent, covering her cold mouth with mine. Her jaw was completely rigid, but her mouth was parted just slightly, allowing me to push air into her lungs.

That's when I started crying. She tasted like death. Don't ask me how I knew what death tastes like. It's one of those things you can't describe or explain but the second it touches your lips you just know.

It didn't stop me, though. All totaled up, I performed shoddy, pointless CPR on my mother's long-dead corpse for an hour and a half. To me, it felt like years. A lifetime.

To this day, I don't know what my father's reaction was when he found his daughter bent over his wife's body on his bathroom floor. I don't know if he screamed or gasped or cried. I don't know if he called 911 before or after pulling me off her.

I do know that, when he grabbed my shoulders and pulled me back, I lashed out with an elbow and socked him in the stomach before returning to my task. I know black spots danced in my vision and sweat rolled off my face and down my neck as I continued the chest compressions. I'd settled on ten. Ten compressions and three breaths. In case you're wondering, that's the wrong ratio. It was supposed to be thirty to two. Fortunately, I guess, it didn't really matter.

I didn't stop until the first responders arrived. Someone big— a cop— wrapped his arms around me and dragged me off her, letting the paramedics swoop in. I collapsed against the stranger, sobbing breathlessly. I couldn't speak. I couldn't even look up. I just clung to my anonymous captor and sobbed.

He wasn't very nice to hug. His uniform shirt was stiff and scratchy and he had a pen in his breast pocket that dug into my cheek. He patted my back, but it was awkward and mechanical, and all he said was 'it's okay' over and over, which didn't make a lot of sense to me because nothing was okay.

I didn't see the paramedics load my mother's body onto a gurney and take it away, but I wish I'd watched it happen. Maybe if I'd seen her go I'd still have the piece of me I left on the bathroom floor that night. That little fraction of me will always be there, sobbing through CPR and begging my mother to live.

My father tried to hug me at some point, but I shoved him away and clung to the cop. Then a female officer came and I let her lead me out of my parents' bedroom to my own. She dried me off and helped me into clean clothes and then walked with me to the bathroom and stood by while I rinsed the taste of death from my mouth.

"We'd like to ask you some questions, Alexandra," she said gently, when I finally finished. "Your father said it was okay, but if you don't want to talk to me you don't have to. Ms. Watterson, here, will sit with us. Is that okay?" She gestured at the gray-haired woman in the polo shirt who stood beside her. I hadn't even noticed her arrival.

"Sure," I mumbled, and let her follow me to my bedroom.

With Ms. Watterson, whoever she was, as a silent witness, I sat on my bed and answered the cop's questions, hands clasped in my lap, eyes fixed on the carpet by her feet. I never looked her in the eye. I can't even recall what she looked like. The questions were brief and fact-based.

"What time did you get home?"

"What time did you find your mother?"

"When was the last time you saw your mother alive?"

"Has your mother exhibited signs of depression?"

"Do your parents get along?"

On and on, and never once did she ask the questions I wanted to answer.

When did you realize your mother was dead?

Why do you think she wanted to die in that dress?

How could your mother leave you all alone?

How did it feel, breathing air into dead lungs?

When you close your eyes, do you see her floating in the water?

It was dark outside when the police officer left. My father tried to talk to me again after that. He knocked on my door and took my silence as invitation. Then he sat next to me on my bed and put his arm around me and I took no comfort in it whatsoever. I'd have rather been hugging the cop with the scratchy shirt and the pen in his breast pocket.

"I asked you to talk to her," I whispered around the tears that hadn't stopped falling. I didn't need to ask if she was dead. I think I'd known the whole time.

"I know, Aly," my father said, tightening his arm around me. "I'm so sorry."

"She killed herself."

"I know, sugar." He tried to hug me against his chest, but I held my body stiff as a board, unyielding.

"You didn't even notice. Did you even ask if she was okay? Even once?"

82

"You're right to be angry."

"You're goddamn right I'm angry!" I yelled, shooting off the bed and rounding on him, red-faced and furious. My father's face blanched. I never got angry at anyone but Nate, and I damn sure never cursed. "Get out of my room."

"Alexandra, please," he said. "Your language… please don't shut me out."

"Get the *fuck* out of my *goddamned* room!" I screamed, heedless of the police who were no doubt lingering in the crime scene that was now my home.

"Aly—"

"Out!" I planted two hands in the center of his chest and shoved him backwards. His face twisted in a strange combination of frustration and despair. I suppose a better daughter would have noticed that his own eyes were red and puffy from tears, and that he was likely blaming himself plenty without my help. I wasn't fit to be a good daughter that night, though. I had my own problems.

"Get some sleep," my father said, shoulders slumping in defeat. "I'll be downstairs with the officers if you need me. We'll talk tomorrow morning."

Then he left, pulling the door shut behind him, and I was alone.

Alone.

I collapsed sideways on my bed, praying for sleep to drag me under, but every time I closed my eyes all I could see was my mother's waxy gray skin and the whites of her rolled-back eyes. I'd brushed my teeth five times and gargled for two minutes with sharp, alcoholic mouthwash, but the metallic tinge of death still lingered on my tongue.

Stifling a cry of despair, I scrambled off my bed, snatched my CD-player off my desk, and ran to the door. I flipped on the overheads, flooding the room with yellow-white light, and slid down the wall by the door, sliding the headphones over my ears and cranking up the volume on the music. Drowning my senses, I wrapped my arms around my knees and stared with wide eyes at my room. My eyes burned from exhaustion and tears, but I couldn't blink. I was afraid to.

I stayed that way for hours. I couldn't have told you what CD I listened to. The songs were just noise, screaming in my ear and drowning out the echoes of my own gasping breath and pleas for my mother to please, *please* wake up. My tired eyes darted around the room, absorbing every detail, jerking open every time they drifted closed into another iteration of my nightmare.

I didn't hear the knock at my window, but I saw the silhouette through my curtains. Since the light was on and reflecting off the glassy surface of the window, all I could make out was the shape of a man, hovering outside. I ripped the headphones from my ears and shot to my feet.

Nate clung perilously to the branch outside my window, hand outstretched and braced on my windowsill. His face, already twisted in concern, seemed to drain of blood when I pulled back the curtains and slid the window open.

"Alex what the hell?" he hissed, leaning forward and poking his head into my room as I stepped back. "Are you okay? What's going on?"

"You shouldn't be here," I said numbly, looking at my feet. "My dad will—"

"Fuck your dad!" he grumbled dismissively, clambering through the window with considerably less grace than I usually managed. "I had a damn heart attack when I saw the police cars parked outside, Al. Please just tell me you're okay."

"I'm okay," I said obediently. It was a lie, but if he needed to hear it I'd say it.

"No you're not. What happened? What's going on?"

He stepped forward, reaching for me, and I stepped back. I don't know why. I think part of me knew that saying the words out loud and letting him hold me would be the final nail in the proverbial coffin. As long as Nate didn't know, I had somewhere I could go that wasn't stained by reality. Once I brought him into it, it'd be real. My mother would be dead. Everywhere and forever.

"Alex, if you really don't want me here I'll leave," Nate said evenly, letting his hands drop to his sides. "But I'm not gonna go until I know you're okay, so just tell me what's going on."

"I don't want you to leave," I blurted, stepping forward and wrapping my arms tight around his waist. His wound around my shoulders, holding me against him as a fresh crop of tears broke loose and rolled down my face. It took me three tries to get the words out, and when I finally said them they were muffled in the fabric of his shirt. "My mom killed herself."

Every muscle in his body locked up and I swear I heard his heart skip a beat. "Shit," he murmured into my hair. "Al…"

"I don't want to talk about it," I said, pulling my head away from his chest and looking up into his eyes so he could see I was telling the truth. He frowned but nodded.

"Okay. You're not hurt though?"

"No." Not physically, anyway.

"Okay. Do you wanna stay here or do you wanna go outside?"

I wanted to go outside, but I didn't think I could handle the climb. My knees were weak and wobbly and my eyes were so sore I could barely see.

"Stay here," I mumbled, tightening my grip and burying my face in his shoulder.

"You got it."

Before I realized what was happening, Nate stooped and hefted me into his arms, walking to the bed and settling against the headboard. He didn't say another word for the rest of the night.

I know I ought to say he took the nightmare away. That's how love is supposed to work, right? You find your soulmate and that person's mere presence eases every trouble you face and soothes every pain?

That wasn't how it worked that night, though. Nate didn't take any of it away. I still saw my mother's body every time I closed my eyes, and I still heard my own desperate pleas in the silence. My stomach still churned and my chest still felt like someone had driven a spike through it. I shattered to pieces that night, and even Nate couldn't hold me together. I cracked and crumbled into a thousand jagged shards, and all he could do was gather them up in his arms and hold them together until the storm blew through.

CHAPTER NINE

NATE

Alex's mom killed herself on Thursday.

On Thursday night, I sat with her until dawn pinked the horizon. She cried at first, but she wasn't hysterical. I think she was too tired for that. She just clung to me, trembling, while silent tears dampened my shirt. At around three in the morning, she finally dozed off, but it was a tense, fretful sleep. She mumbled and cried out and jerked awake periodically, despite my efforts to comfort her. It broke me to leave her in the morning, but I didn't have a choice. She said she understood, and curled on her side, watching through puffy eyes while I climbed gracelessly out the window. She looked so alone that I almost stayed— work and siblings and her reputation be damned.

On Friday night, I returned and found her in the same spot I had left her. She hadn't even changed clothes. I don't know what worried me more— the fact that she didn't even twitch as I climbed into her room or the fact that she'd stopped crying.

"Hey, Alex," I said. She was facing away from me and didn't roll over or sit up as I stretched out on the bed beside her without invitation.

"Hi," she said, her voice a strange, gritty monotone.

"How are you feeling?" I knew it was a stupid question, but I didn't know what else to ask.

"Fine."

"Do you want to talk about it?"

"No."

So I held her in silence for the rest of the night. I was beyond tired and she must have been too, but neither of us slept. Her lights were still on, so I stared at the ceiling, listening to her breathe in a tense, staccato rhythm. At dawn, I left with a promise to come back. She didn't respond.

On Saturday night, Tim and Marsha got drunk. They started the day early and Tim was in a rage by the time the sun went down. Paul managed to spill a glass of milk on the counter at exactly the moment Tim was walking into the kitchen to retrieve another beer from the case in the fridge.

I was in my bedroom and heard the commotion, but by the time I made it to the kitchen Paul was crumpled on the floor and Tim was towering over him, screaming obscenities.

Paul was hunched over on the floor, covering his head with his hands, and he peeked through his arms at me as I entered. A trickle of blood oozed from the corner of his mouth and that spot of red expanded into a haze that clouded my vision.

"Go to bed, Paul," I growled, stalking forward as Tim turned to me, fists clenched at his sides, face purple with rage.

The kid couldn't obey fast enough, scrambling past me to our bedroom, where I hoped Ronnie would take care of him.

Tim and I fought for what felt like hours. I was getting stronger, and I think Tim knew it. He didn't just flail about with his fists, anymore, because he knew I could outmaneuver him. Those days, he'd taken to grappling, using his bodyweight to pin me to the ground. He'd also taken to face shots, since I was practically an adult and had such a reputation for fighting. He knew every teacher, counselor, and peace officer who saw me with a busted lip would sigh in exasperation and ask what I'd gotten myself into. Nobody would ask about home.

We traded punches, bouncing around the kitchen, crashing into furniture and driving each other into counters. Then he took me to the floor and I couldn't even breathe against his weight, let alone buck him off. When I got my breath back, he'd already landed a few good blows. I could barely see for the stars in my eyes and my ears were full of staticky ringing.

Panicking, I managed to elbow him in the face and he sprawled sideways, clutching his bleeding nose. I scrambled to get on top of him, but at that moment Marsha entered the room, staggering drunkenly to her husband, who went limp when his wife appeared, playing the victim.

"How dare you!" she screamed at me. Her backhanded slap didn't hurt that bad. Unlike her husband, Marsha didn't gain freak strength when she drank. She just got clumsy. Even so, her stupid wedding ring caught me on the cheek and I felt blood drip down the side of my face.

"He hit Paul," I said as I backed away, although I knew it was pointless.

"You're a liar!" Tim roared, letting his wife help him to his feet.

"Ungrateful little monster," Marsha hissed, slinging Tim's arm over her shoulder. "Don't think I won't be calling your case manager."

"You let her do that and I'll tell her everything!" I yelled at Tim's retreating back and was satisfied by the way his shoulders stiffened. Nobody would be calling my case manager. Our tense, miserable equilibrium would survive another day.

I found Paul on Ronnie's bed, holding a hand to his mouth and crying silently. Ronnie sprawled beside him, reading a car magazine I'd brought home from the shop.

"Ron, what the hell?" I ground out, plucking Paul off his bed and carrying him to mine. I sat on the edge and placed the kid on my knee.

"He's gotta grow up," Ronnie said flippantly, without looking away from the magazine. "We're not gonna be around to coddle him forever."

I ignored him, too drained to argue or scold. "Let me see it, buddy," I said to Paul, and he cautiously lowered his hand, still crying.

"It hurts," he moaned.

"I know, kid. I'm sorry. I'm just gonna take a look, okay?" He nodded, his breath hitching as I inspected the injury. It wasn't that bad. Just a little slice on the inside of his lower lip. You wouldn't even know it was there from looking at him, and by tomorrow he'd forget it was there.

"Tell you what," I said, using the collar of his shirt to wipe the trickle of watery blood from his chin. "I'm gonna go get some ice for you, okay? That'll make it feel better."

"A Band-Aid too?" Paul asked, probing at the corner of his mouth with a finger.

"You want a Band-Aid inside your mouth?" I asked, raising an eyebrow at him. He giggled and shook his head.

"Okay, just ice then. Wait here."

The rest of the night was an agony of waiting. Paul didn't stop crying until the sandwich bag of ice was a leaking sack of water. Tim and Marsha didn't go to bed until after midnight. The house didn't go completely silent until after one in the morning. After that, I waited another thirty minutes just to be safe. Then I crawled out of bed and reached underneath to pull on my shoes.

Alex didn't get up to let me in when I tapped on the glass, but her light was still on. I wrestled the window open myself and poked my head inside.

"Al?"

The figure beneath her covers shifted and she rolled over and blinked at me. She *still* hadn't moved. Still hadn't changed. Had she even eaten?

I practically fell over the windowsill in my haste to get to her. My beautiful, vibrant girl looked halfway dead. Her face was pale and puffy around the eyes. Her hair was a matted mess. She'd been wearing the same clothes for three days. Her bloodshot eyes were sunken into her face and surrounded by dark shadows.

"Sorry I'm late," I breathed, crouching beside her and covering her hand with mine.

"It's fine," she mumbled. "You don't have to come over every night." Then her eyes focused on my face and her brow furrowed in a weary semblance of concern. "What happened?"

One of Tim's blows had caught me in the eye and, although I didn't think it was going to swell shut, I could feel the bruise rising. Plus, the slice Marsha's ring had left on the side of my face probably would have warranted stitches. I'd scrubbed it out and stopped the bleeding but it was still nasty-looking.

"Just a fight," I said with a shrug, and the shadow of my Alex sighed and shook her head against the pillow, her weary disappointment gouging at my heart.

"I hate when you fight," she said.

Me too, sweetheart. "You need to shower," I returned, effectively changing the subject.

That earned me a glare, and I had to fight not to smile at the familiar sight of her annoyance. That glare was a glimmer of hope that Alex was still there somewhere, buried beneath the shock and the grief.

"I'm serious," I goaded. "You don't smell good. Why don't you go clean up and grab some food on your way back? I'm starving." Even if she wouldn't take care of herself, I knew she'd be hard-pressed to resist the urge to feed me.

"I don't want to," she said, shaking her head and rolling over so her back was facing me. "You can leave if I'm grossing you out."

"You're not grossing me out," I said, sitting on the bed and pulling at her shoulder until she reluctantly flopped onto her back. "And I'm not leaving. But you do need to take a shower. Nothing is gonna fix things, but you'll feel a little better once you're clean and have some food in you."

Alex didn't answer. She just stared at the ceiling as tears welled in her eyes and trickled over her temples. I reached out and caught one with the back of my finger.

"Alex?"

"I don't want to take a shower," she said firmly, still staring at the ceiling. "She…" she trailed off, shaking her head minutely, and more tears broke loose. She drew a deep, shuddering breath and let it out, finally looking me in the eye. "She was in the tub when I found her," she said, her voice back to stony and monotone, and I felt my heart drop into my stomach.

Alex was the one who found her? *Fuck. No wonder…*

"Okay," I said, trying not to let my own shock filter into my voice. "Okay, I hear you. But you can't go the whole rest of your life without using the shower, right? Would it make you feel better if I came with you?"

She mustered up a feeble glare, and I realized she probably thought I was just trying to see her naked again. Or, worse, angling to talk her into having sex. That realization took another chunk out of my heart, but there wasn't any room that night for my hurt feelings. There wasn't space in that big empty house for anything but the roiling, disturbed mass of Alex's grief.

"I won't look," I promised. "I'll just sit on the counter with my eyes closed and be there in case you need me, okay?"

She hesitated, searching my gaze like she always did for some sign of dishonesty. Finally, she sighed.

"Fine."

The fifteen-second walk to the bathroom and back were some of the tensest seconds of my life. The house was pitch black, and I hung onto Alex's shoulder, trusting her to guide me through the unfamiliar hallway and praying her father wouldn't choose that moment to rise for a nightcap or something. Surely he wasn't sleeping well, either?

We made it to the bathroom without incident, and I did just what I had promised. I sat on the bathroom counter with my eyes closed, listening to the splatter of water on the floor of the tub. I don't know if I actually did any good. I've always been better at the physical. I'd rather have stood between Alex and a gang of Tim clones a thousand times before doing something like this. How could I guard her against her own memories?

After she showered and dressed, Alex led the way back to her room, left me there sitting on her bed, and returned five minutes later with clean sheets bundled under her arm and a plastic grocery bag full of snacks.

"You said you were hungry," she said emptily, tossing the bag at me.

I was, but I didn't eat the food. Instead, I helped her strip the bed and put the new sheets on. I tried not to look at her because in spite of everything she was still too beautiful to comprehend. She wore short running shorts that left her long legs bare and a white t-shirt with no bra. Her wet hair was piled in a messy bun on top of her head, and loose tendrils clung to her neck. She took my breath away, but it felt wrong to be affected by her. Her mom was three days dead, Alex was the one to find her, and all my stupid dick could think about was how to get her out of those shorts.

Maybe she was right not to trust me. Maybe I was some kind of pervert.

With the bed made, Alex slipped beneath the covers, but sat against the headboard instead of curling up on her side like she had every other night. "Are you going to eat or not?" she asked, gesturing at the discarded grocery bag I'd dropped on her desk.

"Sure," I said, retrieving the bag and sitting down on top of the covers beside her. The bag contained a bottle of water, a fork, a box of crackers, and a container of some kind of casserole.

"You know that cliche about people bringing casseroles to the grieving?" Alex said wryly as I pulled the casserole out of the bag. "I guess that's true. There's at least ten in our refrigerator. I guess the stupid church is really coming through."

There wasn't an ounce of gratitude in her voice. Nor should there be. I knew how Alex felt about her father's job. His parish was his real family. She, Tom, and her mother had always been made to feel like an unwanted side job.

I pulled the lid off the casserole and used the fork to shovel up a small bite. It wasn't bad, even cold.

"This is actually pretty good," I said, handing her the fork. "Want some?"

Alex took the fork and delivered the tiniest portion to her mouth before handing it back to me.

"It's okay," she mumbled.

We sat in silence for a while, taking turns with the fork and working our way through the casserole. My silence was uneasy. I worried any minute she might realize that I had tricked her into eating. Her silence was thoughtful. Her eyes were far away and I could sense that she was trying to find words. Alex always got a specific kind of tense when she was struggling to piece a thought together into a coherent statement or question. Her right foot always wiggled a little and she twisted a lock of hair around her finger.

Half the casserole was gone when she finally spoke again.

"I'm angry," she said, looking over at me as she passed the fork back. "That's wrong, right? I should be sad. I was sad, at first. Now I'm just angry." She took the fork when I offered it and took another bite of casserole, chewing thoughtfully.

"Why?" I asked, because I'm not a damn grief counselor and it was the best I could do to keep her talking.

"I'm angry at her for cheating," Alex said, staring at the prongs of the fork. "That's what she did. Life got hard and instead of getting help she just cheated. She dumped everything on the rest of us and took the easy way out and you shouldn't get to *do* that if people love you." Her voice broke, but she shook her head and rubbed the tears out of her eyes.

"I'm angry at my dad, too," she went on, handing me the fork back. I took it but didn't take another bite. For the first time in my life, I didn't feel very hungry. "He knew something was wrong. We all knew something was wrong. He just didn't care enough to look after her. He'll bend over backwards for anyone in the church. He's a saint. He just can't seem to understand that we didn't sign up to be saints with him, you know? Momma didn't want to be a martyr for his cause. She wanted to be his wife."

"It's okay to be mad," I offered feebly.

"Is it, though?" Alex asked. "She's dead, Nate. Is it really okay to hate her

91

so much when she can't even defend herself? And Daddy's sad too. He may have been a bad husband but he's not a bad man. He doesn't deserve for me to hate him right now."

"Well, what's gonna make you feel better?"

That sounds like a smart question, doesn't it? Sounds like wise words from a kid trying to coax someone he loves into taking care of herself and thinking about her situation holistically. That's not what it was, though. It was just me, panicking, begging her to tell me how to fix things for her.

"I don't know," she said.

After we finished the casserole in silence, Alex let me turn down the lights. I set my watch alarm and kicked off my shoes before climbing beneath the covers with her. Aside from the occasional, accidental nap out at the spot, we'd never slept together. I read once that's supposed to mean something— sharing a bed with someone and just sleeping. It's a kind of intimacy that goes beyond the physical.

We slept together for the first time that night. I don't know if it was sheer exhaustion, the shower, the food, or the makeshift confessional that finally put her at ease, but Alex was asleep in minutes. She curled up on her side and when I lay behind her she shifted so that her back was against my chest and her perfect ass was torturing me to a slow death.

"Sorry," I mumbled into her hair, because there was no way she couldn't feel my wildly inappropriate physical reaction to her innocent request for comfort.

In lieu of response, she just wiggled closer, reaching behind her and pulling my arm around her waist. Sending up a prayer of gratitude for my incredible good fortune, I pulled her tight against me, measuring my breath against hers as our shared body heat created a cocoon of warm comfort beneath the covers.

"She left me here alone," Alex said sleepily, her voice thick with exhaustion-muddled emotion. "How could she do that, Nate?"

"I dunno," I said honestly. "But you're not alone. I swear I'll never leave you."

It was a silly, childish thing to say, made all the worse by the fact that immaturity has never been one of my vices. Naive promises and foolish optimism were beaten out of me before I was old enough to know what they were. I'm smarter than that, not to mention stingier with promises. I don't swear lightly, because when you're born into a life like mine all you've got to stand on is your reputation and your honor. I never go back on my word.

Never willingly, anyway.

CHAPTER TEN

ALEX

I woke to warm sunshine glowing against my eyelids. I didn't wake with a start, or drenched in sweat. I drifted, languid and smiling, into wakefulness with the smell of Nate in my nose and the memory of his body curled around mine. I lingered for a moment, half-awake and smiling, blinking blearily at the ceiling as I breathed deep of the thick peace that wrapped around my head, making me giddy.

Then it all came back.

It was like a fragment of ice lodged in my chest and every ounce of blood in my body suddenly, painfully crystallized around it. I became cold and stiff. My breath caught in my chest. Memories floated in my vision and I squeezed my eyes shut against them, only to find the pictures seared into my eyelids in sharp relief.

"Momma," I moaned, curling up on my side and pulling a pillow to my chest.

I cried for ten minutes. I guess eating and sleeping had replenished my tears because I soaked my pillow. I sobbed so hard I gave myself the hiccups and black spots floated in my tear-blurred vision. I begged the stars to give my mother back because that morning— waking up content and rested— was the first time I really felt she was gone.

She wasn't in my parents' room sleeping. She wasn't downstairs in the kitchen. She wasn't out running errands. She wasn't even some paralyzed dead thing on the bathroom floor.

She was just gone.

As suddenly as it had started, my crying jag ended. Awash in eerie calm, I sat up, wiping away my tears, and drew three deep, calming breaths, listening to my heart ease its frantic rhythm.

Then I got out of bed.

I went to the closet and picked out a set of work clothes.

I showered. I dressed. I put on a light layer of makeup to disguise my puffy eyes and tear-burned face. I plucked my star earrings out of my jewelry box and stuck them in my ears. Then I stood, head canted sideways as I stared at my reflection in the mirror. I was wearing my gold cross. Momma and Daddy had gotten it for me when I turned 10. Even though I didn't necessarily believe, I'd always worn it because, for me, it wasn't a symbol of God's love but a symbol of my parents' love.

Grinding my teeth, I wrapped my fist around the little gold cross and jerked my hand, snapping the chain. Fresh tears rose in my eyes as I tossed the broken necklace into the small trash can by the toilet.

No more pretending. I vowed not to punish my father, nor to curse my mother's memory, but I was done conforming to their view of the world and their plans for my future. There comes a moment in every child's life when he or she finally realizes that adults aren't omniscient and omnipotent. Then, much later, there comes a moment when he or she realizes that adults aren't just flawed. They're broken and weak, and none of them are in a position to blaze another's trails or protect another's interests. Not even parents.

It was time to grow up.

.. .. ..

My father must have still been in bed when I left for work, because his car was in the drive but the house was silent.

It was just past eight when I closed and locked the door behind me. The sun was still working its way into the sky so, although the air was sticky and damp, it wasn't yet obscenely hot. The sunlight was clear and cheerful, flickering through the trees that lined the sidewalk and dancing on the emerald-green grass. Birds sang, playful and free, in the branches over my head as I walked to work.

Gemma's face went white when I knocked on the glass door of the ice cream shop. Eyes wide, she scrambled around the counter and hurried to unlock the door, pulling me into her arms as soon as I stepped over the threshold.

"Aly I'm so sorry," she said into my shoulder, squeezing me so hard I could barely breathe. "Are you okay? Oh my god, that's a stupid question. Of course you're not okay. What are you doing here? We covered all your shifts. Bob says you've got your job when you feel okay to come back but you don't have to anytime soon. Why are you here? Oh my God, Aly, I'm so *so* sorry."

Tears hovered in her eyes when she pulled back, holding onto my shoulders with her hands as she peered into my face as if she could ascertain my welfare by eye contact alone.

"I'm fine," I said, pulling out of her grip and fixing my best fake smile on my face.

Gemma frowned, crossing her arms over her chest. "You can't be, Aly. You really don't have to be here, you know."

"I'm tired of lying in my bed," I said truthfully, leaving her by the door and skirting the counter, pulling my apron off its hook and slipping it over my head. "I just want to pretend like things are normal for a few hours, okay?"

My friend frowned, and I could tell she wanted to argue but I won by virtue of pity.

.. .. ..

My father was at the kitchen table when I returned home, and for once there was no Bible or theological text in site. Instead, the maroon tablecloth was littered with papers. Bills, I imagined. Death ought to be cheap. It ought to be free. Nobody should have to pay for the privilege of bidding a loved one farewell.

It's not cheap, though. It's damned expensive. You know a decent casket runs for around $1000? Did you know the average burial plot costs $2-5,000? Ambulance rides are expensive too, regardless of whether the patient is alive on arrival. Then there's the fee to have the body all dressed up and beautified. Hearse and funerary services charge by the hour.

It's a racket. I figured when it was time for me to die, I'd just go into the woods and crawl into a hole so nobody would have to pay for my passing.

"Aly," my father greeted hoarsely as I entered the room and set my bag down, pulling out a kitchen chair and sinking into it. "I saw your note. You know you don't have to go to work, sweetheart. I called the shop."

"I know," I said woodenly. "I wanted to go."

He nodded as if he understood, and for a moment there passed between us a flicker of comradery.

I sat in my chair and picked at the ruffled edge of the tablecloth. My father sat in his and stared absently at a piece of paper, tapping his pen against the tabletop. I wished he would try to apologize again. I wanted to forgive him. My outburst was weighing heavily on my soul and I needed absolution. He was a preacher. He should have understood that.

"I haven't told Tom, yet," he said, instead.

"He comes home on Friday." Tension crawled up my spine as I felt us settle into our new roles. My father sank into guilt and silent contrition and I into new responsibility. He would wallow in remorse and I would hold the remains of our family together.

"I know," my father said. "He needs us there. He can't find out over the phone or from a stranger. He needs to hear it in a controlled environment."

"We'll tell him on Friday," I said numbly, standing up. "I'm going to go to bed."

.. .. ..

According to my morbid research, my mother probably took about thirty minutes to die. I have to assume she botched the job a little like most such suicides do. She probably didn't slice clean through the veins, so it would have taken a little while for her blood loss to become critical.

She'd have laid there for a while in the tub as the warm water grew colder and darker with swirls of crimson. She'd have had time to think of us. If her life had really flashed before her eyes, surely ours did too. Surely she remembered the days Tom and I were born. Our first steps. Our first words. Surely she closed her eyes and remembered happy Christmas mornings and chasing us with the hose during long, hot summer afternoons. She'd have remembered reading to us at bedtime, our heads tucked against her chest as her voice soothed us into sleep.

It took my mother thirty minutes to die, but me? I died over the course of months.

I died at an agonizing pace, moment by moment, as my mother's decision grew smaller in my rearview and the festering wound it left behind grew larger and more necrotic.

I died a little bit when we picked up Tom from camp and drove him home. He chatted away in the back seat and my father and I sat in tense silent up front. I tried to engage, to give him a few more minutes of joy, but my soul wasn't in it. When we got home, we sat him down on the couch. My dad said that mom was in heaven, but Tom looked at me with watery eyes and I couldn't hide the truth from him fast enough. He saw the scorn on my face before I could wipe it away, and he knew what I knew— that heaven was a lie and our mother was gone.

I died a little bit when we buried her. My father preached the service, and the crowd was standing-room-only. Nobody had ever cared much for my mother in life, but my father was revered.

Tom and I sat in the front pew and I hugged my brother as he wept noisily into my chest. Everyone had something to say to me, afterwards. Old ladies offered unwanted hugs and cried for my motherless soul, as if their tears might somehow help me. Young women frowned and cooed and patted my shoulder. Men, young and old, offered empty condolences and gripped my shoulder to convey their manly strength and wisdom into me by touch.

I tried— really tried— to cry. I dug deep, calling upon grotesque images and fleeting memories of fear from the day I found her, but my soul had retreated behind a wall of bulletproof glass. I saw the world around me, but it couldn't touch me. I was isolated, both from comfort and from pain. I was dying a slow, cold death and I didn't care.

Summer wore into fall. Momma's body decomposed beneath the earth in a cemetery called "Hope's Fall Memorial Garden" out on the edge of town. Her headstone was a gray-black marble monstrosity with blocky lettering.

Marissa Winger
August 17, 1964 - July 26, 2001
Beloved Mother and Wife

Once a week, Tom and I took fresh roses to her grave and sat for a while in the shade of a towering oak, visiting with her absence. Tom cried into his knees and begged her to come back. I patted his back and stared, dry-eyed, at the inscription on the headstone. It was odd that my holy, poetic father couldn't come up with something less generic to commemorate the mother of his children and the supposed love of his life.

Every evening, I snuck out of the house and visited the spot. I didn't use the window, anymore. I saw no reason to hide my actions because my father's opinions of right and wrong no longer held any sway with me. I knew that I didn't care what he thought, and I knew if he caught me sneaking out or in, I'd have only to level a stare at him and he would let me do as I pleased. Daddy's guilt was like a noose around his neck. All I had to do was kick the chair out from beneath him and he was loath to give me opportunity to do so.

Even Nate and the magic of our spot failed to stall my slow slide into living death. It wasn't Nate's fault. He tried. He coaxed me into games that used to make me laugh. He talked for hours into the warm, dark air, trying to lure me into conversation. He held me close and endured my silence. I felt like I was watching his efforts through a television screen. All of my emotional responses were lukewarm and tangential. I experienced dull remorse that I was so unresponsive, and listless gratitude for the fact that he cared enough to try. Beyond that, though… nothing. No real, gut response.

Nate couldn't fix me. Nobody could. I was cold and dead, and I liked it that way. Cold and dead were far safer and more comfortable than the harsh, blinding sensations of life. Maybe there was a lesson about Momma in that, but at the time I was too numb to see it.

When school started, things got worse. My grades were fine. I poured myself into classwork with the monotonous discipline of the walking dead. With no pleasure, or desire therefore, it wasn't hard to devote my time and energy to work.

My classmates largely avoided me, and I knew they were whispering behind my back. The gossip machine is bad enough for the average joe. It's twice as vicious when your father is the preacher at a prominent church, your brother is mentally handicapped, and your mother took her own life.

Of all my friends, only Gemma stuck by my side, but even she began to drift away when her best efforts at friendship were met with apathy on good days and sharp rebuke on bad ones.

That just left Nate and, gradually, that relationship turned sour as well. He was just *too* steady. *Too* patient. *Too* understanding. The more reliable he was, the more frustrated I became. The angrier I got, the worse I acted, and the greater my confusion grew. I didn't understand what compelled him to stand by my side. The question started as a nagging itch in the back of my mind, growing over time into a suppurating sore. Every nice thing he did made me sick. "Just stop!" I yelled one night at the spot, when he reached out to pull me to him. "Can't you leave me alone for five goddamn minutes?" I knew as I said it that I was wrong. I wanted him to call me a bitch and leave. Instead, he just scooted away, tucking his hands beneath his legs.

"If you don't want me to touch you I won't," he said quietly. "But I'm not leaving. If you really wanted to be alone you wouldn't have come here."

"I came here alone all the time before *you* showed up."

"That was five years ago, Al. Just talk to me."

"No," I snapped, seething. "*You* talk. I'm sick to death of talking about my parents. Tell me about yours."

Even in the moonlight I could see the blood leave his face.

"What?"

I sneered. "Tell me about your parents, Nate. You want me to talk about my dead mom and my asshole dad, why don't you tell me about yours? All I know is that they're not around. You won't tell me anything more." I'd veered wildly off course, but now that I had started there was no stopping. I was so angry, and even in the heat of the rage I know I wasn't angry at Nate. But there he was, right in front of me…

"What's your secret?" I asked, leaping off the rock and whirling to face him. "What are you hiding? You go digging for every secret I've got, but you refuse to give me any of yours. You call that a relationship?"

"Al," he sighed, shoulders hunching. Damn him, for making me feel so guilty when all I wanted to feel was rage. "This isn't about me, angel."

"Yes it is! It's about both of us! We're a couple, you asshole! We're supposed to talk to each other. Why am I the only one who has to spill her guts?"

The funny thing is that I was right. Right for all the wrong reasons, and maybe if I'd been right for the *right* reasons I could have helped us avoid a lot of heartbreak.

Unfortunately, I was right for the wrong reasons, so his defeated silence didn't move me to gentle my touch and cajole him into talking to me.

It made me cruel.

"That's what I thought," I snapped, crossing my arms over my chest and lifting my chin. "Tell you what. You want to talk about my mom? Let's talk about yours. My mom left me because she was so depressed she couldn't bear to be alive any longer. What was your mom's excuse? Was she depressed too, or did she just realize you're an annoying asshole and she'd be better off without you?"

I didn't mean it. Of course I didn't mean it. I wouldn't have said it if I thought it was true. I was just trying to rile him up.

My words had the opposite effect than intended. He didn't yell at me. He went deathly quiet, utterly still, fingers wrapped around the edge of the rock as he studied the dark woods.

"You're lashing out," he said eventually, dropping his gaze to his dangling feet. "You're being a jerk, Al, but if you're trying to piss me off it isn't gonna work. You're just sad. I'm not gonna be mad at you when you're sad."

"Fuck you." Jerking around, I stalked into the woods without a backwards glance. I thought I heard him following me, but I didn't look back. I didn't *go* back. Not that night or the next. I stayed in my room, nursing my anger and telling myself he deserved to be alone out there the way I had been all those nights he bailed without any explanation.

A week later, he cornered me in the hallway at school.

"What the hell are you doing?" I hissed, looking both ways down the empty hallway to make sure nobody could see us. I don't know why I still cared. Instinct more than anything, I suppose. Or maybe I was just trying to hurt him enough to drive him away.

"You haven't been to the spot in six days," Nate whispered, bracing his hands on the wall beside my head and leaning in close. "Where the hell have you been?"

"What, so you can disappear for days on end but I can't?" I challenged him, placing my hands against his chest and pushing him away. I tried to leave, but he pulled me up short with a hand on my arm.

"No, you can't," he growled. "You never have before. Can you please just talk to me, Alex? Tell me what's wrong."

"*You* are what's wrong," I snarled at him, ripping my arm out of his grip. "Just leave me the fuck alone."

With that, I stalked off down the hallway. My cold, dead heart pulsed once as I walked away, sending a spear of regret through my chest. It was gone as suddenly as it appeared, but it was enough to force me to look over my shoulder before I turned the corner.

Nate stood in the center of the hallway, watching me leave. His face and body were a mess of conflicting emotions. His shoulders were slumped in defeat, his hands clenched in anger, his brow furrowed with concern, and his mouth turned down in a thoughtful frown.

It was his eyes, though, which told the true story. They were fixed on my retreating form, shining with blatant need. A few months prior, I'd have called that look love. Sweet, hopeful Alex would have succumbed to the draw of his affection, sucked in by her own reciprocal adoration.

I wasn't that Alex anymore. I was cynical Alex with a cold, still heart and the taste of death on the back of my tongue and I didn't see love in Nate's eyes. I saw lust. Everyone I cared about was pulling away, driven back by my gnashing teeth and cruel tongue. Only Nate stuck around, and in that moment I realized why...

He wanted me. More specifically, he wanted my body. I turned the corner, striding down the hallway with a refreshing energy. I had a mission. My chest burned warm with excitement and I felt almost dizzy as plans turned over in my head.

All Nate wanted was sex. Once he'd had it, he would leave. I would be alone with the gray-toned peace of my apathy. No more guilt. No more shadows of love or echoes of hope and the fierce pain that always accompanied them. Just safe, frigid nothing.

Pre-calc was my last class of the day. Nate was in there with me. Our seats were assigned based on last name, so I sat in the back row and he sat two rows ahead and one column to the left of me. I stared at the back of his head for the entire, fifty-minute stretch of class, hatching my plan.

It was a simple plan, built on a foundation of truths I thought to be immutable: that Nate was a horny teenage boy and wanted nothing more than sex, and that I was a dead-inside girl who wanted nothing more than solitude.

We all know what happens to plans that are built on faulty foundations. Sooner or later, the whole thing crumbles.

CHAPTER ELEVEN

NATE

"Dude, where the fuck is your head at?" my buddy Kyle asked, shoving me in the shoulder so hard I nearly spilled the carton of milk I was absently raising for a sip.

I use the term 'buddy' loosely. Kyle lived in a trailer park out on the edge of town and he and his old man made a living pushing drugs. Prescription drugs, specifically. Oxy, hydrocodone, that kind of shit. Opioids were the driving force that had torn my life to shreds, and deep down I hated Kyle almost as much as I hated Tim.

Why, then, did I sit with him every day at lunch, smoke cigarettes with him between classes, and refer to him as a 'buddy?' If you have to ask that, you've probably never had the privilege of knowing that you're human trash. Kyle was a loser, sure, but so was I. We weren't friends so much as we were colleagues. Fellow lowlifes.

The only exception to my keep-to-your-own-wretched-kind rule was the source of my distraction.

Alex sat in a corner across the cafeteria, picking at a brown-bag lunch and scribbling notes while she read from a textbook. Our conversation from the hallway had scared me more than it hurt me. She was spiraling hard, and I felt like the only person in the world who was trying to save her. From what little she'd shared with me, her father had retreated to his bubble of guilt and work, her friends had largely moved on without her, and Tom had become little more than a source of stress. She was all alone in the world, bearing up beneath her grief and her anger with her father and responsibility for Tom.

She needed help, and I was woefully unqualified to give it to her. Hell, if I tried to shrink her brain I'd probably end up hurting her more than I helped.

"Nate!" Kyle shouted in my ear, punching my arm so hard I nearly fell off the edge of the bench. I recovered my balance and slugged him back. His hand was on his tray, so my punch sent tater tots scattering over the table. The teacher on lunch duty straightened at the commotion, glaring at us from her position by a column in the center of the cafeteria. I lowered my face and helped Kyle gather up his scattered food.

"Sorry, man," I said without a lot of remorse.

"Fuck you," Kyle said with a parallel lack of anger. "Where are you at, though? You're staring at Aly Winger like you wanna fuck her or something." He slapped my shoulder with the back of his hand, laughing. "That prissy bitch doesn't put out, man, everyone knows that." He paused to leer at Alex, and my blood began to bubble and fizz in my veins. "This dead-mom-goth-chick thing she's got going now is kinda hot, though. Hell, maybe she'd want to try both of us—"A primal growl formed, deep in my chest, rumbling, powerful as a building earthquake. My fists clenched and my breath came hot and fast, heart thundering in my ears. I blinked and found myself on the ground with Kyle, his legs still tangled with the bench as I pinned him down. My muscles worked independently of my mind, raining down punches that sent his head snapping from side to side, blood spraying from his mouth and nose.

Fighting Tim always felt like a sprint uphill. Fighting everyone else? I'd never been skiing, but I figured this was what it felt like. This blissful, rapid glide, answering the call of gravity. Gravity, rage, whatever it was—this force that tugged at me every minute of every day, and *finally* I was answering it. Flying downhill, muscles burning as every second took me farther from that agonizing pinnacle of trapped emotion.

As suddenly as it had started, it was over. Deb got between us, fake nails digging into my shoulders as she pushed me back. She was the only person brave enough to interfere. We'd been in foster care together on and off for nearly eight years. She was well-acquainted with the storm that lived inside me, and she was one of few people who knew the only way to tame it.

"Nate, stop!" she said, cigarette-breath fanning my face as she leaned in close, the pitch of her voice and her soft features effectively dousing the fire and dropping me back into my senses. "What the hell is wrong with you?"

"I'm good," I croaked, shoving her hands away and pushing myself up. Kyle lay at my feet, groaning, rolling his head from side to side as he fought his way back to consciousness. We'd drawn a crowd, but it was already dispersing as teachers and our school's lone security guard pushed to the front. I craned to see Alex, but she had disappeared from her table.

Deb disappeared, replaced by stern-faced adults who split between me and Kyle. I was escorted from the cafeteria. I'd likely face suspension, or even expulsion, and a sound beating when I got home. Despite my grim near-future, the only thing I regretted was that I hadn't finished my pizza.

.. ..

I was stretched out on my bed, nursing a splitting headache, when Deb found me. My vigilante justice against Kyle had cost me a week of suspension. They'd called my 'parents' to come pick me up, but Tim was the only one around because Marsha was out of town on a bowling trip. Tim was pleasant with the administrators as he picked me up, and silent on the drive home. The second we walked through the door, judgment day arrived.

The good news was, I won the fight. With the kids at school and Marsha gone, there was nobody to interfere. For the first time, we fought to the end of the line. I learned that, where Tim still had the advantage in strength, I had the advantage in stamina. The fight ended when, winded and weak, he found himself pinned to the ground, unable to even lift his hands to defend himself as I pummeled the shit out of him.

I stopped as soon as I felt the victory. That fight wasn't like the one with Kyle. There was no passion in it, or fury. I was calm and collected and I almost— almost— had fun with it. With nothing at stake but my own well-being, I found I liked the thrill of the battle.

"Stop fucking with me, old man," I said as I climbed to my feet, leaving him sprawled on the living room floor. It took everything I had to stride confidently out of the room. He didn't need to know he'd landed a couple hard blows that had my head pounding and my left shoulder throbbing angrily. That stupid shoulder was a damned inconvenience. I'd dislocated it when I was five and it had a tendency to slip in and out of the socket at the slightest touch.

So that was how Deb found me— sprawled on my bed with a bag of frozen peas on my shoulder and a forearm pressed against my eyes to ward against the light coming through the window. It was a migraine kind of day.

I didn't look up as she opened the door and stalked across the room, sitting on Ronnie's bed. I could tell it was her from the stench of cigarettes and the weight of her step.

"What the hell got into you, today?" she asked without preamble, her voice slightly slurred and tinged with a blissful inflection. Her words were stern and demanding but her tone was damned near euphoric.

"Are you high?" I asked, arm still pressed to my eyes. I sensed her bristle.

"Fuck you," she slurred. "I don't need judgment from a psycho like you." She giggled at her lame insult and I heard the springs creek as she dropped back onto Ronnie's bed.

"What are you on?" I asked, pushing myself up and studying her. She lay on the bed with her arms out to the side. She was wearing a mini skirt that rode dangerously far up her thighs and a tight white wifebeater over a hot-pink lace bra. Her brown hair was streaked with flares of pink and platinum blonde.

Deb broke my heart. When we first met, she was a lot like Trish— sweet and innocent. Quick to cry and laugh. Nearly a decade later, she'd become a living embodiment of the phrase 'lost cause.' She was hard and mean, with a temper nearly as short as mine. She had unprotected sex with every guy she could pin down, and I'd spent more money on Plan B than I had on food. Twice, I'd found her passed out in the bathroom in a puddle of vomit, and she'd been to the ER once for opioid overdose.

I loved her, though. She was the closest thing I had to family. Where parents and other siblings came and went, Deb and I had managed to stick together. I was the last person left on earth who knew the quality of Deb's soul. I was the only one who remembered the little girl who loved to sing and tucked her mangy stuffed rabbit into bed every night, kissing it gently before she crawled beneath the covers herself.

Deb had been a sweet little girl, which made who she was becoming that much more painful. I couldn't even remember when she'd started using, and maybe that was the problem. If I'd noticed when it started I might have been able to stop it, but I hadn't. I'd let her down. Just like I was letting Alex down. Just like I would eventually let Trish down. Ronnie. Paul…

"What are you on?" I asked again when she answered my initial query with silence.

"It's none of your business," she slurred. "You don't give a shit."

"Deb, don't be stupid," I said, pushing to my feet and sitting on Ronnie's bed beside her. She sat up with a groan and we both stared at the opposite wall.

"I *am* stupid," she said clumsily, her voice suddenly thick with tears. I swallowed a sigh. Deb on drugs was always a rollercoaster.

"You're not stupid," I said, nudging her with my shoulder. "You just gotta stop saying stupid shit, that's all. You know I care about you."

Deb shrugged, sniffing loudly and picking at her acrylic nails.

"You care more about *her*," she said finally, her voice barely more than a whisper. My stomach lurched.

"Who is 'her?'" I asked, cautiously shaping my voice into a tone of amused nonchalance.

"Nevermind," Deb groaned, dropping back onto the bed once more. I knew I should press, but I was afraid to. What if she knew?

"So are you gonna tell me what you're on, or not?" I asked, poking her in the leg.

"Just some shit Kyle gave me," Deb said with a defeated sigh. "It's good stuff."

"Oxy?"

"Maybe," she said listlessly. She dug in her pocket and pulled out a small baggy of assorted pills, eyeing them blearily through the dust-coated plastic as if to decipher the little symbols. I knew she couldn't. Deb couldn't tell the difference between Vicodin and Advil. She just knew what it felt like to be high. That was what she paid for. "He gave me a discount for pulling you off him."

I snatched the bag out of her hand and pushed myself up, stalking toward the door and flinging it open so hard it bounced off the wall. Deb's muddled mind caught up with her and she scrambled after me.

"Don't you fucking dare!" she shrieked, tearing after me as I marched to the bathroom and slammed the toilet lid up.

"You gotta stop with this shit, Deb," I said, shaking her off as she clawed at my arm, reaching for the baggy. I upended it, depositing the contents into the stained toilet bowl.

"You fucking asshole!" Her nails gouged at my arm, but I ignored her and reached out, flushing the toilet. Deb stilled as the water swirled, washing away her high. We both watched in silence, listening to the thirsty gulp of the toilet as it swallowed the pills.

"God, I fucking hate you," Deb whimpered, clinging to my arm as she swayed, her knees half-buckling beneath her. I tried to support her, but she shoved me away. "Why are you so goddamn convinced you have all the answers?"

"I don't!" I whisper-shouted back, worried that raised voices would pull Tim from his drunken stupor in front of the television. "But I do know that this is wrong and so would you if you'd pull your head out of the sand for five seconds. You're gonna end up killing yourself, Deb. That's the only way this ends."

"Fuck you!" Her hissed words were punctuated by the crack of her palm against the side of my face. I staggered back a step, blinking away stars that were caused more by shock than the blow. Deb had never hit me. We lived by a code. A twisted, broken code, but still… there were rules. We'd suffered enough at the hands of the system, so we vowed, years ago, never to hurt each other.

Deb left the room, and a few minutes later I heard the front door slam. She was gone for the night— off to seek comfort with a guy who would, if she was lucky, supply her with the high I'd just stolen.

My instinct was to be hurt. She'd broken a sacred rule. Our code had carried us through years of hardship and abuse. It was our foundation of faith— a thread of good that reminded us through everything that there was something that would never betray our trust. Her slap hurt more than any blow Tim had ever dealt, because I didn't expect it. We never — *never* — hurt each other.

Then again… I stared at the empty toilet bowl, thinking of what she'd said about Alex. Maybe I was the one who'd cast the first stone.

.. .. ..

After Alex's outburst in the hallway, I didn't expect her to be at the spot. That didn't stop me from sneaking out, though. I couldn't bear the thought of her showing up, needing me, and being alone because I was too busy feeling sorry for myself to be there for her.

My heart leapt into my throat when I entered the clearing and saw her sitting there on the rock, leaning back on her hands, face tipped up to the sky.

"Hey, Al," I said cautiously, hopping over the stream.

"Hey," she said easily, still staring up at the stars. I couldn't help but notice that she was dressed a little differently than usual. She seemed to be splitting the difference between daytime Aly and my Alex. She'd traded her dirty cargo shorts for cut-off jeans that left most of her legs exposed, shining in the moonlight. Instead of a t-shirt, she wore a tank top, the straps of her bra peeking out to tease me. Her hair was back in a loose braid rather than hidden beneath a baseball cap. Her feet were bare, heels drumming gently against the side of the rock.

"I, uh…" I cleared my throat, unexpectedly nervous. "I didn't think you'd be here."

"I've been thinking," she said, lowering herself onto her back.

"Okay…"

"Come lay with me?"

Hesitant, I hoisted myself onto the rock and stretched out beside her. She shifted naturally into her usual position, canted a little sideways with her head on my shoulder. The faint, floral scent of her shampoo filled my head and my mouth grew dry with need.

"I've been a jerk lately," Alex said.

"No you haven't. You—"

"Let me finish," she cut me off, her voice gentle but firm. I clapped my mouth shut and eyed the stars, trying to find a constellation. She'd showed them to me a thousand times but I still had trouble finding the shapes.

"Okay."

"I've been a jerk lately," she began again, turning onto her side and pressing her hand to my chest. "I've been having a lot of trouble since my mom died, and I've kind of shut down. I'm sorry for snapping at you, today. I know you were just trying to help."

Her hand slid slowly down to my belt buckle and began fumbling with it. I swear I nearly had a heart attack.

"What are you doing?" I asked, jerking away from her and hopping off the

106

rock, putting as much distance between us as I could. Something felt terribly wrong. Of course, in a sense, something also felt incredibly *right* and my dick was screaming at me— cursing me for pulling away.

Mostly, though, it felt wrong. Alex was bold, but she wasn't unceremonious. Everything she did made sense. Her every move fit like a puzzle piece into the dance we'd created together. There was a rhythm to it— a heartbeat— and her sudden, unexpected advance-apology combo was completely out of sync. It made my skin crawl.

"I want to have sex," Alex said plainly, sitting up. I took a step back from the dead look in her eyes. *No you don't.*

"No you don't," I said aloud, shaking my head. "What's going on with you?"

"I want to have sex," Alex repeated, hopping off the rock and stalking toward me until I stood at the edge of the island with nowhere else to go. She threw herself against me, her hands possessively groping at my ass as she pulled me tighter to her. I felt dizzy— my mind and heart in violent disagreement with my body.

"No you don't," I said again, my voice muffled at the end as she reached up with one hand, her fingers gripping my hair hard as she pulled my head down and pressed her lips to mine.

I shouldn't have returned the kiss. I *knew* something was wrong. I *knew* she was up to something. There was something about the sharp pain of her fingers in my hair, though, that broke me wide open. I was a shaken-up can of beer and she'd just cracked the top. My need for her spilled over, and suddenly the tables were turned.

I kissed her back hard, plundering every inch of her mouth. I pulled the elastic out of her hair, shaking it loose, and buried my hand in the tangled locks as I walked her backward. When her ass hit the rock I lifted her onto it, following her as she tipped back. I kept my left hand behind her, cushioning her head, and allowed my right to roam as I kissed her. I released the button on her shorts— an unspoken promise for more— before moving north beneath her shirt.

Her bra was a hindrance, so I lifted her up just enough to worm my hand beneath her back and unclasp it. As soon as it popped loose I let her back down, breathing a sigh of relief as I curved my hand over her chest. Alex sighed too, her back arching slightly, arms linked around my neck as if to hold me to her— as if I had any intention or ability to leave.

"I love you," I breathed against her lips, the words as involuntary as they were true. She moaned in response, her breath coming faster as I kneaded the soft flesh in my hand.

The sense of wrongness was still there, but we'd evolved around it. The clumsy misstep of her blunt forwardness had become part of our dance. We were being rough with each other— rougher than we'd ever been. Her teeth grazed my lip as she kissed me and her legs wrapped around my waist, locking me in. Her hands gripped my shoulders so hard her nails bit into my skin.

I wasn't sparing her, either. My weight must be driving her against the hard granite, scraping her bare skin against the rock. I felt pebbled flesh beneath my palm and rolled it between my finger and thumb, pinching. She gasped in pain and pleasure, her legs tightening around me, and a jolt of electricity shot up my spine.

Suddenly, Alex was pulling away, shoving at me. I stumbled back, equal parts frustrated, confused, and afraid. Tears glistened in her eyes as she sat up, and disgust at my own weakness turned my stomach over. I'd known it was wrong. I'd known she didn't really want it. I'd let my dick act on my behalf, and I'd hurt her.

"Shit, Al," I groaned, taking another step back. "I'm sorr—"

"Shut up," she hissed, ripping her shirt off in one smooth motion. Her bra, already unclasped, slipped down her arms and she tossed it aside. It landed half in the stream. Her watery gaze was fixed on mine as she slipped off the rock and shoved her shorts down her legs, kicking them away. She wasn't wearing underwear.

Shit.

"Al—"

"You talk too much," she said, stalking forward, her body on full display in the moonlight. I swallowed hard, my head swimming with an uncomfortable combination of lust and concern.

"Alex, just tell me—"

"We're done talking," she said, hammering her point home by throwing herself at me, tackling me to the ground.

We landed in a mess of limbs at the edge of the island, cold water licking at the back of my head and the nape of my neck. Alex straddled my waist, her hands tangled in my shirt as she bent down, pulling the protest straight from my lungs with a kiss that had me seeing sound and tasting color.

Again, my body took over. Something about being tackled off my feet flipped a switch inside me and instinct rose up, demanding that I find my way to a position of advantage. I rolled, pinning her beneath me without breaking the kiss, and she made no effort to stop me. The only sign she gave of awareness was the feel of her hands, which let go of the front of my shirt and found their way to the hem, tugging restlessly until I sat up enough for her to tug it up and off.

Cool, fall air brushed across my skin as Alex tossed my shirt away. I pushed my hands into the rocky ground, staring down at her. She lay pliant beneath me, her hair drifting and swirling in the water of the stream.

"Don't think," she whispered, reaching between us, working at the clasp of my belt and unzipping my jeans "Please just don't think."

I almost disobeyed. There was something about the desperation in her voice that set off alarm bells in my head. I opened my mouth to ask her what was wrong, but all that came out was a groan, as she chose that moment to slip her hand down the front of my boxers.

"Fuck," I gasped, dropping down to my forearms and capturing her lips with mine, trying to distract myself from the sensation of her small fingers milking me of every last shred of resolve. "Alex," I breathed against her mouth. "You can't—"

"Shut up," she whispered, and when I tried again to protest, she bit my lip. Hard. "I told you to stop thinking."

The wrongness was hovering, mixing its steps into our dance, tripping us up, singing a discordant, arrhythmic song that made my heart stutter and stole the breath from my lungs. I was a slave to its pull, following the whitewater current as it bashed me about until I couldn't have told you which direction was up.

I could hardly breathe as I pulled back, gently tugging her hand away.

"What the fuck is wrong with you?" Alex hissed, sitting up as I stumbled to my feet. "I'm trying to give you my fucking virginity, Nate. Do you want it or not?"

"Of course I want it," I hissed back, fumbling in my pocket for my wallet. My fingers shook so hard I struggled to pull the foil wrapper from its place, nestled in the lining. "You wanna be a teen mom?"

My jeans went the way of my shirt, and I tossed my wallet on top of them. I found my shirt in a heap a few feet away and shook the sand out of it before spreading it over the rock. Alex was still sitting on the ground when I turned around and tugged her to her feet, my other hand still clenched around the wrapped condom. I kissed her so deeply her back arched, her soft body melding against the surface of my chest. Her hands were like twin brands, burning into the skin of my back as we drank each other in.

"You're sure?" I asked, pulling back. Tears streamed down her face and the slithering, dissonant hum of wrongness crescendoed.

"I'm sure," she whispered, nodding, and suddenly I was at war with myself. My hands lifted her up, carrying her to the rock, completely at odds with my mind which screamed at me to stop— *stop*, before I committed some terrible, irreversible wrong. Then her legs tightened around me, and my body throbbed with a fierce need that battled back my heart, which burrowed, trembling and wary, into my chest.

Stop, stop, stop!!! The voice in the back of my mind screamed the words at me as I tugged on her ankle until she loosened her hold, letting me step back, appreciating every inch of her perfect body. My fingers shook as I reached out and brushed sand off her belly and thighs. Her muscles tensed beneath my touch, and her chest rose and fell jerkily as she fought to stifle her sobs.

"Alex…" I couldn't find my words. I felt trapped— caught between two horrible futures. In one future, I walked away. I put my clothes on and left her alone, just like everyone else had done. I couldn't stomach that thought. In the second future, I took what she was offering and, for the rest of her life, she would think back to the night she lost her virginity and remember nothing but pain and tears. Frustration and anger.

"Just shut up," Alex moaned, pushing herself back on the rock. She braced her feet to either side of me and let her legs fall open. I damn near passed out at the sight, but at the same time she let her head drop back against the rock, staring up at the sky as if begging the stars for guidance.

"Alex just tell me truth," I choked, leaning over her, blocking her view of the sky. Since the night I met her and she had begun teaching me the constellations, Alex had embodied the stars for me—brilliant and unattainable. Just this once, I wanted to be the same for her.

Her eyes met mine and, in an instant, the wrongness evaporated. We fell back into the smooth steps of our dance and the music rang clear. Tears matted her eyelashes together and trickled over her temples. Her hands, suddenly gentle, came up to frame my face.

"I want you," she whispered, and I could hear the truth in her voice. Her words weren't stern or angry or desperate. They were deeply, achingly lonely. "Please, Nate. Don't leave me alone. I just want you."

"Okay," I managed, bending to press a kiss to her lips. She closed her eyes with a shuddering sigh, and I kissed her eyelids, too, tasting the salt of her tears. I kissed the bridge of her nose and the curve of each cheekbone. My clumsy tongue wasn't capable of sweet words, so I worshipped her with my lips, because she had to know. She had to know that I wasn't taking. She was giving and she needed to feel the gratitude that coursed through my veins.

"Please," she moaned, arching her hips against me, and I reached between us, slipping two fingers between her legs. She gasped as my fingers slid deeper. She was slick and warm… ready.

I groaned, grabbing her hand and guiding it between her legs. She seemed to read my mind, taking over for me as I eased my fingers out of her. She touched herself, her heels digging into the back of my thighs as I pushed away just far enough to shove my boxers down and grab the condom off the rock by her hip.

I tore the wrapper open with my teeth and made quick work of rolling the condom on, my eyes locked on her face as her own squeezed shut in pleasure as she kept herself ready.

I hated the condom. I'd never minded them before, but this was Alex. For some reason, it felt like blasphemy to deprive either of us of even those scant nanometers of contact.

I pushed Alex's hand aside, smothering her moan with a kiss as I took over for her. "You gotta look at me, angel," I whispered, stilling my fingers until she opened her eyes, glaring at me. "Are you absolutely sure?" I asked, reaching between us and guiding myself into place, nudging against her so she knew exactly what I was asking.

There wasn't even a second of hesitation. Her hands gripped my hips, digging in painfully. Her lips parted and fiery eyes met mine, glassy with need. "Yes," she said, her voice hoarse. "Yes."

I didn't think it was possible to love her more, but the second I entered her I learned what love really meant. She gasped and cried out, contracting around me, and I fell. I fell so fucking hard I forgot my own name. I fell and spent the rest of my life waiting to hit the ground.

CHAPTER TWEVLE

ALEX

I expected the pain. I'd read about it, so the aching pressure didn't surprise me, nor did the sudden, awful tearing sensation. I cried out, digging my nails into his skin, but I wasn't surprised.

What really took me aback was the slow burn in my chest. It had started in the moments before he pushed inside me— when I met his eye for the first time that night and saw, not animalistic lust, but pain and love. The burn only grew as my body opened up with that terrible ripping pain. Fresh tears rose up in my eyes, but Nate's shaking fingers pushed the hair back from my face and soft kisses landed on my temples, soaking up the tears.

"Okay?" he asked breathlessly, and I nodded, the burn in my chest growing to a roaring fire. It melted the ice inside me like a blowtorch and all of a sudden every pain and worry that I'd stifled and preserved in waking death came back to me at once. I cried. Not silent tears, anymore, but heaving, gasping sobs.

"Al, what's the matter?" Nate asked, and I felt him pulling back, sliding out of me. My limbs acted on their own, legs locking around his hips, hands gripping his back.

"Don't stop," I gasped. Overwhelmed. I opened my eyes and blinked away tears, letting him see the truth in my eyes. "Please keep going. I need…" What did I need? I needed *this*. I needed *him*. "I need to feel alive, Nate. Please."

Strain twisted his features, making him look much older than we were. He hesitated, jaw clenched so tight I was surprised I couldn't hear his teeth cracking.

"Please," I said again, letting my body take over. I didn't know exactly what I was doing, but I let the muscles inside me clench around him, and the tension on his face fell away, replaced by something akin to rapture. He bit out a groan and dropped his head, stealing a kiss from my lips.

"Stop that, Al," he breathed.

"But it feels good," I whispered back, truthfully. I did it again, and small fireworks of aching pleasure burst deep inside me.

"Fuck," Nate choked. "Stop it, Alex. You're killing me."

"Then kill me back," I moaned, frustrated.

Would you believe me if I told you we came at the same time? Would you even believe me if I told you I came at all? That's not normal, right? A girl's first time is just a technicality. It's a thing that has to happen to prepare her body for the real adventure.

I guess I attribute our success to Nate's infuriating fear of hurting me. My body had time to get used to him before he started moving. I had time to learn what those muscles inside me could do and how my use of them affected both of us.

Nate moved like a machine— slowly at first, then faster, responding automatically as I tightened and released around him. That was all I got from him that first time, though— movement. I got no loving words, no eye contact, no attention. He braced himself on his forearms and buried his face in the crook of my neck, breath hot and irregular on my skin. I asked him, later, what his problem was, and he admitted that the second he pushed inside me it took everything he had— every ounce of energy and concentration— not to explode like a 'two pump chump.'

I, of course, found a way to be his opposite. He was stiff and mechanical and restrained, and I cut loose. I was alive, for the first time in months. Stars exploded behind my eyes and my body writhed and bucked beneath his weight. Those clever inner muscles of mine pulled him deeper inside me until I felt perfectly, wonderfully full and complete. His every movement tore a whimper of pure relief from my lips, pounding home that sense of wholeness until there was no more room for it inside me.

I laughed a little as I came. I watched the stars, and my laugh turned to a primal scream as every muscle in my body escaped my control. The gritty surface of the rock abraded my skin, but the pain fed the fire of my pleasure, withering and dissolving into the flames. My hips rose to meet his as I threw my head back and arched off the rock, tears of bliss streaming down my face.

The colors exploding in my eyes faded, my muscles relaxed, and I collapsed against the rock. Nate was still moving inside me, and aftershocks of agonizing pleasure rose within me in response to his thrusts. I shuddered with each one, counting four before he grew suddenly and extremely still. His muscles shook and a growl rumbled, low in his throat. Where my orgasm was a white-capped wave of pleasure, his seemed to be more of a sudden release of pressure. One second he was shifting tension, the next he was near deadweight on top of me, barely able to support himself on shaking arms to hold his body off of me.

We stayed that way for I-don't-know-how-long. Me, sprawled on the rock. Him, bent over me, still buried inside me. When he finally spoke, he didn't lift his face, and I struggled to make out the muffled words.

"You okay?" he mumbled.

"Yeah," I whispered, smoothing gentle fingers over the indentations my nails had left in his skin. "Yeah, I'm good."

He nodded against me. Then, after a bracing breath, he slowly straightened, pulling out of me. His departure left me feeling cold and empty, fresh air sweeping over my sweat-coated skin. I felt alive, but now that the distraction of his presence was gone, all the hurt that had thawed in the fire hit me full force.

I wept. Sprawled on the rock, naked as the day I was born, I scrubbed my hands over my face and sobbed. Distantly, I heard splashing as Nate cleaned up in the stream, and the sound of cloth on skin as he slipped back into his jeans. Then his hands were on me, gentle but firm, pulling me to my feet.

I stood, swaying, tears dripping into the sand by my feet, listening to the gentle splashing sound as he rinsed his blood-stained t-shirt in the creek. The cloth was icy and rough as he used it to clean the sticky combination of blood and arousal from my legs. He dunked the shirt a few more times in the creek, scrubbing it clean, before ringing it out and spreading it on the rock to dry.

All I could do was cry and comply as he helped me back into my clothes, with the exception of my bra which had washed away. When he took me in his arms and sank down beside the rock, I followed him willingly. I curled up in his lap and pressed my face into his shoulder and cried until I was empty.

I felt hollowed out when the tears finally stopped, and I must have drifted into sleep for a few minutes, because the gentle jostling of Nate's arms brought me startling back to wakefulness.

"We gotta get you home, soon, Al," he whispered in my ear, but I didn't want to move. I tipped my head back so I could see his face.

"I'm sorry I…" how could I even describe what had happened? *I'm sorry I gave up? I'm sorry I forgot myself? I'm sorry I froze?* "I'm sorry I left," I said, finally, hoping he'd understand. Or, rather, *knowing* he would understand and hoping he would hear how much I loved him for that alone.

"You're back now," he said softly, trailing a finger down the bridge of my nose. There was a hint of question in the statement. A hint of fear.

"I'm back," I affirmed, snuggling deeper into him.

Of course, coming back hadn't been my intent. My intent was to seduce him, use him, and send him packing with the one thing I thought he wanted. I hadn't expected the desperate fight to make him take what I was offering, or the bonfire our coupling had ignited in my chest. I'd set out to free him so I could die in peace. Instead, he'd brought me back to life and we were more inextricably bound than ever before.

"You need to get home, Al," he said reluctantly, holding up his watch to show me. "It's almost five."

It was, indeed. Which meant I must have slept for hours, not minutes.

We found our feet, and Nate pulled on his still-damp t-shirt. The woods were almost perfectly silent. Those minutes just before dawn belong to rebels, defying the rules of nature and society. The nocturnal animals sense the coming sun and scamper off to bed. The daytime animals slumber on, waiting for dawn. Even the wind goes still and the air settles close to the ground, misty and thick.

Those minutes were just ours. We belonged to neither the night nor the day, but to each other. We abided by no rules beyond the sacred, unstated truth of *us*. I grasped Nate's hand and strode through the misty air, my heart beating strong in my chest, my blood coursing with newfound strength and energy. Sadness dogged my footsteps, as it would for the rest of time, but it no longer controlled me. I'd domesticated my grief— tamed it so that it slouched behind me, weak and defeated, snapping futilely at my heels.

We stopped at the treeline and stood in perfect silence, watching fog drift over the pristine expanse of my neighborhood's back yard. Swings hung silent and unmoving in their chains, and three houses down a light was on in the kitchen— some early morning jogger having a bite to eat and waiting for the sun to rise.

Nate's fingers twitched in mine, and he turned toward me, cupping my cheek in his free hand. He opened his mouth as if to speak, but no words came out. He just studied my face, like he could read our future in the curve of my lips and the bloodshot whites of my eyes.

"Please don't go away again," he said finally, his voice barely more than a breath of air. "I can't..." he broke off, shaking his head and lowering his gaze to the dirt beneath our feet. When he raised his face, there was frantic desperation in his eyes. He pulled his hand from mine and framed my face. "You're the only good thing, Alex," he said hoarsely. "I can't lose you."

There was terrible truth in his words, fear in his eyes, and a swift undercurrent of pain in his voice. He'd been my unflappable pillar of strength and support since the day I turned twelve. It scared me to see him wavering, just as it thrilled me to know *I* was the one who'd set the earth to trembling beneath his feet.

"You won't," I said firmly, stepping into him, offering comfort and absorbing it at the same time. His arms wrapped around my shoulders, squeezing tight, like I'd dissolve into the air if he let go. "I won't leave again," I said, my hold on him just as tight and just as desperate. "I promise I won't leave again."

It wasn't the first or the last time I lied to him, but it was the most significant lie I ever told. The one that would come back, again and again, to haunt us both.

115

Even if I'd known, though, how many times it would hurt us, I'd still have said it, because the really important part was the one that came next. The one that I kept to myself.

Even if I do leave, I vowed to the stars, *I'll always come back.*

That was the truth.

.. .. ..

Nate tried to walk me to the front door, but I stopped him by the old oak beneath my window. He frowned at the branches above us.

"I thought we were over this, Al," he said, brow furrowing as he turned his gaze to me.

"I am. I was…" I trailed off, looking up at my window. "I just… I feel good tonight," I said lamely, leaning back against the trunk of the tree and tipping my head back against the rough bark. "I want this night to feel more like the beginning. I don't want it to feel like the last few months. I want to go through the window like I still have it in me to care if I get caught."

Nate sighed.

"Fine," he said, dropping to a knee and linking his hands together for me to step in. "Be careful, though."

"Always!" I said brightly, letting him boost me up to the lowest branch. I straddled it and, wrapping my arms and legs around the limb, tipped sideways, letting myself drop and hang like a koala. I giggled at Nate's sharp gasp and hung my head backwards to see him on his feet beneath me, arms out, ready to break my fall.

"You're an idiot," I said, hanging onto the branch with one hand and reaching out with the other to pull him close by the front of his shirt. He grudgingly accepted my kiss goodbye and stepped back, crossing his arms over his chest as I swung back up onto the branch and started climbing.

I've talked about fear before— about my theory that we are born fearless. Every anxiety is just a lesson learned. I imagine the wisest, most experienced people are also the most afraid. Somewhere deep down, beneath the serenity of understanding and acceptance, there must be a suffocating miasma of terror because they know every *way* every *thing* can hurt us.

I learned to fear water when I was four. It's one of my earliest memories— sitting forgotten in the grass while my father pulled Tommy's lifeless body from our neighbor's pool. He was gray and limp, and even after they got him breathing again something was missing. I was too young to understand the nuances of oxygen deprivation and brain damage, but I understood enough to know that

116

water had hurt my brother. I understood that water demanded respect.

I learned to fear cars when my childhood cat, Mr. Bug, escaped the house and ran out into the street, just as a shiny red sedan came tearing around the corner. I was chasing my wayward pet, but Momma snatched me up just before I reached the curb. Mr. Bug wasn't so lucky.

I was always wary of small spaces, but that one makes sense too. Momma once told me I was born with the umbilical cord around my neck. I'd bet I have some deep, instinctual memory of being trapped, condensed, and suffocating before I even knew what it was to breathe.

I learned to fear falling on the night I lost my virginity. It happened as I was reaching for my window, legs and one hand wrapped around the bobbing branch, left hand outstretched, shoving the window up.

I heard the crack and froze on instinct, my mouth suddenly bone dry. Nate was saying something, his voice taut and frantic below me. The branch bounced with my weight, leaves rustling above me. I didn't even breathe as another sharp crack rent the air.

Then I was falling. Falling through slapping leaves and stinging branches. Falling through time. My left arm hit a branch and I cried out as sharp pain lanced all the way up to my shoulder. Then my head struck something hard and I was falling through eternity, spiraling and plummeting through white light into inky darkness.

I never even felt myself hit the ground.

CHAPTER THIRTEEN

NATE

I caught her.

Not that it did much fucking good. I should have insisted she use the front door. Hell, it was probably my fault the branch broke, too. I weighed more than her, and I'd used it every day for a week when her mom died. The constant strain of my weight had probably weakened it.

Everything happened in slow motion. I heard the branch crack, and saw her freeze. Then there was a snap and she was falling, screaming, her limbs flailing as she tumbled through leaves and branches.

Then there was a sharp crack of what sounded like wood on wood, and she fell terribly, deathly silent as she plummeted toward the earth.

Somehow, I got beneath her, arms outstretched like an idiot. Her weight carried us both to the ground in a tangle of limbs. Her elbow struck me in the nose and I saw stars, every molecule of air crushed from my lungs as I landed on my back in the grass, her deadweight sprawled across my chest.

"Alex," I choked, sitting up and cradling her head as her weight slid into my lap. Her eyes were closed and blood coated the side of her face, oozing from a terrifying gash on her temple. Her right arm flopped to the side, bent strangely between her elbow and her wrist. White bone glistened at me—an accusation.

"Alex wake up," I pleaded, holding my hand beneath her nose. When a puff of warm air hit my skin I gasped out a sob of relief. She was alive. Still alive.

I scanned her body for further injuries, but the broken arm and the head wound seemed to be the extent of it. Not that those weren't enough.

"Please, angel," I said, gently slapping her cheek. "Please open your eyes."

She didn't. She remained limp and motionless in my arms, her breathing so slow and shallow I could barely see her chest rise and fall in the darkness. I pressed shaking, bloody fingers to her throat and her pulse hammered against my fingers, racing against time.

"What the hell is going— Aly!"

I had lost all awareness of my surroundings when Alex fell, and hadn't even noticed the light spilling out over the front lawn as the front porch light flipped on. I hadn't heard the front door slam, or noticed her father circle around to the side yard. Startled, I looked up when I heard his voice and was blinded by a beam of light shining directly into my eyes.

"Get away from my daughter!" the older man yelled, stumbling towards us. As the stars cleared from my eyes, I saw that he was wielding a kitchen knife in one hand and a heavy flashlight in the other.

"She fell," I tried to explain. "She hit her head. You need to—"

"I've called the police," he snarled. "They'll be here any second. Get the hell away from my daughter!"

Part of me appreciated his ferocity. I saw a little of Alex in his glare. The middle-aged, pot-bellied preacher raised his knife, ready to commit a cardinal sin to protect his daughter, and it almost made me smile. I'd tell her about this when she woke up. This aggressive display couldn't make up for years of terrible parenting, but she deserved to know how much he loved her in a pinch.

"Okay," I said. "I'll move."

As slowly as I dared, and as gently as I could manage, I lowered Alex to the ground and backed away, hands held up by my head as her father scrambled forward, dropping to his knees beside her.

He dropped the flashlight but hung on to the knife, brushing the hair off her face with his free hand and scanning her body, as I had, for injuries. He cried out when he saw her broken arm, his panicked tears splattering against her bare skin.

"What happened?" he moaned, bending over her, stroking her hair. "What happened?"

"She fell," I tried to explain, but he cut me off with a glare, brandishing the knife.

"Stay back!" he ordered. "What did you do to her? What did you do?"

He was weeping openly, his body curled protectively over hers, and my dumbass brain finally caught up with his. I'd been so preoccupied with her fall and my own fear that I hadn't even thought of what this must look like.

Her father had heard her scream and run outside. He'd found her, apparently beaten and bloodied, in the shadows by his house. He saw her scant clothing and sex-matted hair. He saw the claw marks on my arms and neck, and my bleeding nose.

He saw his precious daughter, hurt and unconscious. He saw the man who had hurt her. *Raped* her.

119

"Wait!" I said, shaking my head frantically. My body told me to run, but I couldn't leave. I couldn't leave Alex unconscious, bleeding into the grass. "You've got it wrong," I said, dropping to my knees, trying to make myself look as harmless as possible. "We're together. We meet every night. She climbs in the window, but the branch broke. I didn't hurt her. I swear to you, sir, I didn't touch her."

But that wasn't expressly true, and he didn't seem inclined to listen. He just waved the knife at me and bent over his daughter, blind with the need to protect. I respected him more in that moment than I ever had before.

Sirens screamed and flashing lights bounced off the walls of the house.

"We're back here!" her father yelled, summoning two uniformed police officers who ran around the corner of the house, hands on their pistols. One of them saw Alex's body and his eyes widened. He reached for the radio clipped to his lapel and called for an ambulance.

Thank God.

"He did this!" Mr. Winger said, dropping the knife and jabbing his finger at me.

I shoved to my feet, shaking my head, arms held up by my head. "She fell," I said frantically. "She fell. I didn't... she fell." I sounded ridiculous, and some intelligent part of me— muffled by roaring panic— told me everything would go smoother if I just shut up and let them take me. But if they took me, we would be separated. I wouldn't be there when she opened her eyes. *If* she opened her eyes.

Panic spiked and I stumbled backwards. "I didn't fucking hurt her!" I said, louder, as the two officers advanced. One of them pulled a Taser from his belt, but I hardly noticed it. My eyes were glued to Alex. A third officer had rounded the corner and was kneeling by her head, gently pushing her father aside. He peeled her eyelids back, one by one, and shined a light in them.

"Get on the ground and put your hands behind your head," someone yelled, but I could barely hear it. The officer examining Alex was frowning, and I didn't know what that meant. Was he just a frowny kind of guy, or had his light-in-the-eyes assessment turned up something unsetting?

"Please let me stay with her," I pleaded, unable to tear my eyes from Alex's still form. "She's my—"

Get on the fucking ground," they told me.

Just then, Alex moved. She groaned, and her head rolled to the side, eyes cracking open. Suddenly it was just her and me. Her good arm twitched, reaching for me, and I staggered toward her, tears of relief breaking loose from my eyes and streaming down my face.

Then something bit into my arm and my chest, and the world turned orange and tipped sideways. A crackling sound clicked in rhythm with the muscle-locking agony that pulsed through every tendon and bone in my body. I hit the ground hard, unable to break my fall. My lungs refused to expand and my body twitched and jerked as electric fire clicked through me.

When the Taser finally stopped I was on my stomach with a bony knee in the small of my back and my arms pulled taut behind me. The familiar feel of cold steel on my wrists accompanied the snapping buzz of locking handcuffs.

My head spun as they hauled me to my feet and ripped the Taser leads out of my skin. Alex was unconscious again, but I heard more sirens and knew the ambulance was on the way. I let the cops march me to the front yard and shove me in the back of a squad car. My left shoulder protested loudly, but I ignored it, pressing my forehead against the glass window and trying to make out what was happening as my two arresting officers jogged back to the side yard.

Flashing lights announced the arrival of the ambulance, and two uniformed medics appeared in my frame of view, dashing toward the side of the house, one of them carrying a backboard.

It felt like an eternity before they reappeared, and in those eons my mind flashed through every nightmare scenario my corrupt imagination could conjure. I envisioned blood in her skull, pressing down on her brain until her heart forgot to beat. I pictured horrific internal injuries bleeding her dry from the inside. I imagined her waking up and crying out in pain, searching for me, and thinking that I had abandoned her. I saw her lungs collapsing in her chest and her breathless gasping as she fought for air.

When a crowd of people rounded the corner of the house, I squinted in the dim morning light, straining to see through the smudged, tinted glass. Alex was strapped to a backboard, a brace around her neck and an oxygen mask over her face. Her eyes were closed, but her breath fogged the mask, and I let out a ragged breath of relief. The cops carried the backboard between them, while the paramedics scrambled into the ambulance and pulled out a stretcher. They secured her, backboard and all, on the stretcher and covered her with a blanket before wheeling her out of sight.

I leaned back against the seat as best I could with my arms twisted behind me. Alex was safe. She was in good hands. She would wake up with her teary-eyed father by her side and know that he cared about her. She'd be okay.

Nothing else mattered.

.. .. ..

I'd been arrested before, but it was always for stupid shit. Shoplifting, fighting, loitering… crap like that. Criminals like me were a dime a dozen, and I fit like a beige couch into the decor of the crowded police station. Nobody ever looked at me twice.

Being arrested for rape and battery of a young girl, though? That gets you some attention. Special treatment, too, dished out in small, easy-to-deny increments.

The first offense were the handcuffs, which were painfully tight. They dug into my wrists hard enough to draw blood, which trickled over my hand and dripped off my pinky finger when they hauled me out of the car at the station.

The second treat came when I 'fell' during the walk from the car to the exterior door of the station. Someone's booted foot tangled with mine and I slammed into the pavement, concrete digging into my chin and drawing fresh blood. Neither officer spoke. They just hauled me to my feet and shoved me forward.

Everyone stopped and stared when they marched me through the station. An elderly woman in a pink sweater— a receptionist— glared daggers at me. Detectives in plainclothes wrinkled their noses. Uniformed officers smirked at my scraped-up face, probably recognizing the evidence of some understood ritual.

I wasn't angry. If I really was a rapist I'd deserve to get roughed up. The only issue was that I wasn't a rapist, I would never hit a woman, and I didn't have time for this bullshit. I needed to find Alex and make sure that she was okay.

They left me in an interview room with my arms still cuffed behind me. I tried to ask about Alex as the officers left, but they ignored me. For an offense this serious, they had to call me a lawyer, right? Maybe I could ask the lawyer to call the hospital for me.

There was a clock beside the two-way mirror on the opposite wall. It was protected by a wire cage, bolted in place. Everything in the room was bolted down. The chairs, the table. The camera in the corner, blinking at me as it recorded my every breath.

The hour hand on the clock was stuck between five and six, and the minute hand had just passed the seven when the police officers left me alone. I watched that minute hand trace its full circle three and a half times before the door finally opened again. A balding man in an off-white button up, stained khakis, and a thin brown tie marched through the door and planted himself in the chair across from me, dropping a yellow legal pad on the table between us. There was a badge on his belt and a compact firearm holstered at his side.

Not a lawyer, then…

The other officers had already read my rights and I'd been arrested enough times to know the drill. I didn't have to say a thing, and I knew the smartest way forward would be silence.

Intelligence is overrated.

"Is Alex okay?" I blurted, my voice hoarse from thirst and disuse.

The investigator glared at me, the bald surface of his head shining in the fluorescent light.

"The young lady you assaulted is in serious condition," he said sharply, jotting something down on the notepad as he spoke. "She has a concussion and the break in her arm will require surgery. She has defensive wounds, and it looks like she got in a few good blows before you rendered her unconscious." His eyebrows drew down and he met my eye, his gaze flinty. "Believe me when I say that we can and *will* bury you in forensic evidence, Mr. Reynolds. The best thing for you to do is cooperate fully with our investigation. If you're honest with us from the start, maybe we can see about reducing your sentence and giving you a chance at parole."

That was bullshit. Smart-sounding bullshit, but bullshit all the same. He didn't have the authority to reduce my sentence. He was just trying to get information. Fine.

"Alex and I are friends," I said. "I would never hurt her."

"Do you care to explain to me why your *'friend*,'" he put the word in air quotes and I wanted to cave his face in with my fists, "would want to hurt *you*?" He waved at my nose which had finally stopped oozing blood. With my hands locked behind me, I couldn't wipe it away, and a film of dried blood cracked and itched on my chin.

"I tried to catch her when she fell," I growled. "Her elbow hit me."

"What a hero," the investigator said sarcastically, chuckling without humor. "What about all the marks?" He gestured at my neck, where her nails had scraped across my skin. "Did her cat scratch you up while you were rescuing it from a tree?"

No way in hell was I going to tell this asshole that my girl turned into a wildcat when I fucked her. Her nails had gouged deep grooves in my back, sides, and neck, and I didn't mind a single bit. I fucking loved it.

"They're unrelated," I said lamely.

"I'm sure they are," he said absently, annotating something on his notepad.

The questioning went on for an hour. I tried to answer honestly, and stayed stubbornly silent for those questions I couldn't answer without telling the asshole things he had no right to know.

He left after the hour, taking his notepad of scribbled condemnations with him.

Minutes turned back into hours. I couldn't feel my fingers anymore, and blood trickled slowly over my hands, dripping onto the tile floor. My mouth was so dry I could barely swallow. My nose throbbed, my shoulder ached, and every time I started to doze or daydream, an image of Alex's lifeless face flashed in my vision and jerked me awake to buzzing, yellow-white fluorescents.

Just after lunchtime, two new officers came into the room and hauled me off to booking. They uncuffed me to print my fingers, and if either of them took notice of the bloody grooves in my wrists, they didn't mention it. I held the placard with my name and the jurisdiction of my arrest while they snapped my photo from the front and both sides.

Once they'd processed me, they took me back to the interview room. They cuffed my hands in front of me, though, which was a considerable kindness. One of them brought a paper cup of water, too, which I guzzled the second they shut the door behind them.

I used the sleeve of my shirt to wipe the bulk of the blood from my face, and then settled in for the wait. The next person I saw was going to tell me about Alex, whether they wanted to or not.

CHAPTER FOURTEEN

ALEX

"Aly, sugar, can you open your eyes for me?"

The familiar voice, while low and soothing, sent jackhammers of pain roaring to life in my skull. I groaned, lifting a hand to my aching head, but my arm was heavy and unwieldy. I let it drop back to my side.

"Is she coming around?" asked another voice, this one louder and unfamiliar. Feminine and chipper. It was more like an icepick than a jackhammer.

"I think so. Aly, can you hear me?" Fingers gripped my hand, squeezing hard, and something told me I needed to squeeze back. I tried, and heard a stifled sob. Something wet dripped on my arm. "Oh, sugar, it's okay. I'm here. You're gonna be okay. I'm right here."

Daddy? I tried to speak, but my tongue was as dry as sandpaper and my throat felt swollen and sore.

"Open your eyes for me, Aly," said the female voice, closer now, and small, cool fingers brushed over my forehead. I thought of Momma and a tiny, weary ache flared to life in my chest. "If you open your eyes you can have some water."

This lady knew how to make a deal. It hurt like hell, but I managed to peel open one gritty eye, then the other. The lights were dim, but I still flinched as shafts of pain seemed to shoot straight through my eyeballs and into my brain.

"Good girl," Daddy said, and his face materialized above me, puffy and tear-streaked. His jaw was covered in stubble, and dark shadows surrounded his eyes. Even so, he was smiling, the corners of his eyes crinkling as he leaned in close and pressed a kiss to my forehead. "You're okay, Aly. I'm right here."

Where is 'here'?

Mr. Winger, why don't you go get Aly some ice chips," the stranger's voice said, and I tipped my head toward her as my father left, with promises to return shortly. A young woman in a purple top with rainbow polka-dots stood on my

125

right side. A stethoscope hung around her neck and there was a badge clipped to her pocket. A doctor? Nurse?

Hospital?

Panic flashed through me, sending a flare of agony through the thick soup of my brain. Why was I here? The last thing I remembered was... what *was* the last thing I remembered? School, maybe? Fighting with Nate in the hallway? Was I in a car accident or something?

"Easy, Aly," the woman said, pressing a hand to my shoulder as I fought the pain in order to rise. "You're safe. You're at St. Luke's and you're gonna be just fine. My name is Maria and I'll be your nighttime nurse while you stay with us. Do you remember what happened?"

I shook my head minutely, aware that any greater movement would set off bells in my pounding head.

"That's okay," Maria said, smiling broadly. "You've got a pretty bad concussion so it's normal to have some memory loss. It should come back."

Should?

I wanted to ask her what the hell had happened, but my father came back, holding a paper cup and a plastic spoon. He settled into the chair next to me while the nurse fiddled with a machine by my bed. All I could do was lay there while my father spooned ice chips into my mouth. They melted on my tongue, soothing my throat, and I nearly moaned in pleasure.

"Not too many," the nurse chided, patting my shoulder before turning to my father. "I'll be right down the hall if you need me. Just press the call button."

Daddy just kept feeding my ice chips, until I weakly pushed his hand away. Tears hovered in his eyes and he kept wiping them away before they fell, like that would somehow keep me from noticing.

"What happened?" I whispered, throat aching.

Daddy's face crumpled, and he let his head drop forward onto his hands, which were wrapped around one of mine. My other arm was in a heavy plaster cast, propped up on pillows by my side.

"I'm so sorry, sugar," he moaned, shaking his head without looking up. "I'm so sorry I let him hurt you."

Alarm jolted through me. "Who hurt me?" I asked, but he was crying, his shoulders shaking. "Daddy, who hurt me?"

"Just rest now," he said, raising his head and offering me a quavering smile. "We'll talk when you're feeling better. Go to sleep, okay? I'll be right here."

I didn't want to obey, but my eyelids were weighted down with tar and every muscle in my body felt battered and bruised. Sleep sounded awfully appealing.

"Where's Tom?" I mumbled, letting my eyes slip shut.

"He's here," Daddy said, letting go with one of his hands and brushing it gently over my hair. "He's out in the hallway with the cops."

The cops? But before I could muster a coherent query, the darkness swallowed me up.

.. .. ..

The next time I woke, it was with one pressing, urgent thought—
Where is Nate?

My father was still by my side, slumped in an armchair by my bed. Tom was curled up on the hospital bed beside mine, the curtain between us pushed back. He was wearing his pyjama pants and a shirt that was on backwards. Now that I paid attention, Daddy was dressed in track pants and a ratty old t-shirt as well. They looked like they'd crawled right out of bed.

But where the hell was Nate?

My memory was spotty, but the important bits had, to my relief, returned. I remembered what we did at the spot. I remembered the walk back. I remembered insisting that I climb through the window. I remembered falling.

Then nothing. Not even a flicker of a clue to what happened after I hit the ground.

My arm was broken. I knew that much by the heavy cast that encased it from elbow to wrist. My head pounded with my heartbeat, and I felt sharp pain and scratchy tape on my temple. Reaching up with my good hand, I probed the area and felt a thick gauze bandage. There was an oxygen tube blowing a trickle of cool air into my nose, an IV in the back of my hand, and a handful of wires protruding from the neck of my hospital gown.

I gathered that I had fallen from the tree. I gathered that I was in rough shape. I gathered that I'd scared the hell out of my father and brother.

But where the *hell* was Nate?

He'd been there when I fell. Had he run off and left me bleeding? No. I knew with absolute certainty that he wouldn't do that. Had he summoned help and then taken off before it had arrived? Maybe, but still unlikely.

He should be by my side. I wanted him by my side, no matter the hell it would raise with my father. Surely Nate knew that. Maybe he was just out in the waiting room because he wasn't family.

"Daddy?" I tried, but my voice came out harsh with disuse. Wincing, I cleared my throat and tried again. "Daddy?"

My father jerked awake, blinking sleep out of his eyes and looking around in bewilderment. When his gaze met mine he shot out of his chair and sank onto the edge of my bed.

"Aly, how are you feeling?" he asked, gripping my hand.

"I'm okay, Daddy. Where is—"

"You must be thirsty," he cut me off, reaching for a plastic cup on the table by my head. It had a straw in it, and he held the straw to my lips. I took three large gulps, grateful for something more than ice chips. When I'd slaked my thirst, I turned my head away and he set the cup back on the table.

"Daddy, where is Nate?" I asked, frowning when his face sagged, fresh tears glistening in his eyes.

"He's nowhere near here, sweetheart. He can't hurt you, anymore. I promise you, you're safe." His hand stroked my face, but I jerked away, confused.

"What? He didn't hurt me!" I exclaimed, astonished. I was so loud in my conviction that Tom sniffed and shifted in his sleep, rolling away from us.

"Oh, sugar, I know you don't remember," my father said, gripping my fingers so hard it almost hurt. "But it's okay. He won't hurt you again." There was steel in his voice, which I hadn't heard in years. In other circumstances, I'd have been thrilled at the life and conviction where I was concerned. The proof that he cared about me.

Maybe later, I'd have time for gratitude.

"Daddy, he didn't hurt me," I repeated, more firmly. "I fell out of a tree, that's all. Where is he?"

"The police have him," my father said, sitting back and frowning down at me. "Sugar, you just don't remember. The doctors say… they say he…. he…" His faced collapsed once more as he fell into shuddering sobs. Realization coursed through me, and I tried to sit up before pain sent me back to the pillows.

"No," I breathed through the pain. "He didn't. He didn't, Daddy. That was consensual. I'm so sorry. I know you're angry, but it was consensual. We…" I trailed off, trying to gather my thoughts. I cast around for a way to explain everything to him without hurting him, but all I could come up with was the truth. I took a deep breath and fell into our story, from the beginning.

By the time I finished, my father had moved back to his armchair and was sitting on the edge of it, hands clasped in front of him, staring at the white tile floor. His brow was furrowed, the only sign of movement his right thumb, which tapped a rhythmic beat on his left. He breathed deep and steady through his nose, absorbing my story.

I'd left out the gritty details, of course, but over the course of ten minutes he came to learn everything I'd been trying for so long to keep from him. He learned about my midnight adventures. He learned about my long-standing secret friendship with Nate. He learned that we'd kissed, and that Nate had been in my room every night after mom died. He learned about my depression over the last few months, and he learned that I had asked Nate for sex last night, and that he'd given it to me.

128

Unexpected shame began to creep over me as I finished my story. I'd told myself I no longer cared about my father's opinion, but that was before I awoke to find him shattered and distraught at my bedside. I didn't regret my actions, but it worried me that he would be disappointed with my wanton sexuality.

"Daddy?" I asked, when my story drew to its conclusion and he didn't respond, still staring at the floor in silence. "Daddy, I'm sorry. I'm sorry I let you down."

"Stop," he said firmly, looking up at me, but there wasn't anger in his eyes. In fact, if I didn't know better I'd say I saw a smile lurking in the tired, glassy blue eyes that were so much like mine.

I snapped my mouth shut, waiting for the other shoe to drop.

"So he didn't..." he trailed off, pulling a deep breath and gathering himself. "He didn't force himself on you?"

"No," I said.

"He didn't hurt you?"

"He'd never hurt me."

"You fell out of the tree?"

"If you go home and look, you'll see where the branch is broken by my window."

He drew a deep, shuddering breath and let it out before standing, brushing his palms against his legs as if to wipe sweat away.

"Never lie to me again, Alexandra," he said firmly.

I waited for more, but that was all he said. I nodded. "I won't. I promise."

"Use the front door from now on. I'd rather you break curfew than break your neck."

"You're not mad?" I asked, confused.

"I'm furious," my father said, sinking onto the edge of my bed and wrapping a hand around my shoulder, leaning close. "I'm furious with you, Alexandra. But I just spent the last twenty four hours thinking my baby girl was raped and beaten. I would prefer ten thousand secret boyfriends and premarital sexual encounters to that. Tell me you understand."

I blinked unbidden tears from my vision and nodded silently. He bent forward and pressed a kiss to my forehead. "I'm going to go talk to the police officers. I need to get your young man out of jail so I can give him the 'wrath of God, hurt her and I'll kill you' speech," he said, pushing to his feet.

Warmth flooded through me as I nodded against the pillow. He squeezed my fingers, smiling down at me, and then left me alone with my sleeping brother.

Everything was going to be okay.

.. .. ..

129

I didn't see Nate the next day.

I gave the police my statement from my hospital bed the next morning, using every opportunity to emphasize his innocence. After they left, I waited all day for him to show up. Surely he would come to visit me as soon as he was released from custody.

He didn't, though. He didn't show up that day, he didn't sneak in that night, and the next morning when my father signed me out of the hospital I still hadn't seen him.

Maybe he was still trying to protect our secret?

Daddy and Tom doted on me endlessly when we got home. I was situated on the living room couch, surrounded by pillows I didn't need and covered with blankets that made no sense considering how warm it was outside. They fed me an endless supply of medicine and food, and Tom insisted that I choose the channel on the TV even though all I did was sleep.

By day three of the coddling, I was losing my mind. I felt good, except for a lingering headache and a persistent but low-grade pain in my arm. I saw no reason to remain chained to the couch, and the role-reversal with the men in my family was starting to drive me insane.

And I still hadn't seen Nate.

With nothing to do all day, my mind wandered to things I'd rather not think about. What had the rumor mill had come up with to explain my absence? How would people look at me when I showed back up? Gemma had brought me my books and homework, but she was evasive when I asked her what people were saying.

Mostly, though, I worried about Nate and fretted over his continued absence. As the days wore on, I convinced myself that my initial assessment had been right. All he'd wanted was sex and now that he had it, he had no time for or interest in me. Gemma said everybody knew he was with me that night. Our secret was out. There was no reason for him to avoid me.

Then, on the evening of the fourth day, the doorbell rang. I rose to get it, but my father beat me to it, glaring at me as he passed by the living room.

"Stay still, Alexandra," he scolded. "You're supposed to be taking it easy."

I sat back, frustrated, only to shoot up again, heart in my throat, when I heard Nate's familiar voice from the doorway.

A few seconds later, my father escorted him into the living room. "I'll be in the kitchen," he said, giving Nate a pointed look before walking away. I rolled my eyes, but Nate just smiled.

"Hey, angel," he said, closing the distance between us and sinking onto the couch by my hip. Before I could speak, he leaned forward and planting a firm, possessive kiss on my lips. When he pulled back, his hands lingered, one cradling the side of my face, the other curved around my side. His fingers brushed the edges of the horrific bruise on my temple. It had turned a mottled purple-green color with a row of heavy black stitches marching up the center toward my hairline. Nate grimaced. "You look like shit."

"So do you," I said honestly. He looked like he'd gone and goaded a grizzly bear into a fist fight since the last time I saw him. Both his eyes were underscored by fading black bruises and an ugly scab sliced through his lower lip. "What happened to your face?"

He grinned sheepishly, and pressed a tentative finger to the side of his nose. "I tried to catch you when you fell," he said. "You clocked me pretty good. Broke my nose."

That didn't explain the purple-red knuckles or the split lip. I wondered if he'd fought the cops when they tried to pull him away. I'd seen the way he exploded at school, sometimes, when his temper got the best of him.

I wanted to call him out on the half-truth, but I also didn't want to fight. Not here. Not with my dad in the next room, probably listening closely.

"Where were you?"

He sighed and shook his head. "The cops released me to my foster dad, and he kept a pretty close eye on me for a few days. Wouldn't even let me at a phone."

"Why?" I asked, confused. "You didn't do anything wrong." *Unless you tried to beat up the cops.*

He looked down and took my hand, brushing his thumb over my knuckles, refusing to meet my eye. "I still got arrested," he said, lifting a shoulder and letting it fall. "Plus the cops told him what I told them, and he's *real* pissed I've been sneaking out every night." He laughed, but there wasn't a lot of humor in it. "Anyway," he said, brightening his tone and looking up, offering me a worried smile. "How are you, really? Don't lie."

"Bored," I said with a sigh. "I'm chained to this stupid couch." I lowered my voice so it wouldn't drift to the kitchen. "My dad is driving me crazy."

"Well, you're supposed to be taking easy, right?" Nate asked, squeezing my fingers. "So he's right to hover."

"You're teaming up on me," I said with a groan, dropping my head back against the pillows and closing my eyes. "It's a conspiracy."

Nate laughed. "Well, when did the doctor say you can bust out? It's gotta be killing you to miss so much school."

At that, a ball of dread dropped into my stomach and I sank back against the pillows, shaking my head.

"I don't really want to go back," I said, voicing worries that had been building up for the last few days, turning to a thick stew of apprehension. "The rumor mill must be having a field day with this."

"Yeah," Nate sighed, and my nerves tripled in volume, twanging away like an off-tune symphony. When he met my eyes, his were full of worry and regret. "Everyone knows about us now, Al. That's my fucking fault, too. I'm really sorry."

I frowned, confused. "How is it your fault?" I asked, nonplussed. "I'm the one who fell out of the stupid tree."

He scrubbed a hand over his face and shook his head, looking up at the ceiling. "I kinda freaked out," he said, lowering his gaze back to mine, his eyes pained. "When the cops took me, I panicked and told them the truth instead of just keeping my fucking mouth shut. They told Tim— that's my foster dad— they told him everything and he came home ranting and raving about it. Deb heard and she told her friends and now everyone fucking knows."

My brain took a second to process his words and their implication.

Everyone knew. *Everyone* knew. Everyone knew that dumbass Aly Winger had put out in the middle of the night in the middle of the woods and then fallen out of a damned tree like some kind of demented sloth. I covered my eyes with my good hand, trying not to cry.

How could I ever go back? I'd be the butt of every joke. The hot topic of every gossip circle. I didn't know what was worse— imagining what the girls would say about me, or imaging what the guys would *do*. Suddenly the thought of staying on the couch for all eternity like my father clearly intended didn't sound so bad at all.

"Al," Nate said hesitantly, his voice an unwelcome lifeline, pulling me back to a reality in which I wanted no part. "Al, c'mon, it'll be okay."

"How?" I moaned, looking up at him and trying like hell not to cry.

He frowned, his eyes pained, but the set of his jaw and the tone of his voice were pure determination. "We'll fix it," he said, nodding as if to affirm his own words. "They'll be obsessed with the story for a couple days, but they'll lose interest. We can publicly break up if you want. You can even slap me or something, but it's gotta be with the good arm. If you hit me with the cast you might knock me out."

He smiled at his own joke, but I scowled, suddenly furious.

"Are you serious?" I hissed, shoving at him. "You think that's what I'm worried about?"

He frowned. "Isn't it?"

"No!" I said, so loud I heard the sink turn off in the kitchen and knew my father was listening in. I lowered my voice to a fierce whisper. "No!" I repeated, glaring at him. "I don't care if they know I'm seeing you. I care that they know we had sex in the middle of the woods, Nate! The girls are all gonna think I'm some kind of whore, and the guys... " I shuddered, imagining what nasty things the guys would think and say."

One of the reasons I hated— and loved— Nate so much was that he never reacted the right way. When I expected him to laugh, he got serious. When I expected him to be sad, he made jokes. When I expected anger, I got sweet words, and when I expected sweet words, I got kissed and caressed until my blood turned to liquid fire.

That day, I expected somber commiseration with the unfortunate state of my tattered reputation. Instead, I got a bright smile that made his eyes dance.

"Alex," he said, trying to smother his smile in serious words and failing miserably. "This is like the bullies, remember? Fuck 'em. The girls who spend their time making up shit about other girls aren't worth your time. And any guy who opens his mouth about you is gonna wake up in the ER, preferably with no memory of how he got there. *And* none of that even really matters, because nobody knows what we were doing. They just know we were together. Beyond that, they'll think what we want 'em to think."

From anyone else, the words would've been trite and worthless. Nate, though? I trusted him with all the fervency that young love dictates. If Nate looked me in the eye and told me aliens had invaded earth I'd have packed up my bags and done whatever he said it would take to survive.

When Nate held my hand with bruised fingers, studied me through blackened eyes, and parted split lips to tell me his foster father *grounded* him? Well, hindsight might be 20/20, but young love and ignorance make a smudged and distorted lens. I believed him.

Such was the extent of my faith, that relief spread through me, making me sleepy, and I relaxed against the pillows, drowsy-eyed and smiling.

"You need rest," Nate said, leaning forward and brushing a chaste kiss over my cheek.

"Can you stay?" I asked. I sounded like a little kid— whiny and needy— but he just smiled and shook his head, pushing to his feet.

"Nah, I gotta head out. I'm not even supposed to be here. Tim is gonna… Oh, hey, you never told me. What day do you go back to school?"

"Next Monday," I told him, a shadow of lingering dread creeping up from my gut and into my throat.

"Okay," he answered, smiling down at me. "I'll be here on Monday morning to pick you up. We'll show up together. You gotta lean into your scandalous new reputation as a girl with a boyfriend." The grin he flashed at me melted my dread to a puddle of warm gooiness that oozed from my chest out into my limbs. Then the grin turned to a smirk, cocky and self-assured, and that warm goo began to spark with something livelier. "Plus, I'm pretty hyped to show up with you on my arm. I dunno if you know this, angel, but you're kinda out of my league."

I rolled my eyes at that, trying to hide the fact that I wanted to drag him down onto the couch with me. In spite of my father's revelation, that kind of behavior would still invite a sermon that I didn't want.

"I'll see you on Monday," I said, trying to hide my grin.

"Love you, Al," Nate said, stooping to give me one more kiss. It was barely more than a peck, but it left my lips tingling, yearning for more.

"Love you, too," I whispered, watching him leave.

Daddy came in a few minutes later, handing me a bowl of soup and sinking into the armchair beside me. He stared thoughtfully at the entryway while I ate.

"You know I'd prefer you were single," he said, giving me a stern look that didn't reach his eyes.

"I know," I said, swallowing a spoonful of soup and smiling. "Too bad I've got a boyfriend."

"You know I'll kill him if he hurts you," he threatened emptily. "I don't care if it's a sin. I'll string him up and cut his heart out, sugar."

"I know," I laughed, following his gaze to the entryway. A strange, uneasy sadness began to form over my head as I tried to conjure up a scenario in which Nate would willingly hurt me. I couldn't think of a single one. "I think he'd let you."

CHAPTER FIFTEEN

NATE

What kind of loser wakes up happy?

I usually woke up pissed off at something. Sometimes it was anger at whatever ghost had visited me in my dreams. Sometimes I was wrapped up in what had happened the night before and sometimes I was worried about what the day would bring. The reasons changed, but I always woke up angry.

Not that Monday, though. That Monday I woke up with a shit-eating grin on my face and a bubble of something I couldn't identify— I'd later come to realize it was sheer pride and happiness— expanding in my chest.

That Monday, I woke before my alarm and fixed breakfast for the kids. Usually I just poured some cereal in a bowl and called it good. That morning, they had bacon and eggs— *purchased* not stolen, thank you very much. I even made enough for Tim and Marsha, and we sat around the wobbly kitchen table and ate like some kind of family. A demented kind of family, where the little kids cringe when the adults reach for the salt and the oldest daughter won't stop glaring at the oldest son.

After breakfast, Deb and I got the little kids ready for school and bustled them off to the bus stop with Ronnie. Then Deb marched off without a backwards glance, but I couldn't even bring myself to worry what stick she had up her ass.

I had to coax my beat-up old truck into turning over, but that Monday the awful clunking sound and the heady smell of diesel didn't bother me.

I pulled up outside Alex's house five minutes early, and there followed one of the greatest moments of my life. My girl— *my girl*— opened her front door, morning sun shining on her face, walked down her drive, and climbed into my car. *My* car. Finally, at long last, we were together in the light of day and let me tell you— Alex in the sunshine is blinding.

Those first few minutes, it was almost like we didn't know each other.

135

"Hey," I greeted as I pulled out onto the road, my heart hammering in my chest like I was picking up some girl I'd never met.

"Hi," Alex answered, equally awkward. She fidgeted with her bag and stared out the window.

"How are you feeling?" The bruise on her forehead was a fun combination of yellow and green, and she wore a small white bandage over the row of stitches. Her cast was covered in doodles, mostly by Tom, but all the rest of her was just as prim and proper as it ever was in the daylight. She wore dark black jeans and a loose white shirt. Her hair hung in shiny curls that I longed to run my hands through.

And why couldn't I?

Glancing between her and the road, I reached out and combed the hair away from her face. "Al?" I asked, brushing my thumb over her jaw. "Are you okay?" She'd never answered my original question.

"Yeah, I'm good." She flashed me a weak, fake smile. "I'm just nervous."

"Don't be nervous," I said, placing both hands on the wheel. "I'm a good driver, I promise."

She reached out and slugged me in the arm with her cast. "You know that's not what I mean. Although you *are* speeding."

I glanced at the speedometer. "Five miles over isn't speeding, Al."

"It's over the speed limit, therefore it's speeding," she argued.

"Christ. Are you telling me you drive exactly the speed limit everywhere you go?"

"Of course! We're not all hardened criminals, Nate. Some of us abide by the law."

I groaned dramatically, shaking my head. "Remind me never to let you drive. Ever."

"Well you won't have a choice after they take your license away for reckless driving."

Just like that we were back to normal.

.. .. ..

Alex was surprisingly confident when we pulled into the parking lot, hopping out of the car before I had a chance to do all that chivalrous, door-holding bullshit I wanted so badly to do for her.

My friends stood in a gaggle by Kevin's shitty old station wagon, and they fell silent when Alex met me in front of my truck and took my hand without hesitating. None of them had really believed that the rumors were true. Except Deb, of course. She knew and, for some reason, it pissed her the hell off. The rest of our friends stood in slack-jawed awe as Al and I walked past them toward the school. Deb glared, leaning against the hood of Kev's car, gnawing on a wad of gum, arms crossed beneath her boobs, which damn near spilled out of her tank top.

I'd have to talk to her at some point. As much as Deb pissed me off, she was family and the rift between us was killing me. Later, though. Deb could wait, because Al was tugging me along toward school, her hand steady in mine and a look of fierce determination on her face.

It was still warm, so students gathered in the grassy area in front of the school, clumped into cliques and clusters while they waited for the bell to ring. The second we rounded the corner, conversation ceased. It was as if we'd sucked the air right out of the yard. Their faces all turned to us as one, eyes wide and expectant. What did they think we were gonna do? Start fucking right there in the grass?

Not a terrible idea.

"C'mon," Alex grumbled angrily, quickening her step. Instead of fleeing into the relative sanctity of the school like I expected, she dragged me to an unoccupied spot by the wall. She dropped her bag and sat down, leaning back against the brick.

"Uh…" I looked around. "What are you doing?"

"I always sit here and read before the bell," she said. The front of the school faced east, so she was squinting up at me in the bright yellow of the morning sun. She raised her good hand, blocking it. "Are you gonna join me or not?"

Grinning, I dropped my own bag and slid down the wall beside her. "When did you get so chill?" I asked under my breath as she pulled a book out of her bag. Heart of Darkness by Joseph Conrad. One of our books for AP Lit, but we weren't going to hit it for months. She must be reading ahead. *What a nerd.*

"The branch I hit must have jolted something loose," she said, bumping my shoulder with hers. "Or maybe you did?"

That unfamiliar swelling sensation in my chest grew even more pronounced, until I felt like I couldn't breathe past it. The stupid, shit-eating grin was back too. Trying to hide it, I pulled out my own book and flipped it open, trying to concentrate on the words and not the fact that I was living in a goddamned fantasy.

"Hey Nate?" Alex asked after a few minutes. I looked up from the page, which I'd read twenty times and still hadn't absorbed.

"Yeah?"

"What're you reading?"

"Cat's Cradle," I said, showing her the cover. I liked Kurt Vonnegut. He was pessimistic as hell, but his words made me laugh. I liked that back then, when I was laughing my way through hell as a matter of course.

"That's not on the reading list," Alex said, frowning. I could see the lecture bubbling inside her, and I didn't even try to stop it. I loved the way her brow furrowed and her voice got hard when she was berating me. It was evidence that she cared. To most everyone else, she was sweet-as-can-be. Not to me.

"I know," I said, goading her.

"We have the test on <u>Wuthering Heights</u> *today*," she hissed, clearly starting to panic on my behalf. "Nate you already sleep through the whole period. Mrs. Parker is going to kick you back to general if you don't do the readings."

"Who said I didn't do the readings?" I asked, making a show of going back to my book. It was rare I had the opportunity to show Alex up. I was going to milk it for all it was worth.

"*Did* you do the readings?"

"Finished them over the summer," I said, glancing over to see her face. She stared at me, one finger stuck in her book to mark her page.

"Don't mess around," she said, clearly frustrated. There was a pencil in her hair, because Alex loved to annotate her books. It felt like blasphemy to me to mark up someone else's writing, but she'd underline passages and make notes in the margins, pouring her soul into the space between the lines. Someday I wanted to see those notes and discover what passages she'd found especially poignant. There was one, in <u>Heart of Darkness</u>, I knew she'd have noted and taken to heart.

"'Even extreme grief may ultimately vent itself in violence—" I quoted, lifting my chin into the air and grinning smugly, "but more generally takes the form of apathy.'"

Alex's mouth hung open as she flipped through her copy of the book, frantically trying to find a page while I watched. Sure enough, that passage was underlined in heavy black pencil with a scribbled, cursive note in the margin.

When she looked back at me, she was scowling. "You let me believe you were flunking the course," she said. "I've been worried all year."

"We're like two months into the year, angel," I teased. "That's not that long."

"Still!" she exclaimed, smacking me in the leg with her book. "Why didn't you tell me you were reading ahead, too? We could have read the books together and talked about them."

I thought of sitting with Alex at the spot, or out here in the shade of our brick school building, pouring over literature and discussing what we loved and hated— what resonated with our lives and what confused us. I'd learn so much about her, that way.

Damn. When had *I* become such a fucking nerd?

"You've already read everything on the list?" Alex asked, and I nodded reluctantly. I wanted to lie and say no so we could have our little book club, but it was too late. "That's okay," she said. "I'll just read what you're reading. I'm far enough ahead already. It's not like I'll fall behind. Do they have copies of your book in the library?" She gestured at <u>Cat's Cradle</u>, which sat forgotten in my lap.

"I dunno," I said. "Mrs. Parker has copies, though, I think."

"Great!" Alex said brightly, just as the bell rang. "I'll start reading it tonight."

.. .. ..

The first week Alex was back at school, I was always on the hunt.

Laying waste to my enemies had always been easy, because I had nothing to lose and acted without fear of repercussion. Suspension and detention were nothing to me, and the more people who saw me beat the living shit out of some asshole, the fewer would come at me in the future.

After Alex and I became public, though, the game got a lot harder. I no longer wanted to be suspended, because I desperately wanted to go to school. I could no longer afford detention, because that would mean less time for work which would mean less money in the bank for my fast-approaching launch into adulthood. I no longer wanted an audience, because then Alex would find out I'd been fighting and I couldn't have that.

So don't fight, idiot, I hear you saying, but you have to understand that wasn't an option. Alex wasn't wrong to be worried about how people would react to us. The girls I left alone, because I didn't know how to fix that particular brand of cruelty. The guys, though? They were different. They might be lascivious and predatory, but to me they were prey, and I hunted them mercilessly.

In crowded hallways and pre-bell classrooms, I stalked and gathered intelligence. My ears picked up snippets of conversation. Certain words drew my attention like a blaring red light, lasering my focus into discussions about 'tits' and 'love to fuck' and 'that ass' and 'pussy.' If those conversations weren't about my girl, I left it alone.

If they were?

I'd been at the same school for years. I knew everyone's voice. So when Lance Curry, five feet behind me and pulling books out of his locker, told his friends he'd 'bend the preacher's girl over a desk and fuck her 'till she cries,' I pretended not to notice, made a mental note, and went on with my day.

Then, after school, I called in sick to work and waited in the near-abandoned parking lot until football practice released. When Lance reached his car, I came up behind him, grabbed him by the back of the neck, and slammed him face first into the hood of his shiny red coupe.

"What the fuck!" he cried out. He was bigger than me, but I had him at a disadvantage, bent awkwardly over the hood with his left wrist in my free hand. I twisted the arm up behind his back like the cops had inadvertently taught me, stressing his shoulder until he cried out in pain.

"I hear you wanna bend my girl over and fuck 'till she cries," I hissed. He tried to rear back, and I let him have a few inches before slamming him back into the hood.

"Fuck you!" Lance growled, cheek mushed into the warm metal.

"All I want is an apology," I said, stressing his arm just a little bit more. He screamed. "And a promise you'll keep your goddamned mouth shut. Give me that and I'll let you keep your arm in working order." I pushed again, glancing around just long enough to make sure we were still alone. We were.

"My dad's a lawyer," Lance groaned, hoarse and breathless. "He'll put you away for years if you hurt me."

"Okay" I said, pretending that notion didn't turn my blood to ice water. Of course, if it was true, backing out now would be the worst thing I could do. If he wanted to play the intimidation game, the only way out was to win. "But even if I'm in jail, you'll still be down a working shoulder. I don't think those scouts are gonna look at you twice for college ball if you're sitting on the bench with your arm in a sling."

Lance went still in my grip. "Fuck you!" he growled again, but his voice was weaker, thick with tears of pain, and I knew I was winning. I layered it on.

"I don't wanna go to jail, Lance," I said, leaning close, smiling at the poetic justice of his position, bent double and crying in pain. "But even if I do, you're fucked. Even if you tell me what I want to hear and tattle on me when I leave, you're fucked. I've got friends in low places and if you go crying to daddy— even if I wind up behind bars— your shoulder is going to be the least of your worries. You understand?"

"Fucking *fine!*" Lance yelled, twitching in my grip. "I'm sorry, alright? I won't talk about her."

"You won't *look* at her," I added, squeezing the back of his neck hard enough to make him squirm.

"I won't look at her."

"And if your friends want to talk shit?"

"I'll tell them to shut up," he said.

"Good job!" I said sunnily. With one last nudge on his strained shoulder, I let him go and took a few steps back.

As expected, Lance launched off the car and came at me swinging. Fortunately, athleticism in one field doesn't necessarily translate to another. Lance was a stellar quarterback with the upper body strength of a gorilla, but he threw a punch like a two-year-old— eyes closed and flailing. I ducked beneath it and darted forward, hammering *one, two, three* strikes into his midsection before slipping away.

Lance collapsed to the ground, curling around his stomach. I pushed at his shoulder with my foot, nudging him onto his back. "You done?" I asked, but he didn't respond. Just moaned and rolled around weakly. "You're done," I answered for him.

I left him on the ground and strode back to my truck. By the time he got up and staggered to his car I was turning out of the parking lot and watching him in my rearview.

And that was how I hunted. One by one, I picked off the predators, until rumor and fear took care of the rest. My days were pure bliss. My grades were improving, I spent nearly every waking moment with Alex, and for the first time in my life I looked at the future and saw something other than a bleak, gray struggle to survive. I felt strong and smart and happy. I guess that's what makes me culpable for everything that came next.

I'm not much of a Bible guy, but I've read the thing a couple times. Once because there was nothing else to read, and once because Alex was reading it and we never stopped loving our book-club-of-two idea.

By and large, I was never a huge fan of the 'Good Book.' It's kind of boring and repetitive in places, and I could never reconcile an omniscient, omnipotent, *loving* deity creating the world in which I lived. Even so, there's one passage that stuck with me as absolute truth, lingering over my life and casting a shadow of foreboding on every happy moment— Proverbs 16:18.

"Pride goes before destruction, and a haughty spirit before a fall."

CHAPTER SIXTEEN

ALEX

"This doesn't make any fucking sense," Nate grumbled, letting his head thunk onto the heavy textbook, open on the desk in front of him. I looked up from my book and glanced around us, but we were the only ones in our section of the library.

"Aw, it'll be okay," I said condescendingly, patting his back. "You're just dumb, that's all."

"I think I actually am, Al," he whined, sitting up and scratching out his latest failed attempt at the math problem. "I've been at this for an hour and it still doesn't make sense."

"It's okay," I said, more serious. "You just don't have the foundation, that's all. This is what you get for sleeping through trig."

He scowled, slouching in his seat. "Trig was dumb and easy. This is hard."

"Trig is the foundation for half of what we're doing in this class," I argued, stealing his notebook and flipping to a blank page. "And it was only easy because you were in the basic class so you didn't have to understand what you were doing. You just had to regurgitate answers."

"Your wisdom doesn't make me any less fucked on this problem set, Alex," Nate snapped, scrubbing a hand through his hair and staring angrily at the textbook like he could intimidate the problems into solving themselves.

"Stop being dramatic," I said, rolling my eyes and tugging on his arm. "Check it out…"

I sketched out a right triangle on my blank page and proceeded to walk him through the definition of sine, cosine, and tangent. Then we moved on to the unit circle. Then we practiced graphing the functions on an x/y plane. By the end of the hour, Nate was flying through the remaining problems and I had my nose buried back in <u>Crime and Punishment</u>. It was Nate's latest pick for our two-man book club. He seemed to have an affinity for godawfully depressing books.

Because I was so far ahead in classes, and Nate so un-fixably behind, we both had study hall during the fourth period, right after lunch. I liked it because the rest of the school population was in class, so we had the place to ourselves. Usually we worked in the library, at this little table tucked back into the corner. Sometimes we sat in the courtyard and read.

I'd gotten my cast taken off weeks prior, and the scar on my forehead had faded from angry red to pink. It would never fade completely, but I didn't really mind. It gave my face character, and every time I saw it I thought of that pivotal night in my life. The night I came back to life. The night I exchanged secrecy for striding purposefully through life with my favorite person at my side. I loved that scar.

Nate liked it, too. Or maybe he just wanted me to know it didn't turn him off. Either way, he treated it like a sacred symbol. He always traced it with his fingertips before we kissed, his eyes warm and fierce with possessive need.

Without moving my head, I looked up from my book, watching him covertly. He was hunched over the table, left hand shoved into his hair while his right flew over the paper, scribbling out solutions that— now that he understood the process— I knew would be invariably flawless.

It almost made me angry how easily he picked things up. The concept I'd just taught him had taken me a week of nose-to-the-grindstone studying to understand. He'd mastered it in less than an hour. I'd never thought he was stupid, but the longer we studied together the more I realized just how much potential he was wasting by not graduating.

"You could be an engineer," I said suddenly, startling him. He jerked his head up, frowning at me.

"What?"

"You're crazy smart," I reasoned, closing my book and setting in on the table before leaning forward, resting a hand on his arm. "You need to apply to colleges. There's still time."

"We've been over this, Al," he said warningly, his voice low, eyes narrow as he studied my face.

"I know," I whined. "It just bothers me. You could do anything you want."

"Maybe I *want* to be a mechanic," he snapped, turning back to his notebook. "Did that occur to you?"

"Do you?" I asked, unphased by his irritation. I think I was the only person in town who didn't fear the infamous Nate Reynolds temper.

He didn't answer, making a show of going back to work, his pencil digging a little too hard into the paper. I smiled. Sooner or later, I'd break him down. He wanted more, just like me, and I'd be damned if I went to the stars and didn't take him with me.

"Shit!" I screamed, shaking out my hand. Every cast iron pan should have the handle painted red so idiots like me don't grab them.

"Don't curse, sugar," Daddy said, his voice mellow. He had his back to me and was bent over the sink, dutifully washing the endless stream of dishes I was sending his way. It was nearly three in the afternoon on Thanksgiving Day. I had gravy on one burner, cranberry sauce on another, a massive pot of mashed potatoes on the third, and a cooling, cast-iron pan of cornbread on the last. That was the pan I'd just grabbed with my bare hand and *shit* it fucking hurt.

Thanksgiving at the Winger house was an affair. Daddy always invited a family or two from his church, so the panicked flurry on Thanksgiving morning was its own tradition.

The difference was that, this year, I was in charge. This year, Momma was gone. Fortunately, I didn't have time to be sad about it because my whole world had become a chaos of beeping oven timers and food splatter.

"They're gonna be here in an hour," I said, blowing on my fingers, although they weren't actually burned, and the pain was already fading. I pulled a stack of plates from the cupboard.

"Tom!" I called, and he bustled in from the living room seconds later, standing at attention. I'd tried to keep him involved with odd jobs all day like Momma used to. He loved to help.

"I need you to start setting the table," I said, handing him the plates and praying like hell he wouldn't drop them. "One at each spot at the adults' table, okay? Come back for silverware when you're done."

By the time I reached a semblance of readiness with the food, I only had five minutes before the guests would start arriving.

"Go ahead, Aly," my father said, ever level-headed. "Me and Tom will finish up, here."

Oh, what heroes, I wanted to snark, but I didn't have time. I needed to get ready quick. Nate and his siblings had somehow made it onto Daddy's charity invite list this year and I couldn't leave my boyfriend alone with the wolves. The gossip circle at the church was even more dubious of our relationship than the one at my school.

I took a quick shower, washing away sweat and flour and splatters of food. Wearing a towel, I wove my hair into a french braid and threw on some mascara. As I dashed from the bathroom to my bedroom, I heard voices downstairs. Nate's wasn't one of them. Was he late? *Shit*. What if he didn't show up at all? *Double shit*. That'd look really bad.

I knew it shouldn't matter to me what other people thought. Nate was all about that— just living your life and not worrying about other folks' opinions. I tended to fret a little, though, especially where he was concerned. I wanted everyone to think as highly of him as I did, but he made it hard, especially back then. Sometimes I felt like he was bound and determined to live up to everyone's awful expectations just to be spiteful.

In my bedroom, I hastily donned leggings, a skirt, and a modest white top with a cardigan, and shoved my feet into my favorite ankle boots. Before leaving, I looked at myself in the mirror on the back of my door. I looked respectable. A perfect little preacher's daughter. Definitely *not* someone who had lost her virginity in the midnight woods to the town's most notorious juvenile delinquent. I grinned at my reflection, tracing a finger over the scar on my temple. *Almost* respectable.

I found our living room filled to brimming with adults, nursing wine glasses and chatting. Daddy had invited two families from his church— the Smiths and the Popoviches. Peter and Jodie Smith were a nice couple with two little boys, aged six and four. Peter got laid off at the paper plant outside of town in September, and they'd been struggling ever since. Jodie had to get a job waiting tables at a restaurant downtown, and Peter was working odd jobs. Daddy said they were good people. They had a strong marriage and had protected their children from the worst of their struggles. They had 'stayed true to God,' whatever the hell that meant.

Neil and Harriet Popovich were an older couple whose children had all left home years ago. My father invited them to dinner because their eldest son, Jack, was overseas, serving in Iraq. They were having a hard time with it, Daddy said, and needed a little distraction, especially during the holiday season.

Then there were my guests, who sat in a corner, looking about as out-of-place as possible in my Momma's pristine living room. Nate sat at one end of the couch. The littlest boy sat in his lap, clinging to his arm and watching the room full of adults with wide, terrified eyes. The little girl sat almost as close, but her eyes were bright with excitement, a half-smile on her lips. The older boy —*Ronnie?* — sat a few feet away, arms crossed over his chest, scowling at everything. Deb wasn't there. I'd made a point of extending the invite to her, but I have to admit I was relieved she hadn't showed up. She hated me.

"You didn't tell me there was a dress code," Nate hissed, glaring at me, when I drew close.

I hadn't. I'd thought it was implied by the occasion. Apparently I shouldn't have assumed. Nate's entire entourage, himself included, were wearing jeans. Nate was wearing a plain gray t-shirt, the little girl a stained pink sweater, and the little boy what looked like a pajama top with a kids' show logo emblazoned

145

on the front. Ronnie hadn't even removed his puffy, duct-tape-patched overcoat.

"You're fine," I lied, trying not to smile.

"No we're fucking not," Nate argued, his voice low as his eyes swept over the room of well-dressed adults. "We look like assholes, Al."

"You sound like an asshole, too," I whispered, leaning close. "Stop cursing."

"Shit, sorry," he dropped back against the couch, clearly overwhelmed. "This was a bad idea."

"Don't be a baby," I said, crouching in front of him so I was eye level with the little kids. "Do you guys want to come see the toy room?"

The little girl's eyes brightened. "There's a room just for toys?" she asked, breathless. Even the little boy looked intrigued, although he still cowered in Nate's lap.

Nate's ragtag crew trailed me as I wove through the sea of adults and led them downstairs to the basement. It was furnished, and my parents had converted it to a sort of den/playroom for me and Tom. Over the years, it had become more Tom's space than mine as I outgrew its appeal. There were Legos and toy cars, a train table, a small trampoline, a TV with attached Nintendo and VCR, a big puffy couch, and bins of dolls and dress up clothes from when I was little.

Ronnie made a beeline for the gaming console, abandoning our group to slump in front of the TV. Tom, kneeling by the train table, looked over his shoulder when we came down the stairs. His boyish face split into a wide grin when he saw us.

"Nate!" he said gleefully, abandoning his game and bouncing up. Nate placed the little boy on the ground to receive Tom's overzealous hug, and then set about introducing each of the kids to my delighted older brother.

One upside of Tom's condition was that he adored kids, and got along with them great. He was low on friends, so any potential new playmate was a delight. He already had the Smith kids embroiled in some made-up story on the train table. I envied the persistence of his imagination—the enduring technicolor a stark contrast to my own fading, sepia-toned view of the world.

"Tom-Tom, this is Paul," Nate said, picking up the boy again. "He's a little shy, so you gotta be extra nice, okay?"

Tom nodded vehemently. The little girl spoke up before Nate could do it for her. "I'm Trish!" she said, holding up her arms as if asking to be picked up. Tom looked at me, and I nodded. He picked her up in one arm and shook her tiny hand.

"I'm Tom," he said. "Do you like to play trains?"

"I don't have trains," Trish said. "What do you do?"

"I'll show you," Tom said brightly, setting her down by the table. He coaxed the Smiths into abandoning their game for a few minutes so he could line up all the trains and tell Trish their names and their jobs. She listened intently, nodding along.

"You oughta join 'em," Nate said to Paul, but the little boy shook his head hard and buried his face in Nate's shoulder. Nate rolled his eyes at me. "C'mon, buddy," he coaxed, kneeling down and peeling the boy away from him, setting him on his feet. "Tom's really cool, okay? He won't hurt you, I promise. Besides, you *love* trains. How many chances are you gonna get to play with real ones? C'mon, I'll come with you."

For ten minutes, Nate and I knelt by the train table, playing along as the little kids guided the trains along the tracks, shouting dialogue at each other and laughing as the senseless story progressed and evolved. Before long, Paul was leaning over the table, grinning and giggling at Tom's sound effects, racing his train along the tracks while Tom guided a Hotwheels car alongside.

Blinded by love as I was, I thought it was *adorable* how good my boyfriend was with his siblings. I thought it was *sweet* how he toted them around and comforted them and coaxed them into playing. I thought it was *sexy* that he was so responsible and grown-up around them. I marveled at the glossy facets of a diamond, too awed by the sparkle to ask about the pressure that had formed it and the steel blades that had cleaved those perfect, smooth edges.

"We oughta make our exit," Nate whispered conspiratorially in my ear. "While they're distracted."

I nodded, grinning, and Nate tapped Paul on the shoulder. "Hey, buddy, I'm gonna head upstairs. Are you okay, here?"

Paul nodded distractedly, pushing him away. Before we headed up the stairs, Nate went to the sofa and stood in front of it, blocking Ronnie's view until he paused the game with an angry curse. Then he bent close, face stern, talking to him so low I couldn't make out the words. When he stopped talking, he stayed there, waiting for something. Finally, Ronnie growled, "Fine!" and Nate sighed and stood, meeting me by the foot of the stairs.

"What was that about?" I asked as we climbed back up to the ground floor.

"I was just telling him not to be an asshole," Nate said casually. When we got to the top of the stairs, out of view of the kids in the basement, he stopped me from opening the door.

"Happy Thanksgiving, Al," he whispered, turning to box me in. His hands grasped the rail on either side of my hips as he leaned in close, pressing me back until my shoulders were flush against the wall.

"Happy Thanksgiving," I breathed, raising my face for the kiss I knew was coming.

He let go of the handrail with one hand and, as always, brushed a thumb over the spiderweb scar on my temple. Then his hand drifted behind my neck, tipping my head up even further as he lowered his mouth to mine.

From somewhere beyond the door, my father called my name and we broke apart— Nate with a stifled groan and me with a giggle. "Serves you right," I said jokingly, pushing him away. "That's what you get for molesting me on this holy day."

"It's Thanksgiving," Nate said sarcastically as he followed me up the last two steps and back into the party. "Since when is Thanksgiving holy?"

"Since you started dating a preacher's daughter," I said over my shoulder. "Now come with me to the kitchen. We gotta get these dishes plated."

It was another half hour before we settled down to the large dining table for dinner. First, I had to put the final touches on the food. Then Nate and I plated them and carried them to the dining room. Then the adults filed through, building plates for their children. Then came the odious task of peeling the kids away from their games and getting them to sit still at the little card table we had set up for them in a corner of the dining room. *Then* Daddy had to make sure all the adults had wine to drink.

My stomach was a growling, aching pit of emptiness by the time we finally bowed our heads for grace. While Daddy droned on about God and gratitude and blessings, I cracked one eye and glanced around the table. The Smiths had their heads bowed, brows furrowed with concentration as they magnified Daddy's words and sent them up to heaven, hoping for some divine intervention in their lives. Harriet Popovich appeared to be on the verge of tears, lips pinched together and trembling, eyes squeezed shut. Her husband's head was bowed so deep his chin was almost touching his chest.

Then there were my guests. Ronnie had dutifully joined hands with Jodie Smith, who sat on his right, but his head wasn't bowed and his eyes were open, glaring around the table like the lot of us were responsible for war and poverty and death itself. Nate was sitting on his left, and both their hands rested on the table, close but not quite touching. Nate's own left hand was wrapped around mine, and his head was bowed slightly, but his eyes weren't closed. They were locked on the kids, who sat squirming at their table in the corner.

"... and finally, Lord, we ask that You continue to watch over us," Daddy was saying, his voice strong and sure as he lead the prayer. He was in preacher mode, guiding his makeshift Thanksgiving congregation to gratitude. "We ask that You challenge us as you see fit, and protect us in our darkest moments when we can't protect ourselves. We ask that You continue to love your children, forgiving our sins and guiding us through our mistakes. We pray that when the world becomes too much for us, and our spirits find our way to your embrace, that You welcome us into Your Kingdom and show us the peace we could not find on earth. Amen."

"Amen," I whispered, eyes stinging as I thought of my mother. Nate's hand squeezed mine before letting go, and I knew he'd heard the pain in my father's prayer and felt the loneliness in my own murmured acknowledgment. Unlike me, my boy never missed a thing.

After the prayer, there wasn't much room for sadness or introspection. Solemn words and silence were replaced with groans of appreciation as the dishes were passed around. Plates filled and were emptied. Filled again and were emptied again. Wine glasses followed suit. Nate's charges appeared at his side four times each with empty plates, tugging on his sleeve until he sent them off with a fresh pile of food to devour. I'd never seen little kids so willingly consume green beans and carrots, but Paul and Trish cleaned their plates of anything Nate gave them.

Unfortunately, the rapidly disappearing wine had a liberating effect on the gaggle of adults, and right around the second helping, they started grilling Nate and I mercilessly.

"So, Aly, the college application deadline is approaching," said Mr. Popovich. He was the dean of admissions at the local university. "How many schools are you applying to?"

"Five, sir," I answered. "I just turned the last one in on Monday."

"Ahead of the game, as always," my father said proudly, smiling at me. Of course he didn't know about the five out of state schools I'd applied to as well. He definitely didn't know about the early admissions application I'd sent to Caltech months ago. We'd been getting on so well, lately, I didn't have the nerve to tell him about my real aspirations. He wanted me close to home, studying to be a teacher or a nurse— something respectable and employable and feminine so I could follow my husband and work anywhere. Daddy's real dream was for me to go off to college and find a good Christian boy to marry. For all that he was kind to Nate and accepted our relationship, it was clear he thought it was some kind of phase. He'd come to grips with the present, but never asked about the future.

"And what about you, young man?" Mrs. Smith asked, smiling at Nate. "Where are you applying?"

"Oh…" Nate paled, setting his fork down on his plate and shaking his head. "I, um… I was gonna—"

"Nate's planning to attend to the technical school in town," I answered for him. "He already has a job at Red's Auto and Services, down on Main Street. He's really good with cars, so his boss promised to foot the bill so he can keep him on as a mechanic after he graduates."

As much as I wanted more for him, I was proud. With no formal training at all, Nate had become an invaluable employee at the shop where he worked. So invaluable, his boss was willing to drop thousands of dollars into his pocket to hang on to him. To me, that was impressive.

Our dinner guests didn't seem to agree.

149

"Oh," said Mrs. Popovich. "That's nice, dear."

"Yes," said her husband, but he was frowning. "I don't suppose it's terribly lucrative, though. How do you intend to support a family with a minimum wage?" He looked pointedly at me, as if asking Nate how he was going to take care of me when I was barefoot and pregnant with our fifth child.

Someone remind me of the year, I wanted to scream. *It's the 21st century, people. We can date without getting married and spewing out children. I can work, too!*

"Neil," Daddy said warningly.

"It's fine," Nate said easily, smiling at my father before turning back to Mr. Popovich. "I'm not too worried about supporting a family, sir. Al's the only girl I have any intention of marrying, and she's gonna be at college for at least four years and I don't think she'll be ready to settle down until a few years after *that.* That gives me plenty of time to save and work my way up the ladder. Plus, she's crazy smart. She'll probably be out-earning everyone at this table within a few years of graduating."

I swallowed a mouthful of turkey and stared at my boyfriend, who had speared a few green beans as he talked.

"Even if she doesn't, though, auto mechanics actually do make a decent salary. Modern engines are extremely complex, and half of what your mechanic does to your car looks more like computer science than grunt work. Red, my boss, requires us to stay on top of our certifications so we can work on a broad spectrum of makes and models, which translates to a considerable bump in our earnings. Not to mention, he's getting old and his kids moved away and don't have any interest in the shop. He and I have been talking about night classes and a business degree in a few years, so I can take over for him when he retires."

Most of that was news to me, so I wore the same slack-jawed look of surprise as the rest of the adults at the table. They were probably hung up on talk of an MBA and business ownership, though. My brain had shorted out at '*Al's the only girl I have any intention of marrying.*'

"But is your boss aware of your criminal record?" Mrs. Smith asked, her voice slightly slurred as she leaned across the table.

"Jodie!" her husband hissed and Ronnie snorted out a laugh, but Nate just smiled pleasantly, elbowing his brother in the ribs without look at him.

"He is, ma'am," he said, nodding. "And I haven't been in trouble since Al and I started dating. She's kind of a taskmaster, with all the studying. I haven't had a spare minute for crime. Not even a little casual shoplifting."

Ronnie barked out a laugh, and I shoved another slice of turkey into my mouth and chewed, trying not to smile.

Unfortunately, Nate's easy answers to all their questions just seemed to embolden them. By the time we finished eating, the adults had exorcised every rude, intrusive question they must have compiled on their drive to our house. I felt like I was escaping some kind of warzone when I finally found a quiet moment to rise and start clearing away everyone's plates.

"Nate, can you help me?" I asked, loathe to leave him alone under the microscope, but he was already on his feet, gathering plates and silverware.

"I'm so sorry," I whispered, as soon as we were in the kitchen and out of earshot.

"It's fine," he said with a grin, setting his armful of plates on the counter and taking mine. "It's normal to be curious, and they're right to worry. I mean look at you." He set my plates in the sink and reached out, pulling me to him with a snap. "You're so sweet and innocent," he teased, leaning in close and brushing my nose with his. "You shouldn't be dating some juvenile delinquent," he whispered as one of his hands slipped down to my ass, squeezing hard.

I choked out a laugh and pushed him away. "Wash your hands and get out a mixing bowl," I said. "We need to make whipped cream."

"Right here?" Nate asked, raising an eyebrow. "In the middle of the kitchen? With your dad and all those adults so close by?"

I stared at him for a long second, confused, before I caught his meaning. "For the pie!" I said, shaking my head in disgust. "You're nasty."

"I just have my priorities straight," he said, dutifully washing his hands.

He did, I thought, as I pulled the carton of whipping cream out of the fridge and cleared a spot on the counter. I'd had it in my head he was still drifting, just taking the easiest path without thinking about his future. It hadn't occurred to me until the adults started grilling him that he might actually have thought about the future.

He didn't want to be a mechanic because it was the easiest option. He wanted it because it meant job security, growth opportunity, and enough of a salary that he could save while I was in college. He wanted to *marry* me, and that idea was more appealing to me than it had ever been.

I'd always hated the idea of marrying young. Even after I fell madly in love with Nate, I still wanted to wait. I wanted to live a single life of adventure and freedom before I settled down and started crapping out grandbabies per my father's wishes. It shouldn't have surprised me that Nate knew that. He knew I wanted to wait, and he seemed like he was more than willing to wait with me.

Suddenly, eternity with a single person seemed less like a looming trap and more like a far-off dream. Suddenly, the thought of four years in California was more daunting than exciting. Four years apart. Would we survive that? Would we even want to?

Yes, I decided with all the confidence and gravitas of the lovestruck teenager that I was. Yes, we would survive. We would *thrive*. I loved him with all of my

151

CHAPTER SEVENTEEN

NATE

For the better part of six months, I occupied real-estate on the heaven-adjacent side of purgatory. My days were divine. My evenings were hellish. My nights were spent in restless sleep, waiting impatiently for the morning to come. For the first time, I did more than just survive my circumstances. Home didn't change, but I no longer defined myself by what I suffered there. I defined myself by who I was and what I did in the daylight.

During the day, I was Alex's boyfriend— the guy whose hand she held in the hallway without a trace of shame or fear. I was a straight-A student, with signs of something called 'promise' and my teachers and counselors talked to me like something other than a disappointing, hopeless statistic. I was a model employee with healthcare and life insurance and this crazy thing called a 'savings account' that was growing every day.

Even at home, I was stronger. Tim was just as mean as always, and Marsha just as useless. I still spent most nights staring at the ceiling, wide awake, trying to discern sloppy, pass-out drunk sounds from rage-filled, predatory drunk sounds. I still slept on the floor by my bed more nights than not, with Trish tucked beneath my covers so Tim wouldn't get her. I still made a habit of goading Tim into fights to distract him from his more dangerous desires.

The difference was in how those fights ended. I was no longer a skinny kid with nothing to lose, curled up on ratty carpet getting the shit kicked out of him. I was man. A man with a girl who loved him, money for food, and a fierce and prideful sense of self. Even on the nights he caught me off guard, I never gave up and took it. I fought like hell, every time. I'd land a few punches, Tim would land a few, and when he got tired we'd walk away.

So the months ticked by, and I marked the time by landmarks.

In December, Alex received a thick packet in the mail from Caltech. She brought it out to the spot that night and we opened her acceptance letter together.

152

She bawled her eyes out, caught somewhere between joy at her success, fear at the prospect of telling her father, and sadness at the knowledge that she'd be leaving me behind. It was adorable.

In January, a massive blizzard blew through town, shutting down schools for a week. Every day, I bundled the kids up in their Goodwill snow suits and drove slowly and carefully across town to Al's house. She and Tom joined us outside, and we built forts and snowmen and had epic snowball fights. Then we'd sit in her living room while our socks dried by the fireplace and drink hot cocoa and watch movies.

In February, I celebrated my first birthday. Fortunately, I thought at the time, a loophole in the rules let me stay with Tim and Marsha until I graduated high school. Technically, it was my eighteen birthday, but it was the first one I remembered celebrating.

When I showed up to pick Alex up for school, she made me come inside and have pancakes with candles stuck in the top. I had to sit still and endure her and Tom's awful, off-key rendition of the birthday song. When Alex went to get her bag, Tom pulled me aside and pressed a small, jagged rock into my hand. In a loud whisper, he described a magical place where he and Alex went when they got sad. A spot where everything bad went away. He told me the rock was from that spot, and that Alex had one just like it.

Alex's present was an uncharacteristic spurt of rebellion. She dragged me out the back door of our school before lunch and we played hooky together— albeit only for the two hours we usually spent at lunch and in study hall. She made me drive out to the lake outside of town and delivered up a surprise BJ right there in the cab of my truck. I could tell she'd done some research, because her technique was… creative. She used her teeth a little more than I would've liked, but in the end who was I to complain? I had a beautiful girl giving me a birthday blowjob in broad daylight. A beautiful girl whose family let me come around in daylight. What's a little nerve-wracking toothiness in the face of all that awesome?

In March, Alex told her dad about Caltech. He was furious. He stopped speaking to her for three days. She was a nightmare to be around, oscillating every few minutes between sadness and anger, hurt and indignation, defeat and determination. At the end of the third day, I skipped out of my last period, drove to her father's church, and stuck my nose where it didn't belong.

I hadn't spent much time in churches as a kid. In fact I could count on one hand the number of times I'd been in one. One of my foster families, way back in the day, were devout Catholics. I remembered the whole affair being very ornate. There were gaudy gold scepters and a dangerous amount of candles, and a man wearing wizard robes chanting from the dais at the front.

Mr. Winger's church was a little more subdued. The only ostentatious feature was the large, stained-glass window at the front of the room. The ceilings were vaulted, but both walls and ceiling were constructed entirely of white plaster and pine beams. The floor was stained cement. Even the preacher himself was a picture of modesty, in jeans and a polo shirt. He was squirrelled away in his tiny office in the basement of the church, which smelled of must and old books.

"I suppose my daughter sent you to beat some sense into me?" he asked with a glare, when I knocked on the open door to his office. It wasn't an unreasonable question, I guess. Tim had gotten in a few good shots two nights ago. Between the scraped up knuckles and the bruises, I looked like exactly the violence-prone asshole everyone thought I was.

"You know Alex wouldn't send me to do her dirty work," I said, letting myself into the office without invitation. "If she wanted to beat you up she'd do it herself."

A smile tugged at one corner of the preacher's mouth before his lips pinched together and the glare returned. With a sigh, he gestured at the chair opposite his desk and I sank into it. All of a sudden, I was nervous. What was I thinking, getting in the middle of their family business? Alex would *kill* me if she found out.

"Alex doesn't know I'm here," I said.

Her father cocked his head, frowning as he studied me. "So you just decided to involve yourself in our private affairs of your own free will, then?" he asked, leaning back and crossing his arms over his chest.

"Uh…" I hesitated. "Yeah, I guess. I mean, yes. I did. She's really upset. I thought—"

"You thought you'd just swing by and talk me out of years of hopes and dreams for my baby girl's future."

"Not really," I said, shaking my head. What in the hell *had* I been thinking? This man loved my girl more than life itself, and he still wouldn't listen to her reasoning. How the hell had I convinced myself that he would listen to *me*, a guy he didn't even *like*?

"So why are you here?" he asked, sitting forward and clasping his hands on the desk in front of him.

"I guess… " I frowned, staring at my hands before looking up and meeting his eye. "I guess I just wanted to tell you that she's really upset. She misses you. But she hasn't once talked about changing her plans. She's going to go to Caltech, with or without your blessing. So if you think freezing her out is going to change her mind, you're wrong. She's already calling around, trying to find work-study programs. She's applied for financial aid. She asked me to drive her out there, if you won't when the time comes. Nothing is going to stop her, and I figured if I was her dad I'd wanna know that. You're either going to send her to California alone, without her family, or you're going to send her with support and a home to come back to during the summer. If it was me about to lose her, I'd want someone to warn me."

Every word I spoke had the voice in my head screaming louder and louder. *Shut up shut up shut up!!!* But I forced myself to finish and then fled in the silence that followed my diatribe. Alex's father stared at me, his eyes stony, and the thick air of the church began to close around my head, suffocating me. I stood, cleared my throat, nodded awkwardly, and left before he had a chance to respond.

That was early March. In late March, Alex and I had our first fight. Two weeks after my talk with her dad, I arrived to pick her up for school and I knew the second she opened the door that I was in trouble. She glared at me across the expanse of her front lawn, and her steps as she marched toward my car were so heavy I swear I felt the earth quake.

"What the *hell*," she hissed, climbing into the cab and slamming the door behind her so hard I flinched. We'd never fought before, and suddenly I was terrified. I knew what a fight looked like— screaming and flying objects and one or both parties leaving in the back of a squad car. Between my dad's death and the day the state pulled us out, mom went through six boyfriends, and every one of those relationships had ended with the first fight.

"What's the matter?" I asked, my mouth dry, praying on the off chance she might be mad about something completely different. Something unrelated to me and my transgressions.

"You talked to my dad without telling me?" she snapped, jamming her seatbelt into the lock and crossing her arms over her chest.

"A while ago, yeah," I said, hurriedly pulling out onto the street. Alex was safety conscious, so long as I was driving, she wouldn't kill me or hit me, and she couldn't leave. I resolved to drive to the end of the earth if that's what it took to see this through without losing her.

"You mind telling me what possessed you to stick your nose in my family business?" she said, tossing her bag on the floor by her feet.

"You were upset," I said lamely.

"Yeah I was upset!" she said, slapping her hands on her thighs to emphasize her point, and it was all I could do not to cringe away from her. What if she got so angry she forgot about safety? My second set of foster parents after Jake left got in a fight on the road, once. We were on the highway, driving back from an appointment with my caseworker after I got suspended for fighting, and they started arguing about whether to keep me. That turned into a larger fight about bills, which turned into her smacking the shit out of him and him shoving her back with a hand wrapped around her throat. The car swerved all over the road and I remember wishing it would just roll over and kill us all.

I didn't want to die today, though, and I definitely didn't want to roll the car and hurt Alex. I wanted her to calm down. I wanted to keep her. "Al, I'm sorry," I said. Whatever she needed to hear, I'd say it. "I shouldn't have gone behind your

155

back."

"You're right you shouldn't have!" she snapped. "I don't need you to solve my problems for me, Nate. You're my boyfriend, not my bodyguard. You can't just run around beating up my enemies for me. That's not how life works."

"I didn't lay a finger on your dad!" I argued, panicked. What the hell? She thought I'd—

"No, but you did beat up half the male population of our school!"

Oh, fuck.

"They were talking shit, Al."

"Yeah, I know. That doesn't mean you had to go all mob justice on them."

"You were worried about what people would say. You told me—"

"Yeah, I was worried, Nate. I had every right to be worried. But I need to be able to tell you my problems without worrying that you're going to try to solve them with your fists. You're like a fucking guided missile with no off switch! I can't even vent to you without wondering if I'm putting people in harm's way!" Her voice was loud, and thick with tears of frustration.

The explosion was coming. The fight had escalated, and now we were reaching the boiling point. I could feel it. My skin prickled as her anger mingled with the diesel fumes in the cab of my shitty old truck. Out of the corner of my eye, I saw her arm move toward me, and I jerked away on instinct, packing myself into the corner of my seat, hands tight on the steering wheel. I needed to pull over so I didn't wreck when she started beating on me, but we were on a four-lane road with no shoulder. Fuck. *Fuck* I was gonna get us both killed.

"Nate, what the hell?" Alex exclaimed. When her fist never hit me, I glanced at her out of the corner of my eye and saw her tucked back into her own side of the truck. Her hand was pulled tight against her chest like she'd just touched something hot.

"Sorry," I choked out. I'd swerved into the left lane in my distracted attempt to get away from her. Fortunately there were no other cars, and I pulled us back into the right lane.

"Pull over."

"We're almost to school," I said, trying to pull a breath into lungs that refused to work. "Can we just finish this once we get there?"

"Pull the fucking truck over, Nate. Now," she said again, her voice pitched low in warning. *Fuck. Fuck fuck fuck.*

I turned off on the next available side street and pulled into an empty furniture store parking lot. As soon as we stopped moving I yanked on the parking brake and let myself out, desperate for fresh air. *You almost got her killed, you fucking idiot.*

"Nate!" Alex chased after me as I strode across the parking lot toward the furniture store. It was still closed, the windows dark. When I reached it, I leaned against the wall, back to the parking lot, pressing my palms to the cool, pock-marked surface of the cinderblock and staring at the chipped white paint. My lungs still didn't want to inflate.

"Nate!" Alex said from right behind me, and I jerked around to face her, pressing my back to the wall. She flinched away, and that was just another drop in the bucket of 'reasons this was never going to work.' "What is going on with you?" she asked, taking a cautious step forward, shaking her head. "You almost got us killed."

I couldn't even find words. Part of me wanted to explain, but I was scared to speak. What if I said something wrong and ignited another fight? Alex and I bickered constantly, but we never *fought*. I'd thought we never *would* fight. I'd thought we were safe from that.

"You're scaring the shit out of me," Alex said, closing the distance between us. Behind her, the truck was still running, loud and clunky. I closed my eyes and tried to breathe in rhythm with the clunks. Three clunks in. Four clunks out. Three in. Four out. Alex's scent filled my nose and her hands settled tentatively on my shoulders. Breathing got a little easier.

"Sorry," I managed, forcing the word through the narrow passageway of my throat. I tipped my head back against the cinderblock and stared at the sky, trying to anchor myself back in reality. Miss Meg had taught me this stupid trick, decades before, and I'd been using it ever since on those rare occasions when I needed to tamp down the emotion instead of channeling it into war.

Yellow clouds against a green-blue backdrop. Sharp morning sunlight bouncing blindingly off the metal bumper of my truck. Cars speeding down the road beyond the parking lot, rushing to work and school and errands.

Finally grounded, I lowered my gaze to Alex's face.

She didn't look pissed anymore. Just scared. "Sorry," I said, again. Was that the only word left in my vocabulary?

"Stop apologizing and just tell me what happened," Alex said, stepping back, hands sliding off my shoulders. "Are you okay?"

I nodded jerkily and wished I had the courage to look her in the eyes. "Yeah."

Her brow furrowed, carving delicate lines into the smooth skin, and she propped her hands on her hips and cocked her head. "Do you get panic attacks very often?"

Humiliation surged through me and I lowered my gaze to the ground. "No," I lied. How could I explain that every fight I'd been in was just... all of that—all of what had just happened in my head—pushed outward? *Every day, angel. It happens every fucking day.*

"Why did you freak out?"

Staring at the toes of my sneakers, I cast about in my head, desperately seeking some way to change the subject. That was the best way to distract her—

ask her about something she cared about more. Tom or her dad or school or something…

Fuck. I couldn't think of anything. My brain was still swimming in a syrupy concoction of fear and humiliation.

"Nate," Alex said gently, like she was luring a feral cat out of a gutter. "Did you think I was gonna hit you?"

I shook my head wordlessly— not a negation so much as an expression of my inability to explain anything I was thinking.

"You know I'd never do that, right?" Alex asked, and I wanted to say yes. *Yes, of course I know.* But I didn't know that. I'd never seen her angry like that before. I'd let myself believe she was just too level-headed to get angry. Even at the height of her depression she was reasonable. *I* was the violent one. *I* was the angry one. Not Alex.

"Would you ever hit *me?*" she asked, and I balked at the question. My words suddenly came back in a rush.

"Of course not!" I snapped.

"Why?" she asked, smiling.

"Because you're a girl." *Obviously.*

"Why else?"

I shrugged, casting around for a truthful answer. "Because I love you?"

"Yeah, and I love you too, remember?"

"It's not the same," I argued, frowning at her. "You were angry."

"Yeah I was angry!" she exclaimed, throwing her hands out to her sides and letting them fall. "But that doesn't mean I'm gonna freaking *hit* you. And even if I was I wouldn't do it in a moving car that *you* were driving. That's crazy!"

"You were really angry," I said stupidly. Why didn't she understand? There's no logic when you're angry. There's no love. There's just a red haze and bloodlust.

"Not everyone solves every problem with violence," Al said, scowling at me. "Are you gonna get like this every time we fight?"

Jesus H. Christ. This is gonna happen again?

I shrugged, and Al rolled her eyes, heaving an exasperated sigh.

"You're impossible," she said with a shake of her head. "Don't go behind my back again to solve my problems, Nate." I shook my head to agree. "And next time we fight, don't try to wreck your car." I hung my head, unable to look at her. Alex was the most well-adjusted girl I'd ever met. How long would it take for her to run out of patience with my bullshit? I ought to have broken up with her right then and there— liberated her of my convoy full of baggage.

I couldn't do it, though. I loved her too much. Or maybe I didn't love her enough. Either way, instead of setting her free I wrapped my arms around her and hugged her until she squeaked, batting at my chest with her hands.

"Let me go, crazy," she mumbled against my chest, and I loosened my grip, letting her step away. She glared at me, but her hackles were down and the air no longer buzzed and crackled with the energy of her anger.

"I'm still pissed at you," she said, bracing her hands on her hips. I just nodded. And that was the end of our first fight. No screaming. No thrown objects. No police involvement. No bruises. Just raised voices and fear.

I could survive that.

.. .. ..

In April, for the first time since we started seeing each other, I took Alex on an actual, honest-to-god date.

I thought maybe I was dreaming when the stars finally started falling in line—

First, Paul left the system. In late March, his maternal grandparents finally got wind of his existence. They were estranged from his mother before she died and had no idea they had a grandson. One day Paul was there. The next he was gone, swept away by the same combination of luck and love that had snagged up Jakey so many years ago.

Trish cried and Ronnie pouted and bitched about his own grandparents, who'd had the gall to die before he was born. I was just happy. I'd fucked it up with Jake, so now any time a kid got adopted out from under me, I made sure to send them off with a smile and a hug. When the loss and petty jealousy inevitably crept up I beat it back with memories of Jake's tear-stained face and I forced myself to be happy. Just happy.

A week after Paul left, Ronnie brought home a permission slip for a sleep-away field trip to the capitol to visit a natural history museum. He didn't want to go, but I talked him into it. Two nights away from Tim and Marsha was a rare opportunity. Not hard to sell. I forged the signature and he took the permission slip back to school the next day.

I damn near cried when Trish came to me two days later, begging to attend a sleepover at her friend's house that Friday night. I didn't even bother to clear it with Tim and Marsha. As long as they knew where we were if the authorities came knocking, they didn't give a shit where we went. I would drop her off and pick her up, so it wouldn't interfere with their drug consumption. Nothing else mattered.

The only person left to worry about was Deb and, if I'm being honest, I didn't worry too much about her those days. She was never at home and, when I did see her, she was invariable stoned out of her mind. I still cared about her. I still wished she would clean up her act. I just didn't have it in me anymore to drag her kicking and screaming back to the light, only to have her dive back into the darkness the second I turned my back.

159

Paul was gone. Ronnie had a field trip. Trish had a sleep over. Deb was never home. For the first time since I entered the system, I didn't have a single person to worry about. Friday night was wide open. I could do whatever the fuck I wanted.

"Do you wanna see a movie on Friday?" I asked Alex, hiding a smile when she gawked at me across our little table in the library.

"Like... sneak out and catch a midnight showing?" she asked, confused. Usually, I was only available during school hours and in the middle of the night.

"I was thinking more like dinner at five and a movie at seven," I said, shrugging like it was no big deal.

"My stars, Nate Reynolds," Al breathed, widening her eyes and pressing her hand to her chest. "Are you asking me on a date?"

"Of course not!" I played along, holding up my hands and shaking my head. I leaned forward, whispering so the library staff wouldn't hear me. "I was just thinking we could get dinner on me and then sit in the back of a dark theater and make out. Then, if you're up for it, maybe we could wander into the woods and have a little sex."

Alex leaned forward and whispered in my ear, warm breath brushing over my skin. "That sounds an awful lot like a date."

"Call it what you want," I said with a shrug. "The offer expires in five... four... three... two..."

"Okay, okay!" Alex exclaimed, pressing a kiss to my lips before pulling back to her side of the table. "What should I wear?"

"I mean the date ends in the woods, so..."

"Ballgown. Got it," she said, smiling as she pulled her book open. I watched her read for a while, and the smile never left her face. It didn't leave mine, either.

.. .. ..

I dropped Trish off at her sleepover at four, which left just enough time to run home, shower, and pull on my newest jeans and least ratty t-shirt. I arrived at Alex's house at quarter to five. I half expected her to be wearing a ballgown just to be funny, but the sight that greeted me when she opened her front door was so much more tantalizing than that.

She wore jean shorts that were probably a little too short for her father's liking, and the same sneakers she always wore to traipse around in the woods. Her shirt was a casual halter top that left her shoulders bare, displaying a smattering of freckles. The only part of her that seemed done up was her hair, which she'd brushed into compliant, shiny curls that hung to her shoulders. I stared at her, wondering if she'd be cool with skipping past dinner and the movie and going straight to the sex portion of the evening.

160

I didn't really want that, though. I wanted to sit in a restaurant with her and buy her food. I wanted to make out with her in a crowded theater. Call me an exhibitionist, but I just really wanted every person in the world to know she was mine.

We ate dinner at Applebee's. I didn't have many options. Our town wasn't exactly at the forefront of Michelin star dining. The only other decent place I knew of was an Italian restaurant that cost $25 a plate and I think Alex would've killed me if we went there. She knew I was trying to save.

So we ate at Applebee's, surrounded by families and loud frat boys getting drunk at the bar, yelling at the game on the screens above them. We didn't talk much while we ate. At that point, Alex and I didn't really have to. We'd long ago reached the point where we primarily communicated via significant looks and off-handed comments. We were two teenagers who had settled comfortably into the rhythm of a middle-aged married couple with kids.

We still had the libido of teenagers, though, and I don't even remember what movie we saw. We sat in the back row, and the second the lights dimmed, Alex's hand was in my lap. By the time the movie started she herself was in my lap and my own hand was up her shirt, wrapped around a bare breast. Twenty minutes into the film, some beleaguered theater worker came by, shined a flashlight on us, and asked us to leave.

We walked back to the truck, laughing hysterically. Alex clung to me, her arms around my waist as we walked, and I kept an arm around her shoulders. Older people stared at us and rolled their eyes, and I knew deep down that we were being obnoxious, but not even a small part of me actually cared.

Instead of taking her home, I drove out to the same secluded spot by the lake where we'd celebrated my birthday. There, I killed the engine and returned the favor she'd done me back in February.

There's some moments that stick with you no matter how distant they become. Most of mine are bad, but that night is one of the rare, *good* persistent memories. I'll burn out with the dying sun, remembering the taste of her arousal on my tongue, and the feel of her hands gripping my hair. I'll remember the smell of diesel and sweat, and I'll remember the sound of her crying out when she came.

For a few minutes after, Alex didn't move. She just slumped against the door, panting, one arm draped over the back of the seat, the other hanging down toward the floorboards. Her hair was matted, her skin shining with sweat, chest heaving as she tried to catch her breath.

Immensely satisfied with myself, I gathered her up in my arms and pulled her into my lap, kissing a trail up her neck toward her mouth. She wrapped her arms around my neck, snuggled close... and *fell asleep.*

I admit, my dick was pissed the fuck off. I did my best to ignore it, though, because this was kind of a dream in itself. I lowered my face to her hair, breathing in the flowery fresh scent, and let my own eyes drift shut. A cool breeze trickled through the half-open windows, drying the sweat on our skin and carrying with it the smell of damp earth and springtime. Alex sighed, nuzzling closer, the warmth of her body penetrating my skin and making me unbelievably drowsy.

I'd dozed at the spot before, with Alex curled against my side. I'd shared her bed in the days after her mother died. I'd never really slept with her, though. Waking up a few hours later, I realized that I'd never really slept at all. Not until that night. That night, I sank into an inky black soup that smelled like Alex, and echoes of the future drifted around me, bright and hopeful. When I woke, it took me thirty seconds to get my bearings. Thirty seconds of groggy vulnerability as I blinked away dreams. That kind of weakness was like a death sentence in my world.

I blinked open gritty eyes, trying to remember where I was. Alex had slipped down so that her head was in my lap, her face turned into my stomach, one arm shoved between my back and the seat behind me. Confused, rubbing at my eyes, I brushed hair off her face.

"Alex," I whispered, smoothing a thumb over the scar on her temple. "Wake up, angel."

It took three more tries before her eyes blinked open, glistening up at me in the dim light.

"I think we fell asleep," I whispered.

She blinked. Then her eyes widened, and she jerked up, looking around. "What time is it?" she asked. I glanced at my watch.

"11:30." Her curfew was midnight. "We've still got time to get you home."

Alex breathed out a sigh of relief, shifting back over to her side of the bench seat. Her shorts were on the floorboards, and I bent to retrieve them, dropping them in her lap.

"Thanks," she mumbled, awkwardly slipping back into them. "Sorry I fell asleep."

"It's okay," I told her, starting the engine. The headlights made me wince, and all I wanted was to go back to sleep—a sleep I'd never known was possible. "I did too."

We didn't talk on the drive back to town, but Alex held my hand, humming along with the crackling music pouring out of my crappy speakers. We rolled the windows down all the way, and the wind played with her hair, whipping it about her face. She was the most beautiful thing I'd ever seen.

I got her home with two minutes to spare, and she kissed me goodbye and slipped out of the truck. I shamelessly watched her ass as she jogged across the lawn. At the front stoop she turned, blowing one last kiss before darting into her house.

I was utterly at peace for the whole drive back to Tim and Marsha's place. Still heavy and listless with sleep, I parked on the curb and hopped the low, chain link fence. The house was dark and I said a silent prayer of gratitude as I slid my window open and climbed inside.

It was strange, being in an empty room. I kicked my shoes off and sprawled on my bed. Without Ronnie snoring in one bed, Paul sleeping talking in another, and Trish tossing and turning in the third, the silence was almost deafening. Little noises rose up in the emptiness and jammed themselves into my ears.

Noises like the house settling. Noises like the midnight train, four blocks away, and the slam of a car door two blocks over.

Noises like the soft sound of stifled sobbing, coming from the room on the other side of my wall. The girls' room. Trish's room.

Deb's room.

CHAPTER EIGHTEEN

ALEX

The day things started to end was appropriately dreary. I woke up to rain falling hard on the roof above me and, although it was well past sunrise, heavy clouds blotted out the sun to give the impression of evening.

Despite the weather, I woke up chipper and cheerful. It was Monday, and I hadn't seen or heard from Nate since our date on Friday. I missed him. Where, to other kids, Monday meant the first day of the slogging school week, to me it meant something different. It meant the first of five days of guaranteed facetime with the guy I loved. Our Friday date had been a rare exception to the rule. Nate worked so many hours, we didn't get afternoons together, and evenings were even worse. His foster parents were way too strict, and he had to wait until after they fell asleep to sneak out.

My father was sitting at kitchen table when I came downstairs.

"Morning, sugar," he greeted, lifting his coffee cup in acknowledgment without looking up from his book.

"Morning, Daddy." I pulled a travel mug from the shelf and mixed my own coffee. I took it with a gallon of creamer and eight metric tons of sugar mixed in. Nate liked to make stupid jokes about how I took my cream with a splash of coffee. I rolled my eyes to myself as I poured the last of the pot into a second travel mug for my boyfriend, who of course took it black.

My father and I had reached a tentative agreement. Loathe as I was to admit it, whatever Nate had said seemed to have worked. I was still on thin ice, but the lectures had stopped and my father had started mentioning tickets to my orientation over the summer and plans for a road trip to drive me out at the start of the school year.

Of course, he never said he was *proud* of his daughter for gaining admission to one of the most prestigious universities in the country. I couldn't hold that against him, though. It was my dream, not his. I was just grateful he was letting me live it.

I barely had time to shove a piece of toast into my mouth before I heard Nate's truck rumble up outside. He honked twice and I kissed my father on the cheek before pulling on a rain coat and dashing through the rain to the truck parked by the curb.

I had my head down against the downpour, and I didn't look up until I pulled the car door open.

I froze.

Rain pounded against the hood of my jacket. My right hand was wrapped around the edge of the door, and droplets trickled down my hand into the sleeve. Nate sat behind the wheel, jaw clenched, right hand wrapped tight around the gear shift. Next to him, arms crossed and glaring at me...

... Deb.

She looked different. Usually she dressed to impress. Or, rather, she dressed to *de*press anyone who liked to think that women were something more than sexual objects. Today, though, she wore jeans instead of her usual short skirt, and her hair was lank and pulled into a sloppy ponytail. There wasn't a trace of make-up on her face, and dark shadows hollowed out her eyes.

Perhaps because Deb and I had always had an unspoken rivalry, or perhaps because I was young and self-centered and insecure, my mind barely paused on the clear evidence that she was going through something. Instead, it went straight to the absence of her usual leather jacket— two sizes too small so that, when zipped, it pushed her boobs up toward her chin. My attention focused on what she wore instead— a sweatshirt that was three sizes too big, swallowing her frail frame.

There was a rip in the sleeve of that sweatshirt, from where it had caught on a branch while Nate had chased me through the woods. There was a stain near the hem from where Tom had spilled hot chocolate on him during the big snow storm.

Correct me if I'm wrong, but there's only one girl to whom a teenage boy should give his sweatshirt.

"Deb, scoot over," Nate growled, still not looking at me. "Let her in."

Shooting me one last glare, Deb shifted over the bench until she sat flush against Nate's side. The sight sent a stab of pain spearing through my chest, and I lowered my gaze as I climbed into the truck, pulling the door shut behind me. I set the coffee I'd made for him in the cupholder, where it remained untouched and unacknowledged.

The ride was painfully silent, and my thoughts expanded and multiplied in the vacuum until I was halfway to tears with despair. Nate was cheating on me.

He'd got what he wanted from me and now he was going to dump me. He'd loved Deb all along. I was just a distraction. As we pulled into the parking lot, I forced myself to calm down. Maybe I was overreacting. Reading things wrong. All I had to go on was Deb's presence and her strange attire. I needed to give Nate a chance to explain.

Unfortunately, he didn't seem to want to give *himself* a chance to explain.

"You go ahead, Al," he said as he put the car in park. "I'm gonna walk Deb to her first period."

Walk Deb to class? Are you fucking kidding me?

"Sure," I said, the pain my chest so powerful I could hardly breathe. I shoved the door open and went to hop out, but Nate's voice stopped me.

"I'll see you in English," he said unnecessarily. It wasn't the words that held me up, but the tone. He sounded almost desperate, and I heard the unspoken plea in the undercurrents. *Please don't be mad. I'll explain.* It was so unlike him, I almost demanded an explanation right then and there. Something was so clearly wrong.

But what?

"Sure," I said, unable to keep the bite of hurt from my voice as I slid out of the car.

First period was AP European History. I don't remember a word the teacher said. Every time I tried to tune in, I got distracted by the memory of Deb's fierce glare and the way she tucked Nate's sweatshirt around her, huddling closer to him while he drove.

Second period was AP Chem. I couldn't really afford to miss a word of that lecture, but I did. I spent *that* class wondering exactly what had happened between his departure on Friday night and his arrival that morning. I'd never felt closer to him than I had on Friday. He'd brought me to a high I'd never imagined, then held me close as I floated back to earth. We'd slept together, our minds mingling as we dreamed. It had felt like the first stone in a path to forever, and my entire weekend had been a series of daydreams, from our first apartment together to our rocking chairs on a sunset-gilded porch.

What had his weekend been like? Had he taken Deb out to that exact same spot and shown her that exact same future? Had he held her as she slept? Had he wrapped his sweatshirt around her shoulders when she began to shiver in the cool night air? Did he make her feel as loved as he made me feel? Was that why she'd abandoned the too-short skirts and the skin-tight shirts and the caked-on make up? Because he made her realize she didn't need it?

Tears blurred my vision and I blinked them back, forcing myself to concentrate on the board as the chemistry teacher scrawled out equations.

I was halfway insane by the time third period English finally rolled around.

166

Nate and I didn't sit together. He insisted on the back of the classroom and I always sat at the front. Sitting with him would have been pointless, anyway. He always slept in Mrs. Parker's class. Shamelessly, too.

That day, he didn't even look at me as he entered the classroom. He kept his head down as he walked by me, and I forced myself to look straight ahead. Even so, I followed him with my ears, listening as he slumped into his seat with a sigh. Anxiety made my stomach turn, and my heart hurt like someone was squeezing it in a fist.

At the end of English class, I let myself get my hopes up again. Nate ate lunch with me and my friends. Always. Every day since we'd come out to the school with our relationship. But when the bell rang, he swept past me before I'd even zipped my backpack. When I reached the cafeteria, my reluctant eyes found him in the corner, sitting with his old crew.

It would have been bad enough if he'd been laughing and joking with his friends. Instead, he sat at the end of the table with Deb, and they ate in relative silence. As I watched, Deb picked up a piece of pizza, then dropped it back onto her tray. She said something, her face crumpling, and Nate wrapped an arm around her, pulling her to his side. He lowered his face, and I could tell he was speaking by the way she nodded occasionally, tucking herself further into his body. I wondered if the soft rumble of his voice made her chest warm the way it did mine.

"What in the actual fuck is going on with lover-boy?" Gemma asked, appearing by my elbow. I realized with shock that I was standing in the middle of the cafeteria, staring. That, and half the cafeteria was watching me, eyes wide, expecting a reaction.

Shame burned in my gut. Even if he wasn't cheating on me, which felt less likely with every passing hour, how could he have so little regard for me? How could he flaunt it for the entire school to see, as if he'd never cared for me at all? Surely he knew what they'd say.

"I don't know," I said, tearing my gaze away from Nate and leading the way to our usual table. I purposefully sat with my back to Nate. If the school wanted a show from *me* they'd be waiting a long time.

"Seriously, Aly, what gives?" Gemma asked, sitting across from me and glaring over my shoulder. "You two are all lovey-dovey one day and the next he's making googly eyes at the sister, which… I know they're not really related but… *ew.*" She made a face that would've had me laughing in different circumstances.

"I don't know," I said again. "I haven't seen him since Friday. I don't know what's going on."

"Ohhh, you had your date, right?" Gemma said excitedly. Then she lowered her voice. "Is that what happened? Did he want you to put out?"

Even Gemma didn't know I'd given away my virginity. I'd oscillated a lot about wanting to tell her, excitement battling with lingering shame. Now I was glad I hadn't. If this really was the beginning of the end, I was glad nobody knew how much of myself I had given to the jackass. Nobody but the jackass himself, and my father. Which… what would he say when he found out I'd been dumped? Would he tell me he saw it coming? My heart couldn't take that.

"Just leave it alone," I sighed, shaking my head and pulling my lunch out my bag. Since October, I'd made two lunches every day. One for me, one for Nate. Two coffees and two lunches. And, like the abandoned coffee in his truck, his lunch sat in the bottom of my bag. I resolved to throw it out on the walk home from school.

"Fine," Gemma said. "But if you need me to beat him up, I will." She flashed me a grin and I tried like hell to return it. "I'm pretty sure I could get a few good shots in."

"If anyone hits him, it'll be me," I said, but my words took me back to the fight we'd had in March. I'd been so angry, but the rage had drained out of me at the panicked gleam in his eye. I'd been reaching out to take his hand, and he'd reacted like he thought I was going to snap his neck. It blew my mind that he thought I'd actually hit him, and the look on his face when I promised I never would had ripped my heart in two. Disbelief. Polite, restrained, unspoken *incredulity.*

And why? Who had taught him that anger and violence were so inextricably bound? His parents, maybe? I'd always wondered why he ended up in foster care. Maybe his parents were abusive…

No. Whatever the reason for his reaction, I knew I could never hit him. Even if he really had cheated on me. Even if he did dump me for Deb. I couldn't prove him right. Not on that count.

.. .. ..

At the end of lunch, I bid farewell to Gemma and made my way to the library for my study hall. Unlike English class and lunchtime, I didn't let myself get my hopes up for the free period. I resigned myself to an hour of lonely studying and silence.

Unable to sit at our usual table, I picked one in the corner behind the bookshelves, pulling out a textbook and setting it on the table. I opened it up but couldn't concentrate on the words. My mind was filled with vivid nightmare daydreams. Deb cuddling up to Nate in the front seat of his truck. Deb and Nate making out in the maintenance hallway between the gym and the auditorium.

Deb in a hospital bed, holding Nate's baby. Deb and Nate, on rocking chairs, watching a golden sun rise.

My heart lurched when movement caught my eye and I looked up to see Nate walking toward me. Swallowing the lump of emotion that had formed in my throat, I lowered my face back to my book and shielded my last shred of dignity behind a wall of false indifference.

I didn't look up when he reached the table. Or when he sat down. He didn't pull out any books, and I knew he was watching me, waiting for me to explode on him.

I didn't.

"Don't you have homework to do?" I asked icily, glancing up from my book.

Again, my heart lurched. I hadn't gotten a good look at him all day, and what I was finally seeing had the soft, weak part of me clamoring for supremacy over the strong, vindictive part.

He looked like shit. I don't know if it's possible to lose weight over the course of two days, but he looked thinner. Rendered down to muscle and bone, the hard lines of his face harsher and more pronounced than usual. His eyes were glassy with exhaustion and rimmed by dark shadows, and the emotion in them sliced clean through my resolve.

He looked lost. The boy who picked and won fights with guys three times his size— who had unwanted answers to every one of my problems— who had held me in strong arms through every crisis— looked unbearably, incurably *lost*.

Was it guilt? The ice returned, encasing my heart behind a thin barrier of apathy.

"What's going on, Nate?"

He shook his head, lowering his face. "It's complicated, Al."

"Is it Deb?" I demanded, my voice barely more than a whisper. I couldn't bring myself to utter the words louder, for fear that they might be true.

Nate nodded, his face still downcast, and my heart broke. The fist that had been tightening around it all morning suddenly clenched, and for a moment I thought I was actually dying.

I didn't, though. My broken heart kept beating, pumping blood to my arms and legs, helping me move as I clumsily shot to my feet, gathering my books and shoving them into my bag.

"Al, wait!" Nate said, reaching out to grab my arm, but I jerked it out of his reach. He stood, blocking my way as I went to leave. Unwilling to touch him, even long enough to shove him away, I turned around and circled to the other side of the table. He met me there, still blocking my exit. "Al, stop," he pleaded, holding his hands out.

"Why should I?" I hissed.

"It's not what you think," he insisted, glancing over his shoulder to make sure we hadn't drawn an audience. But the library was still and empty— colorful shelves of books and rows of unused computers hanging in stasis beneath the scent of dust and carpet cleaner.

"You're not… *with* her?" I hissed at him. "Because it sure looks like you are, Nate."

"No!" he exclaimed, before lowering his voice. "Of course not, Alex. I'm with you. I'm yours. I swear. I just…"

He trailed off, shaking his head and pushing trembling fingers into his hair.

"Just what, Nate?" I asked, stepping forward. I desperately wanted him to set me straight. Call me foolish, but I'd have believed anything he said. All he had to do was give me *something*. "I love you so much. You know I do. But how can I trust you? You never talk to me. Just give me something to work with, here. *Anything*."

"I can't, Al," he moaned, sinking back into his chair and burying his face in his hands.

"Can't what?" I asked, trying so damned hard not to cry. *You can't admit you cheated?*

"I can't explain," he said into his hands. "I want to, angel, but I can't. Please just trust me. I swear there's nothing between me and Deb. I swear on my *life*. It's you and me."

"How can I believe that if you won't even *try* to explain what's going on?" I asked. I desperately wanted to sit down and take his hands and tell him everything was alright, that I forgave him, that I believed him. He needed to hear it. I could tell by his hunched shoulders and the desolation in his voice. My heart pleaded with me to fix it— to fix *him*.

My brain knew better.

"You're not giving me anything to work with," I said, my voice remarkably even, considering I could hardly think over the screaming in my mind, *begging* him to help me understand. "I want to trust you, but you have to understand how it looks. All of a sudden, out of nowhere, you're driving Deb to school and hanging out with her between classes and eating lunch with her and your old friends. What else am I supposed to think?"

"Just trust me, Al," Nate said, looking up at me. The raw need in his eyes should have ignited more sympathy, but instead it sent a chill up my spine. What had he done? What was *so* bad that it had shaken *Nate*? "Once I explain you'll understand. I will explain. I just can't yet. Please just trust me. Give me time."

"You have a week," I said, reason and self-preservation buckling beneath the weight of my love for him. "I'll give you a week."

I gave him two.

Because I'm weak, I gave him two weeks to pull himself together and tell me the truth. The only time I saw him during those two weeks was in class and at study hall. I couldn't bring myself to go to the spot and sit with him beneath the stars, suffocating beneath the silence and the weight of his secrets as they snuffed out every good memory we had made there.

To this day, I wish I'd gone. It wouldn't have been pleasant, but I wish I had subjected myself to that uncomfortable silence and the shame of loving him when I knew I shouldn't. I wish I'd let him hold me and suffered through the agony of passion and hurt his touch ignited. If I could go back, I'd go to the spot every night and put myself through all that pain. It would be better than the pain that came later, when I learned that he went there every night. That he waited for me until dawn kissed the horizon. That I'd wept tears of angsty teenage hurt into my pillow while our last moments of youthful love and relative innocence were trickling through the hourglass.

I like to think that, with the gift of hindsight and the knowledge of how limited our time really was, I'd have gone to the spot and let him love me so we both had something to carry into the years that followed.

But I didn't. I saw him only at school, and what I saw there only buried me deeper in doubt and heartbreak.

He was slipping. Quickly. Snowballing back into the boy he was before we started dating— before he jump started my life and let me breathe hope into his.

He slept through our classes together, and stopped turning in his homework. He sat with his old friends at lunch and cut class with them to smoke cigarettes in the parking lot. Deb was with him nearly every moment of every day, stuck to his side like a leech. She never smiled, but I caught her watching me with warning and loathing in her eyes. Maybe he'd given her the same lines—that she was his one and only. Maybe she trusted him as little as I did.

Once, I looked up in the cafeteria and she caught my eye. While I watched, unable to look away, she linked her arm through Nate's. He flinched away from her, confusion on his face. Then he looked up and saw me, and his expression twisted in anger. He pulled his arm from hers and spoke words I couldn't hear over the din of the cafeteria. I don't imagine there's anything he could have said to her that would have stopped my heart from breaking. Because even if they weren't together— even if she was marking territory that wasn't hers to claim— he still didn't walk away. He still chose her over me, and no matter how much it hurt me.

Ironically, Deb wasn't even involved when the powderkeg finally caught a spark and the whole thing went up in flames.

It was the end of the day, and I was heading home. It was a fifteen-minute walk, but with the way everything was going I didn't mind the time alone to think. It was a little piece of normalcy, undisturbed by the shift in my relationship with Nate. Even before things went south, I walked home because my boyfriend had work after school.

That day was a Friday. I remember everything about it, from the weather to what I was wearing. Sunny and unseasonably cool; jeans and a sweater.

A car pulled up beside me as I turned the corner and started walking through the residential neighborhood surrounding my school. The neighborhood looked a lot like mine— white picket fences. Green lawns. Tire swings and minivans and rose gardens. It was lovely and idyllic and fake. What skeletons were these homeowners hiding? How many of these housewives quietly wanted to slit their wrists and bleed their lives into lukewarm bathwater?

"Hey, Aly!"

I looked up, and saw Isaac Campbell leaning out the passenger side window of a shiny red BMW. Without stopping, I stooped and saw Lance Curry behind the wheel. Both were leering at me as Lance idled the car along the side of the road, gong just fast enough to keep up with me.

My gut churned and I wanted to flee, but I forced myself to keep my step even and raised my chin, ignoring them.

"Oh, sweetheart, don't be a bitch!" Isaac said, thumping gently on the side of the car with his open palm. "We just wanted to see if you need a ride home?"

"I'm fine, thanks," I said sweetly, but with a hint of heat. Chile-laced chocolate.

"I heard you and Reynolds broke up," he said, a sneer in his voice. "That's a shame. You must be real lonely."

"I'm fine." *Leave me the hell alone.*

"Oh, I doubt that. It's okay to be sad, sweetheart."

Don't call me sweetheart! "Well, I'm not, so you can leave me alone."

My stomach clenched when the car pulled over at the curb and Isaac hopped out, blocking my path on the sidewalk.

"C'mon, Aly," he crooned, cuffing me in the shoulder. "Just let us give you a ride home."

"Leave me alone, Isaac," I said, pushing past him only to have him circle around in front of me once more. Dread grew to cannonball in my belly when I heard another car door shut, telling me that Lance had gotten out of the car as well. His heavy footsteps approached me from behind and the skin on the back of my neck stood on end. Surely someone in one of these big, beautiful houses would see what was going on and interfere.

Maybe none of them were home, because nobody did. I kept walking, in lurching five-foot increments, each spurt of movement halted by either Lance or Isaac. Their words were kind but their eyes were lecherous, unabashedly roaming my body, and their fingers dug into my arm every time they stopped me.

I felt the barest shred of relief when I heard the familiar clunking of Nate's truck approach and draw to a stop on the curb beside us. Then I panicked. What were the odds he'd just ask them politely to leave? I quickened my step in a vain attempt to drag Isaac and Lance with me and outrun the problem.

"Get the fuck away from her," accompanied the sound of a slamming door, and suddenly Nate was blocking the sidewalk, towering in front of me, fists clenched at his sides, every muscle locked. He glared over my shoulder at Lance and Isaac, who had stumbled to a halt at my back.

"It's not a big deal," I said weakly.

But it was as if he was beyond hearing. He moved around me, his body seeming to expand into the cloud of his own anger as he placed himself between me and the others. I turned as well to see Isaac and Lance both back away a step. But they didn't leave.

"We were just trying to give her a ride," Isaac said, glancing nervously from Nate to his friend. Lance just glared, puffing out his chest, drawing himself up. My mouth went dry with dread. There was only one way this ended.

"Nate, it's not a big deal," I said again. "They were just trying to give me a ride."

"Did you want a ride?" he asked over his shoulder.

"No, but—"

"Did you tell them that?"

"Yeah, but—"

"Then it's a big deal, Alex. Go wait in the truck with Deb."

What the hell did he think I was? Some kind of distressed damsel?

"I'm fine here," I said, crossing my arms over my chest, although his back was to me so I suppose my defiant stance was wasted on him.

"You fucks have two seconds to get the hell out of here," Nate said, reaching behind to push me back, and I rolled my eyes in spite of myself.

"Ease up, man," Isaac said, holding up his hands. "We thought you were done with her. Just a misunderstanding."

"Done with her?" Nate echoed, his voice quiet but sharp with venom. Isaac and Lance each took a step back. "I'll never be 'done with her.' And whether I am or not shouldn't matter." He was walking forward now, driving them back along the sidewalk. Nate was neither short nor scrawny, but the two football players each had him by a good fifty pounds. So it was strange that, from where I was standing, he seemed to dwarf them. "She told you she wanted to walk. You

173

harassed her. Alex doesn't like violence, so I'm giving you five seconds to get the fuck out of my sight. After that, whatever happens is on you."

I'd never heard his voice like this— all chilly and hard. It made my spine tingle, and not with pleasure. With fear. Base, animalistic fear that told me to flee to the hills from the predator standing before me. Apparently Lance had no such instinct for self-preservation.

"You know what, man? Fuck you!" he said, stepping forward, his face beat red. "I'm sick of you lording around school like you own the place. You're just some piece of trash with an anger management problem who dipped his stick in the preacher's girl and caught a god complex."

I didn't even see the punch. One second Lance was standing there, chest out, face red, flecks of spittle flying from his mouth as he yelled in Nate's face. Then I blinked, and when I opened my eyes he was on the ground, holding his jaw, and Nate was shaking his hand out at his side.

"How about you?" he asked, turning to Isaac, fists flexing at his sides. "You want some, too?"

"Goddammit, you pussy!" Lance yelled at his friend. "Fucking do something!"

Isaac's eyes flicked from Lance to Nate, then back to Lance. I saw resignation, and before I could scream a warning he was barreling into Nate, tackling him onto some unwitting family's manicured lawn.

As they rolled around on the ground, it occurred to me that I'd never actually seen Nate fight. I knew it was happening, of course. I couldn't remember a day since I met him that he wasn't bruised up in some way or another, and he was always getting suspended for starting shit at school. I knew it, but I'd never actually *seen* it.

It was terrifying.

I don't know who that boy was, but he wasn't *my* Nate. My Nate was sweet and thoughtful and annoyingly in control of not only himself but every aspect of the world around him.; He was smart and mature and had the answer to every problem.

The guy trading punches with Lance and Isaac wasn't any of those things. He was vicious and reckless and… feral.

I stumbled back as they rolled from the grass back onto the sidewalk, nearly knocking me off my feet. Before I could find the brainpower to be anxious about the outcome, Nate was on his knees, straddling Isaac's chest, driving fist after fist into his face. His teeth were bared and I swear his eyes— normally the color of a stormy sky— were glowing red with bloodlust.

Then Lance was up, launching himself forward. Before I could blink he had Nate by the back of the shirt and was hauling him off of Isaac. Instead of toppling off balance like I imagine Lance intended, Nate used the momentum to his advantage, letting Lance pull him to his feet and turning as he rose, driving an elbow into the side of his assailant's face.

"Stop it!" someone screamed from behind me, but I couldn't move. My feet were rooted to the sidewalk as I watched Lance drop to the ground with Nate on top of him.

"Keep…" Nate growled, wrapping a fist in Lance's shirt and pulling him up so they were nose to nose.

"Your…" he shoved him back to the sidewalk.

"Fucking…" Lance's head snapped to the side with the force of Nate's blow.

"Hands…" Another punch.

"Off…" Behind me, footsteps were slapping the pavement, but I couldn't look away from the carnage before me.

"My…" Blood spattered the cement.

"For fuck's sake stop!" Deb screamed, streaking into my field of vision. I reached out on instinct, snatching at her arm. She was going to get herself hurt. But her shirt sleeve slipped through my fingertips and she threw herself into the fray like she was bulletproof. "Stop it!" she yelled, grabbing Nate by the shoulder and pulling him back, leveraging herself into the space she created between the two men. "Stop!" She shoved him back, hands on his chest, and by a divine miracle she survived.

It was like someone flipped a switch. The fire went out, his fists unclenched, and he didn't offer any resistance as Deb pulled him to his feet, dragging him away from his victims with a hand around his wrist.

"If any of you go to the cops about this," she hissed, glaring at Lance and Isaac, who were struggling to sit up, then at *me*, "I will tell them you tried to rape me."

"You're a lying slut," Lance said, and Nate lunged, held back only by Deb, who placed herself between the two like some kind of perverse force field. Her hands were on his chest, and I wasn't even jealous. His lips were drawn back in a snarl, his expression so fierce I barely recognized him.

"I might be a slut," she said over her shoulder as she marched Nate away from the carnage he had caused, Lance and Isaac still sitting on the sidewalk with blood-streaked faces. "But I don't make empty threats, and you don't want to test me on this."

The fight had carried us ten feet from where Nate had parked his truck. They were halfway to it, Deb dragging Nate by the wrist, before he planted his feet, pulled free, and marched back to where I still stood. My body was still frozen as my mind struggled to process everything that had happened.

"I'm driving you home," Nate growled, reaching towards me, and I flinched away. I no longer recognized him. This wasn't my boy. This wasn't the man with whom I wanted to raise children and grow old. What little trust I still had in him dissolved in the face of his uncontrollable violence. For the first time, I feared him as much everyone thought I was supposed to.

His hand dropped to his side like I'd burned him and his eyes went hard as granite, but he didn't turn away.

"I'm not leaving you here, Al," he said, jerking his head toward the truck. "Either come with me or I'm walking you home."

Isaac and Lance were weaving unsteadily as they helped each other stand. As much as I feared Nate, I feared them more. Plus, Deb would be there. She could sit in the middle—a barrier between us.

Feeling utterly powerless, I turned and followed the stranger to his truck.

CHAPTER NINETEEN

NATE

"What the hell were you thinking?" Deb hissed as I leaned out the window to check for passing cars and pulled back onto the street. Alex sat scrunched against the passenger door, hugging her backpack to her middle and staring out the window.

"Leave it alone," I snapped at Deb, probing at my lip with my tongue. I'd bit it when Isaac's weight slammed me into the ground. That was my only injury aside from the requisite bloody knuckles.

"Fuck you," Deb hissed. "You just put us all at risk. What do you think happens if you go to jail?"

"Shut the fuck up, Deb," I growled, glancing over at Alex. She was still staring out the window, but I knew she was thinking about me. I knew she was terrified. I could feel her scrutiny and fear down to the marrow of my bones. I knew what she was thinking because it was exactly what I wanted her to think. She was asking herself who in the hell I was. If she even knew me. If I was too dangerous to be around. If I was some kind of monster who couldn't control his anger.

All those years, I'd hid this part of myself from her because I'd known what would happen when she learned the truth. She'd be repulsed, she'd run, and I'd never had the strength to let that happen. Alex was an open door in a dark room, and when she left she'd pull that door shut behind her and I'd have nothing left but the darkness. I'd been a coward and an idiot, letting her light up my life and exposing her to darkness that had no business touching her.

That was why I'd finally let her see it. She had to leave. I didn't deserve the light. People like me can't just waltz into heaven. We have to do penance. Mine wasn't even near to complete, but that hadn't stopped me from pouncing at that open door and the light spilling through it. I'd stepped into heaven, and when the universe came to collect my entrance fee, it wasn't me who paid it.

It was Deb.

On Friday night, I'd gone on a date I couldn't afford with a girl I didn't deserve, while Deb got high on pills. I ate more than my share of food while Deb's boyfriend drank more than his share of beer. I'd laughed more than I thought possible while, somewhere across town, Deb's boyfriend dumped her because he was too drunk to get it up and it was easier to blame her.

Then I'd driven out to the lake while Deb stumbled back to Tim and Marsha's house.

I'd tasted heaven while she curled up on her bed and tried not to listen to the sound of Tim drunk-fucking his wife.

I'd listened to the sweet sound of Alex screaming my name while Deb screamed my name too— screamed my name and hammered on the wall that joined our bedrooms, begging me for help while she clawed and bit and punched and made every futile effort to stop Tim from forcing himself on her.

Then, for hours, I'd slept like a baby, safe and content, while Tim pulled himself out and stumbled off to bed. While Deb curled up on her mattress and cried, unable to move, too scared and humiliated and shocked to pick up a phone and call for help.

I'd done that. My world was dark and ugly and filled with innocent people, like Deb, who didn't deserve to be there. Protecting them was my job— my only hope at redemption— and my negligence had cost Deb what little innocence she had left.

Alex thought I was cheating on her. I wasn't. I would never sleep with Deb. I loved her, but she was a sister to me. A charge. Everything about her screamed 'fuck me' to the world, but all I ever saw in her was a scared little girl who needed protection.

In a sense, though, that was worse. I'd die before cheating on Alex, but what had happened to Deb made me realize that I had to choose: the kids or Alex; redemption or happiness. I wanted Alex. I needed her like I needed air to breathe. But I couldn't turn my back on the kids, and I couldn't have both.

Alex deserved someone who was all there. Someone with whom a regular date was the rule, not the exception. Someone who didn't keep half of himself locked away from her out of necessity. Somebody who, when all was said and done, could join her on the gold-paved roads of heaven instead of abandoning her to rot for his sins in hell.

It took me two weeks to talk myself into letting her go. No, not letting her go—driving her away. Two weeks to work up the fortitude to accept a future without her. Two weeks to come to terms with the fact that I couldn't be both the brother Deb needed and the boyfriend Alex deserved. It was one or the other, and the sad truth was that Alex would survive without me.

Deb wouldn't.

I had a whole break-up speech planned, and merely reciting it in the mirror had taken rusty sawblades to my insides. I planned to lie to her, one last time. *"I'm with Deb. I'm sorry. I loved you but I don't anymore."*

Call me a coward, but I'd been relieved when Lance and Isaac had given me an easier out. Why put the weight of another lie on my soul when I could just show Alex the truth and let her do the dirty work for me.

So I let her see the real me— violent and cruel and mean, and as I drove her home I felt a weary sense of satisfaction. Alex was too smart to stick with me after that display. She'd dump me so I wouldn't have to do it. She'd get on with her life. She'd pull the door shut behind her and leave me where I fucking belonged.

It was exactly what I wanted. It was the right thing to do. Which is why it was so strange that, the closer we came to her house, the more agitated I became. It was like an off-key note, screaming in my ears, louder and louder, multiplying into a chorus of dissonance that had me wincing.

The sense of wrongness grew to nauseating levels when I pulled into Alex's drive and shifted into park.

"Thank you for the ride," Alex said woodenly, fumbling to push the door open and slipping out of the car. She was painfully composed, pushing the door shut instead of slamming it. She met my eye through the open window, ignoring the heat of Deb's sideways glare. "You don't, um…" she broke off and crossed her arms over her chest, looking down at the ground. "I think maybe we shouldn't… I don't want…"

"Just spit it out," Deb snapped, resting a possessive hand on my thigh and gripping so tight I felt the bite of her nails.

Alex flinched and nodded jerkily, raising glassy eyes to mine. "I don't think we should see each other anymore," she said quickly. "I'm… I'm done. I can't do this."

Those words were what I expected. They were what I *wanted*—for her to say them so I wouldn't have to.

But how could I have known the way they'd hit me? For six years, I had taken her for granted. All those years, all those homes, all those fights, and I'd assumed I'd survived them because I was strong.

It had nothing to do with strength, and everything to do with the fact I'd had somewhere to go. I'd had the quiet noise of the woods, and the cool water of the creek, and the breadth of the stars, and a girl who held my hand and brought me food and loved me even when I gave her nothing.

Before I could stop myself, I was shoving my own door open and throwing myself out of the truck, jogging around the engine block and chasing her across

179

the lawn. My mind wanted to let her go, but my heart wouldn't let it happen. My soul knew better than I did that I wouldn't survive without her. She was it—the only good thing—and my selfish fear of losing her won out over my desire to set her free. Disgusted at my own weakness, I circled around her and placed myself between her and the house, effectively stopping her progress. I didn't dare reach out and touch her. Watching her flinch away again would kill me.

"Alex, wait," I gasped, breathing like I'd just run a race. It was like my mind's resistance to my soul's desperate striving for her had sucked the energy right out of my body. I couldn't seem to catch my breath.

"What do you want, Nate?" Alex asked, her composure cracking slightly. Her face was stern, but her eyes were bleeding heartbreak that burned me like acid.

"Please don't go," I begged, trying to keep up with the words that spilled out of my mouth and barely managing to stop the ones that so desperately wanted to follow. *Please don't go. I don't know what to do. I need help.*

My convictions and self-damnation crumbled under the force of her pain. Of *my* pain. I had to explain. I respected Deb's need for privacy, and my life was almost too humiliating to put to words, but Alex needed to know. If I was going to break her heart, and condemn myself to a life without her, I'd do it with the truth. The full truth. I couldn't send her out into the world alone without making sure she knew exactly how much I loved her. It wouldn't be fair. And what if there was a chance she'd still want me? We'd find a way. Maybe I could pay off my debt without living in hell. Maybe I could look out for the kids and do right by Deb without bailing on Alex. If there was a way, she would help me find it.

"You've had two weeks' worth of chances," she said, taking a step back. I felt a desperate urge to drop to my knees and plead, but I just stood there, rooted to the ground, as tears sprang into her eyes. "I can't do it anymore, Nate."

I can't either. "I know." I shook my head. Of course I knew I didn't deserve another chance, but this was Alex. She'd always been better to me than I deserved. "I know I fucked up. I'll tell you everything. I'll explain it all. Just give me one more chance. Please, angel." *Please, help. I need help.* "I..." my own voice cracked and I ground my teeth together, fighting for a brand of strength I'd never had. I sucked in a deep breath and squared my shoulders and met the sharp distrust in her eyes. "I need help, Alex. Please..."

I watched her resolve falter. Her lips trembled and a single tear broke loose and tracked down her cheek. It took everything I had not to reach out and brush it away. She drew a shuddering breath and crossed her arms over her chest.

"Fine," she said, her voice hard. It wasn't hard like steel, though. It was hard like plaster, cracking and flaking away, unable to mask the technicolor pain that lay beneath it. "Explain."

I almost did. Right there, standing in the lawn. But it wasn't the time or place. We needed time, and privacy. Over her shoulder, I saw Deb scowling at us from the open window of my truck.

"Meet me at the spot tonight," I said, the words spilling out in a frantic rush as I watched frustration and resignation rise on her face. "I swear I'll tell you everything. *Everything*. It's just… not the way you think, but some of it's got to do with Deb, and it's a really long story. We need time and we need to be alone. Please meet me at the spot."

I saw the hesitation on her face. More importantly, I saw the fear. Now that she finally knew what I was, she was scared to be alone with me. That hit me like a one-two combo to the gut. My feet moved, carrying me backwards.

"I can come here if you're more comfortable with that," I said, struggling to talk around the pain in my chest. "After your dad and Tom turn in. That way if… if you feel uncomfortable there's other people around."

Alex steeled herself, raising her chin and clenching her jaw. So brave. So perfect. "I'll meet you at the spot," she said. "But this is it, Nate. If you don't… I can't keep doing this."

It was a miracle she'd stuck with me for as long as she had, considering the dishonesty. The secrecy. She wasn't stupid. She must have noticed I'd evaded all her questions. It must have hurt her, all those nights throughout the years when I hadn't showed up at the spot and hadn't given her shit by way of explanation. But she'd stuck around. Trusted me even when I didn't deserve it.

"I know," I said, nodding as I backed away. I had to escape before she changed her mind. "I'll be there. Thank you, angel. I love you."

She didn't say it back, but I didn't need to hear it. I heard it loud and clear when she agreed to meet me. Alex loved me, I loved her, and I had one more chance to prove it. I couldn't squander it. If protecting the kids was my job, Alex was the home I came back to after doing it. If I didn't have her, there was no point to redemption. Without her and the light she gave me, I wouldn't be alone in the dark. I would become it.

.. .. ..

Deb didn't speak to me all evening. I think she knew what I was planning to do. When we got home, she marched off to the bedroom I shared with Ronnie and threw herself down on the unclaimed third bed, turning her back to the room. The girls' bedroom was just a formality by that point. Deb couldn't bear to be in there, and Trish— although ignorant of the cause— fed on Deb's anxiety and refused to spend time there as well.

So, every evening, the four of us would pack ourselves into that one little bedroom and distract ourselves from whatever was happening beyond the door. We played shitty board games and told stories and listened to music on Ronnie's thrift-store boombox. I'd bought it for him for Christmas the year before. In true Ronnie fashion, he'd called it a piece of shit, bitched that it didn't have a CD player, and then proceeded to treat the damn thing like a priceless ancient artifact. None of us were allowed to touch it, and he put more love and attention into cleaning and maintaining it than most people put into caring for their children.

At around six, Trish and I tiptoed to the kitchen to make dinner while Deb and Ronnie stayed behind. We'd long since figured out that traveling in smaller groups meant less noise and presence, which in turn meant less likelihood that Tim and Marsha would take notice of us.

Our 'parents' were in the living room, yelling at some pre-recorded baseball game. They were distracted, but not yet drunk enough for their awareness to fade, so I tried to make a game of avoiding their attention. When Trish dropped a butter knife on the ground, I hid my cringe and nudged her in the shoulder.

"That's one point for me!" I whispered, pressing my finger to my lips. She grimaced dramatically, displaying two missing baby teeth, and nodded.

When the plates clattered as I pulled them from the cupboard, she grinned at me in triumph and held up one finger.

By the time we made it back to the bedroom with four hastily-prepared turkey sandwiches, Trish had three points and I was still at one.

"I win!" I sing-songed, nudging the door shut with my heel.

"It's no fair!" she complained, sitting on the edge of my bed and taking a sloppy bite of her sandwich. "You're bigger."

"Yeah, that should make me louder, silly," I teased, sitting by Ronnie and prodding his hip until he tossed his magazine aside and sat up, accepting the plate I handed him. "I think you're just clumsy."

Trish spat out her tongue at me, and I faked disgust at the lump of half-chewed sandwich in her mouth. Deb's disgust was real enough. "Shut your mouth while you're chewing," she scolded half-heartedly. Her shoulders were slumped and she stared with disinterest at the untouched sandwich on her plate. She wasn't eating enough, rapidly shedding pounds she couldn't afford to lose.

I'd always thought there must be some kind of limit for how much a person could worry. I imagined at some point you just ran out of brainpower and couldn't fit any more items on the list of shit that stressed you out.

I was out of brainpower, though, and the list just kept growing. Tim's predation. Alex's heartbreak. Deb's deterioration. Trish's perilous innocence. Ronnie's distance. Money. Food. Assholes at school creeping on my girl. Said girl's imminent departure for college. My looming exit from the foster care system. The question of how to look after the kids after I aged out and couldn't

182

live with them anymore. Deb's refusal to go to a doctor after Tim raped her. My own culpability in allowing it to happen....

Earlier that day, Mrs. Parker had pulled me aside after class and told me she was concerned. "You haven't been turning in your homework," she had said, brow furrowed. "You've been doing so well, Nathan. You owe it to yourself to see this through."

I wanted to scream at her— to take her by the shoulders and shake her until the blinders she was wearing fell off and she realized my world and goals and priorities didn't look the same as hers. That I had real problems that a quality essay on Chaucer wasn't going to solve.

Instead, I'd just nodded and made an empty promise to 'try harder.'

It was Friday, so Tim and Marsha were up a little later than usual. At 8, we tucked Trish into my bed and switched to more subdued activities. Deb read a magazine. Ronnie plugged headphones into his boombox and listened to music. I sat by the door and tried to concentrate on my book. I'd already finished *Pride and Prejudice*— Alex's ooey gooey love story selection for our two-man book club— and had moved on to the *Fellowship of the Ring*. I usually wasn't much for fantasy, but the last two weeks had necessitated an unprecedented degree of escape.

The book wasn't bad. Given a choice, though, I'd prefer to escape to Alex than to Middle Earth.

By nine, Ronnie was out cold. Deb gently pulled the headphones off his ears and shook a blanket out over him.

By ten, Deb had fallen into restless sleep, curled up on Paul's old bed. As she did every night, she wrapped herself into a ball, twitching and mumbling at every yell and laugh that came from the living room. I switched off the lights and retrieved Ronnie's boombox from beneath his bed. I had my own stash of cassettes and found an old Beatles album, plugging that in and turning the volume down low. Background noise usually helped when one of the kids was having trouble sleeping.

I wouldn't have had any trouble sleeping at all. With the lights off and the kids asleep, my own eyelids grew so heavy I had to fight to keep them open. I sat with my back against the door and tried to read by the dim streetlights, but my eyes kept sliding out of focus. The nauseous fear of drifting off and missing my last chance at redemption only made me more tired.

So I stood. I paced. I did push ups and crunches. I silently rehearsed my speech. I'd have to start at the beginning. If I'd learned anything from living half my life between the pages of a book, it was that context is important. I couldn't just tell her. I had to show her.

It wasn't until midnight that Tim and Marsha shifted to the bedroom. By the time I heard them moving I was suspended awkwardly between consuming anxiety and pressing exhaustion. My heart was pounding, but I couldn't keep my eyes open. My brain was firing on every synapse, but my head felt stuffy and too heavy for my neck.

I did another set of pushups and then stood, leaning against the wall and trying to listen to the Beatles instead of Tim and Marsha going at it in the room down the hall. Outside, a car drove by and bright white headlights slid across the room, illuminating the kids. They all slept peacefully, and an unexpected bubble of hope swelled up in my chest. I don't know if it was the exhaustion making me stupid, or the knowledge that I was about to tell Alex the truth after over a decade of going it alone, but I felt *good*. I could do it. I could keep them safe and hang onto Alex. I could support myself when I left Tim and Marsha's. I'd find a way for the kids to spend their time with me. I'd figure it out. With Alex in my corner, I'd make it work.

I was so caught up in the delusion, I almost didn't catch the sound of Tim rising from bed and stumbling down the hall. A year or so ago, that sound would have sent chills down my spine. That night, I just felt annoyed.

About time, old man.

He was fumbling with the girls' doorknob when I slipped out into the hall.

"Go to bed, Tim," I said, leaning against the wall. We'd long since abandoned our back-and-forth. He knew exactly why I was confronting him. It was almost refreshing. Tim was the one person with whom my relationship consisted of no secrets or lies. No false smiles. We hated each other, pure and simple and honest.

"Fuck off," he slurred, turning back to the door.

Sighing, I pushed myself off the wall and approached, shoving him back. "I said go back to bed."

The cracking backhand came faster than I would have expected, slamming me against the wall. My head rang, my mouth filled with blood, and the familiar, comfortable red haze dropped over my vision.

I punched him in the face, so hard he dropped back against the opposite wall, giving me room to circle around so we were no longer crowded. I had the empty hallway behind me— room to maneuver.

He came back swinging, but I ducked beneath the blow and plowed a shoulder into his stomach, driving him back. He stumbled away until he hit his own bedroom door, at the end of the hallway.

That was my fatal mistake.

Pinning Tim against the door with my weight, I pounded my fists into his sides, grimacing in satisfaction at the sound of his grunts of pain. Then something happened. Maybe he finally got his arms up and brought an elbow down on the back of my neck. Whatever the cause, the world went unpleasantly colorful and

184

my legs dropped out from beneath me. When I got my shit together, I found myself face down on ratty carpet with all of Tim's weight bearing down on the knee he had pressed between my shoulder blades.

My right side was pinned against the wall and my left arm was trapped beneath me. Tim had a hand on the back of my neck, shoving my face to the ground, hissing obscenities at me. If he was smarter, or had the gift of hindsight, he'd have knocked me out cold while he had me vulnerable. Instead, he just took the opportunity to wax poetic.

"You're a useless little faggot," he whispered venomously, pressing his weight into that knee until it was all I could do not to scream.

"Fuck you," I gasped, struggling to get my left arm free.

"Maybe I will. Just like I fucked that slut you love so much. Teach you a little something about defying me."

I didn't even bother replying. With a gargantuan effort, I managed to leverage my body up just enough to free my left arm and swing it back blindly. My elbow met with the side of his thigh, just above the knee.

That little lump of muscle and nerves is more vulnerable than you realize if you've never been hit there. Tim didn't exactly collapse in overwhelming pain, but he did cry out, and his weight shifted as he instinctually moved away from the blow. It wasn't much— just enough to get my arms beneath me and shove up, bucking him off.

Tim dropped back against the wall, struggling to keep his balance as I scrambled to my feet, clumsily batting away his punches. He was panting hard already, his booze-drenched muscles failing him. Just a minute more— maybe less—and I'd have him.

I was too confident. Too oblivious to my surroundings. I drove Tim back, dealing three times as many punches as I took, so consumed with my looming victory that I didn't even hear the door open behind me, or Marsha approaching at my back. All I knew was Tim, and the fact that I had him. He was stumbling backward, nose and lip bleeding, panting raggedly as he struggled to fend off my blows.

Then, in a flash, my skull was splitting open, spilling me off the surface of the earth and causing time to blink and swirl together. I felt my body hit the floor, and Tim's weight straddling me, and the flashing pain of meaty fists pounding into my face. I heard Marsha's voice.

"Get him, baby!" she screamed. I must have woken her up when I slammed Tim into her door. Back in the day she'd have stopped us fighting, but she knew that with my record it wouldn't be Tim the authorities suspected. Especially now that I was eighteen. He'd be cited with self-defense and I'd be carted off to jail. She wanted this fight.

My arms didn't want to respond as I fought to get them up in front of my face, fending off Tim's blows.

Holy shit. Is this how I die?

No way in hell. Alex was waiting for me. Gritting my teeth, I pulled my arms up, blocking my face while I screamed at my legs to come back to me as well. If I could buck him off I could get the upper hand. He was still tired. I could still win.

"Get off him!" someone screamed, and my blood froze. The voice wasn't tinny or raspy from years of chain smoking. It was young. Crisp. Terrified.

Trish.

Her round, innocent face appeared behind Tim's shoulder, her skinny little arm wrapped around his neck. Her free hand was balled into a fist and she pounded it against his back with righteous fury. "Get off! Leave him alone! Get off!"

Tim shrugged her from his back like she weighed nothing. With a growl, he tossed her against the wall and she slid to the ground, stunned, and that was that.

I snapped.

It wasn't just Trish that did me in. The sight of her sprawled against the wall was the straw that broke the camel's back, but the real weight was in the build-up. It was in the years of suppressed hatred— blows I pulled for the sake of the kids. It was in the fury over what he'd done to Deb. It was in the heartache over the thought of losing Alex. It was in the sheer exhaustion— mental and physical and spiritual— that had dogged my footsteps for as long as I could remember. In the looming darkness and the fear of what would happen when it finally closed in around me.

Ultimately, though, it was a choice to break. Somewhere, deep down, I still had a kernel of strength—a fraying string wrapped around the rage that I chose to cut. That red haze deepened and spread from my vision to my whole being, and I made no effort to stop it. I welcomed the transformation. The surrender. My blood was fire. My bones were steel. My muscles were the frothing waters of a raging sea. I was power. Lethality. I was unstoppable vengeance.

With a roar that tore itself from my throat like a living thing, I rolled, throwing Tim off me against the wall opposite Trish. He slammed into the drywall, and I followed and pinned him to the ground, all trace of weakness gone as power surged in my veins. I wrapped my fingers around his throat, squeezing with intent to kill. It wasn't enough to choke him to death. I wanted to rip out his trachea and watch his blood stain the carpet.

Marsha was screaming, and I felt her approach. Without looking, I sensed the same heavy object in her hands with which she had clubbed me earlier. One hand still wrapped around Tim's neck, I reached out with my free hand

and grabbed her ankle, yanking hard and bringing her to the ground. A lamp thumped to the carpet beside her. With one heave, I dragged her drug-wasted form into reach and shifted my grip up to her neck.

"You're next," I snarled, and she whimpered as I released her neck and shoved her away. Never mind that it was an empty threat. Even in the rage, I couldn't hit a woman. Not even her. But Marsha didn't need to know that, and from the way she scrambled away I knew she believed me.

Tim was choking and gasping, his eyes bugging out of his head. His hands scrabbled feebly at my wrist before shooting up to my face. I smacked them away before he could dig his fingers into my eyes. When he kept clawing at me, I hauled back and slammed my fist into his face.

It felt good. Better than it ever had before. I felt the distant pain as the tiny bones in my hand jammed against each other and my knuckles met with the hard surface of his cheekbone. I felt the squish of skin and muscle giving out beneath the force of the blow. I felt blood, thick and warm, coating my skin. I hauled back and hit him again. His hands dropped away.

"You don't touch them," I heard myself scream, my voice raw. I let go of his throat so I could hit him with both hands. I needed to feel his skull cave. I needed his blood on my hands. I needed to know— beyond the vaguest shadow of a doubt— that he was gone. I couldn't share the earth with him. I wouldn't survive another day breathing his air.

"Stop!" someone was screaming, and there were hands on the back of my shirt, pulling. I barely felt them. My life began and ended with taking Tim's. I hit him again and again and again, watching his head snap back and forth with the force of my blows. The air tasted like blood, and I pulled it deep into my lungs with each ragged breath, savoring the tang. I felt his presence leave the earth with each punch, each drop of blood, and I knew I had to keep going. I had to finish it or nobody would be safe.

The hands tugged harder. "Stop!" someone new screamed, and another set of hands latched onto my right arm. Reality shot through the fog. Trish's tiny, cold hands wrapped around my wrist, and I knew I couldn't shake her loose without hurting her.

Fuck.

"You gotta stop, Nate," Ronnie said in my ear, his arm wrapping around me from behind, pulling back. Then Deb was there, her face filling my red-clouded vision.

"Stop," she pleaded, pushing me back, and I didn't have a choice. They were all over me, sucking the fight out, their desperate fear like a bucket of water on the flames of my bloodlust.

187

I let Ronnie pull and Deb push me away from Tim's body, staggering to my feet. The kids let go and fell away from me, grouping together and staring at me as I stumbled back. When my spine hit the wall my knees buckled and I slid down until my ass met the ground. Tim lay in the center of the hallway, arms and legs sprawled out to the sides. His eyes were open, staring at the ceiling, and his face was a puffy, ruined mask of blood. His chest was still.

My eyes burned, and my gasping breath began to wheeze with helpless sobs. Hot tears burned their way down my face and I couldn't find it in me to make them stop. I'd just murdered a man. I should have been flowing over with fear, remorse, and disgust. All I felt, though, was peace. Like the clouds were finally parting. Like the noose around my neck was finally loosening.

Irony is a bitch, huh? I had just thrown myself bodily from the frying pan into the fire, and all I could do was weep with relief.

Deb broke away from the group and knelt by my side. I tipped my head back against the wall and blinked at the ceiling, waiting for her to slap me. Berate me. Cry. Something.

Instead, she just wrapped an arm around my neck and pressed her forehead to my temple in an awkward approximation of a hug. When she pulled back, her eyes met mine and I saw my own relief reflected in her gaze. She tipped her chin up and nodded slightly, and I knew that there was more to the bloody corpse than solace. Revenge permeated the air.

Then Trish was there, pushing past Deb and worming her way into my lap. "It's okay," she said, with all the weight and wisdom of a woman ten times her age. Her hands wrapped up in my shirt and she buried her face in my chest, but she didn't cry. It was like some sort of twisted role-reversal. My kids, my charges, dry eyed and strong while I melted into the respite of Tim's absence. "We're okay."

Ronnie didn't look at me, but he slid down the wall by my side, pulling his knees close to his chest. His jaw was locked tight and his eyes were wide, watching the hallway down which Marsha had disappeared. Ronnie was a smart kid. He knew what was happening— a silent changing of the guard. My watch was ending. His was just beginning.

Beyond the thin walls of the house, I heard sirens. Trish tucked herself tighter against me, Deb huddled on my right with her arm linked through my mine, and Ronnie sat silent vigil on my left. Tim lay lifeless in the hall, his blood congealing in the carpet. Marsha cried and screamed in the front lawn, railing at whatever poor 911 operator had the misfortune to answer her call. Just miles away, miles that felt like lightyears, Alex lay on the rock and stared up at the stars. Alone.

Even though I wasn't there, I could feel her giving up on me. I felt the last sliver of light disappearing as she walked away and pulled the door shut behind her. Even if I'd had the chance to tell her everything, she couldn't forgive this.

Could she?

I was eight when I took my first life, eighteen when I took my second, and felt no remorse on either occasion. I was drawn tight as a bowstring my whole life— both a product and a perpetrator of a ruthless, barbaric brand of violence. Pain was my natural state. Blood was my medium for artistic expression. Cruelty was my native language.

I was a tough little shit, is what I'm saying.

The cops knew that. They knew who I was. I suppose that's why they showed up guns drawn, faces red, eyes popping as they screamed at me. "*Get on the ground, asshole! Hands behind your head! Cross your feet at the ankles! Don't fucking move!*"

They probably didn't expect to find me sitting against the wall, face buried in my knees, crying like a baby. I'd sent the kids back to Tim and Marsha's room the second the sirens drew close and flashing lights bounced off the walls from the bedroom windows. They were safe, so I didn't feel much compulsion to obey the cops' orders. I just sat there and sobbed— marooned in a sea of consuming relief and plunging darkness.

Alex was gone. Somewhere, worlds away, she was walking home with moonlight shining off her tear-streaked face. Walking away from me. Away from the pain I brought her. Away from the darkness I carried with me.

I should have been happy. She deserved a good life. A man who didn't have blood on his hands. A life of certainty and light. My arrest was giving that to her, forcing her away when she might otherwise have kept coming back— offering me chance after chance to set myself straight.

I'm a selfish fuck, though, and I wasn't happy.

I just wanted her back.

CHAPTER TWENTY

ALEX

I wish I could spell it all out for you. That it was simple and straightforward. *I was sad at first, so I cried. After two weeks and three days, I became angry. I left town. I forgot he ever existed.*

But it's never that simple, is it? Emotions don't arrange themselves neatly for us to hurdle over on our race to the finish line. They're a murky, muddy mess. They're a waist-deep pit of sludge and prickly vines. When one lets go another grabs hold, and sometimes you're a victim to everything at once. When that happens, it's all you can do to keep from sinking below the surface and letting them drown you just so you can get some freaking peace and quiet.

The first few days weren't the hardest, either. They should have been. Time heals all wounds, right? I'd lived that adage with my mother. Not that I was 'over' her death, so to speak, but the wrenching agony had faded and become more livable.

It didn't work like that with Nate. Perhaps because he wasn't dead. Maybe if he was, I'd have been able to get over it. The first few days would have been the hardest, and then I'd have moved on and found a way to live without him. But how do you learn to live without something you may never have had in the first place?

The first few days were straightforward sadness. Defeat. Betrayal. All I knew was that he'd begged for another chance, made me a promise, and then abandoned me at the spot. I waited until dawn and then stumbled home in tears, curled up in a corner of my bedroom, and wept until the sun was high overhead. Daddy was away at a conference and he'd arranged for Tom to stay with some folks from the church so I wouldn't have to look out for him. All weekend, I wandered about in a haze, alone in an empty house.

On Monday, it got worse. So much worse.

Gemma picked me up, as she had for the past two weeks. Her face was unusually pale as I climbed into the front seat of her two-door coupe.

"Aly, I'm so sorry," she said mournfully. Her concern matched my broken heart, but it didn't make any sense. I hadn't told her that Nate was supposed to meet me, or that he'd squandered his last chance to make us right. How did she know to pity me more today than any other? "My mom told me what happened. Are you okay?"

Her mom told her? "Uh…" I frowned, so perplexed I momentarily forgot my sadness. "How the hell does your mom know?"

Gemma rolled her eyes as she backed the car out of my drive. "Her latest boy toy is some cop," she said. "And you know mom's nosey as hell, so she's always prodding him for info on his cases. He responded to the call on Friday night."

"The call?" Fear slithered up my spine, even before Gemma's eyes widened, mouth parting in a silent 'o'.

"You don't know," she breathed.

"Don't know what?" I asked, my heart thundering in my ears. An amorphous, nameless terror had taken over my body, and it took all my strength to ask the question and validate my fear.

Gemma flipped her hazards on and pulled over to the side of the road— the vehicular equivalent of telling someone they should probably 'sit down' to hear whatever was coming next. My stomach dropped like so much lead into the pit of my stomach and my heart hammered so hard I could feel it pounding against my rib cage.

"Gemma, what happened?" I asked again as my friend put the car in park and angled herself so she was facing me. Her right hand clutched the gear shift, nails digging into the false leather.

"Aly, your boy was arrested," she said, looking down at her lap and shaking her head. "He…" she trailed off before looking up at me. "Didn't you think it was weird you didn't hear from him all weekend?"

"I never hear from him on the weekend," I shrugged impatiently. "He doesn't have a phone. Gemma, please just tell me. What did he do?"

He got caught shoplifting. Loitering. Fighting. Driving too fast. Is speeding an arrestable offense?

"He killed his foster dad," Gemma said, her voice barely more than a whisper. "Beat him to death with his bare hands."

I stared at her, uncomprehending. My mind frantically tried to make sense of her words. It threw memories at me in rapid fire. Holding his hand the first night we met. Laying on the rock with him, staring at the stars. His arm around my shoulder, offering comfort. His gruff, reassuring strength, holding me together after my mother's death. The lost look in his eyes when I promised I would never hit him. His voice, firm but gentle, talking me down off of cliff after cliff throughout six years of loyal, intimate friendship.

"No he didn't," I breathed, unable to reconcile Gemma's words with my truth. He *wouldn't*. My Nate wasn't a murderer. But just as soon as the words left my mouth, I remembered the feral gleam in his eye during Friday's fight. I thought of the endless bruises, cropping up and fading on his skin, and the tough, silvery scar tissue on his knuckles. Perhaps *my* version of Nate wasn't a murderer, but it was past time I finally accepted that *my* version wasn't the *only* version. Somewhere out there was a version for whom fighting was a way of life— who slept with pseudo-siblings and apparently beat people to death.

Perhaps if it hadn't happened so abruptly, and if I hadn't been so mired in heartbreak, I'd have been able to see past the shock and ask myself why there were multiple editions of the boy I loved— what external circumstances had broken him into so many unknowable pieces. Maybe if he hadn't kept himself so closed off from me I'd have realized there weren't multiple versions at all. Just one. One boy and more secrets than anyone should have to keep.

But it *was* abrupt and my heart *was* broken and some instinct for self-preservation rose up from my subconscious and wrapped me tight in a shield of disgust and self-absorption. There was no room in my heart for empathy.

"Aly?" Gemma asked, resting a gentle hand on my arm. "Are you okay?"

"No." All I could feel in that moment was my own hurt. Shame that I hadn't seen who he really was. Humiliation that everyone would know that Aly Winger shacked up with a murderer and was therefore either stupid or irreconcilably broken. Disgust that I'd given so much of myself to someone so twisted.

"Do you wanna cut class?" she asked kindly. "We could go get coffee. Or go back to my place. My mom's at work. We could get day drunk."

That sounded wonderful. I'd never had more than a glass of wine, but I relished the thought of drowning my sorrows in humanity's favorite numbing agent.

"No," I said again, trying to make my voice stronger. My relationship might have been a sham, but the version of me it created was better than the one before. I was no longer one to cower. "Let's go to school." The best path forward was to hold my head high and make myself impervious to the whispers and rumors. Shrinking from reality and getting sloppy drunk wouldn't help at all. I would walk into school and act like nothing phased me and maybe, if I kept up appearances for long enough, I would start to feel as strong as I acted.

The next few weeks were an exercise in discipline. Nobody confronted me directly, perhaps because of the persistent rumor that I shared the relentless sociopathy of my erstwhile boyfriend. I still heard them talk, though. Whispers and snippets came together into a conflicted, dramatized legend, and it was a fresh pain that I had no more idea of what was truth and fiction than the rest of them.

"I heard he flipped out on the guy for looking at him funny."

"I heard he's in foster care because his dad's a murderer too. You know there's a theory that crazy is genetic?"

"I heard he beat up one of the kids, too. A little girl."

"My mom is friends with the foster mother. Apparently, he tried to force himself on her and that's how the fight started."

"Well, I overheard some of the sister's friends in the bathroom. I think the dad was a pervert and Nate was just trying to stop him."

"My dad says he's gonna get the death penalty."

"I heard the other kids got carted off to a different city for their own safety, in case he gets out and comes after them too."

"He tore the guy's head clean off. Blood everywhere."

After then, somehow, it got worse.

"You hear his sister is pregnant? The slutty one I mean."

"Apparently they were fighting over her. I saw her at the mall. She's definitely got a bump."

"The baby is his. He tried to get her to abort it but she wouldn't so he tried to beat it out of her. The dad intervened."

The pain didn't get better. It was bad, then worse, then unbearable. I desperately wanted to know the truth and, just as desperately, to forget Nate had ever existed.

Then came the letters.

The first was in a business envelope. My address was scrawled across the front in Nate's sloppy chicken scratch, and the return address was a stamp from some law firm downtown. *I went inside and opened the envelope and pulled out two pages of lined legal pad paper. Happy tears trickled over my cheeks while I read his story. His truth. My father took me to visit him in jail. We pressed our hands to the plexiglass between us and said 'I love you.' His case was dismissed. It was all a misunderstanding. He followed me to California and we got married and spent the rest of our lives together. Happily ever after.*

The End.

Of course not. Life isn't a fairytale, Nate wasn't a prince, and I was not a sweet and gentle damsel.

I sat for hours that night, cross legged on my bed with the envelope on the comforter before me. I stared daggers at that paper— light as a feather but heavy with possibilities. I picked it up and held it to the light above as if I could somehow see his intent through the envelope. I raced through possibilities, his voice reading my theories straight from the wrinkles of my brain, as real as if he was sitting right next to me.

"*I'm not a murderer, Alex. He killed himself and framed me.*"

"*It was self defense, Alex. He hit me first.*"

"*I had to kill him, Alex. He was going after Deb.*"

"*I never loved you, Alex. You were nothing but a game.*"

In the end, I never opened the letter, but not for the reasons you think. I wasn't afraid he would say the wrong thing and break me further. I was afraid he would say the right thing and pull me back in. Whatever the reason, he had killed a man. He had beaten a living being unconscious and then kept beating him until he no longer drew breath. Whatever the reason, he had suddenly, out of nowhere, abandoned me for Deb. Deb who, according to a particularly consistent rumor, was pregnant with Nate's baby.

You've heard the theory of Occam's Razor? If there are two explanations for an occurrence, the simpler one is usually better?

The bottom line was that Nate was violent, he was dishonest, and he was about to go to prison for a very long time. My Nate was gone. Dead and buried, if he ever existed at all. The letter was just a whisper from the other side. An artifact from a life I desperately wanted to leave behind. All it could do was hurt me.

So why did I keep it?

.. .. ..

I graduated high school on June 8, 2002. I was the valedictorian, and I wrote a charming, loquacious speech about hard work and friendship and bright, happy futures. I printed it out in triplicate for the class president, the English Department head, and the vice principal to proof for grammatical errors and inappropriate content. They said it was lovely and vice principal told me how brave I was for overcoming everything I'd been through.

When the day came, I stood in front of 112 students and their corresponding families and delivered a speech that was thirty seconds long. I tapped my three pages of drivel on the podium, leaned toward the microphone, and squinted against the spotlights into the dark, packed auditorium.

"Gemma Roberts," I said, trying not to cringe as my voice echoed out through the loudspeakers. "You're an amazing friend. I'm going to miss you next year. Daddy," I said calmly, as the faculty seated behind me on the stage started to shift. They knew I was going off script. "Things haven't always been easy, but I know you love me. Thank you for forgiving me when I didn't follow your rules. Tom-tom," somewhere in the audience I heard my brother *whoop* and I smiled in spite of myself. "You're my favorite person on earth. I love you more than life. Mrs. Parker," I turned around and smiled at the English Department head. "You're the kind of teacher who changes kids' lives for the better.

"All the rest of you," I finished, gripping the edges of the podium so hard my fingers were turning white, "can go fuck yourselves."

The crowd went wild. Some people laughed. Some people cheered. It was the most support I'd ever received from my classmates, and I barely heard it. I walked backstage, and nobody followed me. I think the faculty were all too shocked. Sweet, quiet little Aly Winger would never do something so outrageous.

My cap and gown were a crumpled-up wad in my arms and I was leaning against the car when my father approached, Tom grinning by his side, five minutes later.

"Did that make you feel better?" Daddy asked evenly, unlocking the car as he approached.

"Yes," I answered honestly, returning Tom's too-tight hug.

"You left without your diploma." I buckled my seatbelt as my father turned the key in the ignition.

"It was just a rolled up piece of blank paper," I said. "We get our real diplomas in the mail in two weeks."

My father hummed thoughtfully and we drove the rest of the way home in silence.

.. .. ..

I spent the summer at my grandparents' lake house in northern Michigan. Tom and I whiled away the longest days of the year swimming and fishing, walking in the woods, and lazing around watching TV. It was only there, hundreds of miles from the pain of the past, that the pain finally began to fade.

Every week on Sunday my father would call and ask us how we were and share trite small-talk from home. Nearly every call ended on the same note.

"You got another one," he'd tell me.

"Throw it away," I'd respond.

"Sugar, you know I hate that he hurt you but maybe you should just read them. Forgiveness is important in the healing pro—"

"Throw it away."

But when I came home in early August there was a stack of letters on my desk. The more recent ones weren't from the jail. They were return addressed to the federal prison on the other side of the state. There were ten of them. Eleven including the first, which was sitting in a shoebox with other treasured items beneath my bed.

I sat for a long time, the letters in my lap, leaning back against my bedroom door and staring at the window through which he had climbed last summer to comfort me. The paper was smooth against my fingertips, and I brushed my fingers over my address, scrawled on the front of each envelope.

I vowed to open them, someday. Weeks or months or years in the future, when my heart no longer ached to see him, I would read his letters and close the door on him once and for all.

In the meantime, they'd live beneath my bed with all the other nostalgic relics of my youth. I knew myself, and I knew my heart. I was an addict, and those letters were a fix that would drag me right back into the hole. If I read them now I'd go back to him. I'd tie myself to a liar and a murderer—a man who did not deserve the best years of my life.

Funny how it was Nate from whom I was running, and Nate who had given me the strength to turn away.

.. .. ..

That evening, I went to the grocery store to pick up the essentials, because apparently my father had been keeping true to the bachelor stereotype in Tom's and my absence. All he had around was a half-gallon of milk and a freezer full of TV dinners.

I was rounding the corner from the canned-veggies-and-soup aisle into the baking-goods-and-spices aisle when I nearly ran her over with my cart.

Deb.

Pregnant Deb.

She was wearing plastic, dollar store sandals, sweatpants, and a worn yellow tank top that molded itself to her rounded belly. Her hair hung limp and frizzy by her face, and her eyes were shadowed.

That I wanted to smack her was no surprise.

That I also wanted to hug her took me aback.

"You're, um…" I trailed off, my eyes sinking to her belly. "Congratulations?"

"Don't be a bitch," she snapped, but there was little venom in her voice. And why should there be? She won. Nevermind that I hadn't even been aware of the competition until the end.

"I wasn't," I said honestly. "I just didn't know—"

"I'm pregnant."

"Right." I tried to steer my cart around her but she side-stepped, blocking my way.

"It's his," she said, glaring at me over my basket of produce and ground hamburger. I felt like she'd reached across the cart and slammed a knife into my chest.

"What?" I asked, my tongue suddenly too big for my mouth. How did it hurt so bad when I already knew?

"It's his. Nate's." She pointed at her belly. "When he gets out, he's going to help me raise it. He's not coming back to you."

"Okay," I said quietly, although my heart was dropping to its knees and raising hands to the heavens, wailing out a drawn out, Hollywood '*Noooooooooooo!!!!!*' at a cruel, remorseless god.

It was the culmination of three months of worrying, agonizing, and second-guessing my decision to cut myself off from him. Three *months* of trying not to imagine the possibility that I was wrong. All that time I'd quietly hoped that I really was the villain, and my Nate wasn't imaginary or dead but holed up in a cell wondering why I'd abandoned him when he needed me most. I'd tried and failed to stop myself from imagining a future where he got out of prison, found me, and berated me for being such an idiot as to question our love.

She fell at his feet and wept her apologies. He pulled her into his arms and kissed away her tears, forgiving her. They rode into the sunset together and lived happily ever after.

The End.

When was I going to learn?

"My dad's church has a program for single parents," I said woodenly. I don't know why I said it. Partly, I think, because of the baby. Deb had never struck me as a mothering sort, and the child didn't deserve to be punished for the parents' shortcomings. Partly, though, it was about Deb. She'd just driven a knife into my heart, but as I slammed into rock bottom, I guess I recognized that I wasn't alone there. She was as broken as I was— perhaps more so. Nate had hurt us both, but at least I could walk away from him. She was tied to him forever.

"Excuse me?" she spat, glaring. "I don't need charity."

"Okay," I sighed. "But it's a good program. They've got donated clothes and car seats and toys. Stuff like that. There's a support group of other moms if you have any questions about any of it. It's not like I'll be around, so you don't have to worry about seeing me. Just think on it."

I rifled through my purse and came up with one of my father's business cards, handing it to her. She took it, eyes scanning my face.

"Thanks," she said, her brow furrowed as she stared at the card.

"You're welcome." I steered the cart around her and left her standing at the end of the aisle with her baby belly and basket of mac and cheese boxes and two liters of soda.

"Hey, Alex?" she called, forcing me to stop and turn around. "I'm sorry," she said hoarsely.

I didn't respond. I guess it's not very Christ-like, but I wasn't quite ready to forgive her.

I finished my shopping, paid for my purchases, and shuttled them out to the parking lot. The August air was thick, and the streetlights buzzed overhead, attracting bugs that slammed themselves repeatedly above the bulb with loud *thwack* sounds as I loaded my groceries into the back of my father's sedan.

I tried not to breathe through my nose as I pushed my cart back to the store. The grocery was bordered on two sides by thick, undeveloped woods and the air smelled like damp earth and sunbaked vegetation. It smelled like long nights spent staring at the stars with my best friend by my side.

It wasn't until I was safely behind the wheel and driving home that the tears broke loose. I cried in anger at the betrayal, in grief at the loss, and in agony at the loneliness. I damn near crashed the car I cried so hard.

I sat in the driveway outside my house for long minutes as the tears poured down my face and the vast and empty world somehow closed in on me, compressing me down until I could barely breathe.

When the tears finally stopped, I sat up and wiped my eyes and pulled the rearview mirror down so I could see my face in the semi-darkness. I looked myself in the eye and made myself a promise.

"That's the last time," I said firmly, glaring at myself in the mirror. "You don't need him. You never did. He's a jackass, a cheater, and a killer. He doesn't deserve your tears, and you will never cry for him again."

Eighteen-year-old Alex made that promise.

Twenty-four-year-old Alex broke it.

ACKNOWLEDGMENTS

Always and forever, first and foremost: Ava Larksen, without whom I would have quit the writing community five years ago and slunk back into my hovel to hunker down and mope atop a hoard of half-finished manuscripts. I don't know what I did to deserve such a talented, kind, hilarious friend, but here we are. This book would not be what it is without her influence. Hell, it might not exist at all. When she's not patiently coaching me through mental breakdowns, she keeps busy crafting her <u>Little Bird</u> series, which is Tolkein-esque in its sprawling inventiveness and Sparks-ian in its heartstring tugging and House Hunters-y in its ceaseless, stirring real-estate porn.

Gigi Laurent. The girl who filled the silence when I first began sharing these ridiculous books. The one who asked for more chapters right when I was running on fumes of motivation and self-confidence. And how delighted was I to find out that this wonderful, consistent, devoted reader was also an amazingly accomplished writer, herself?! Gigi's <u>Bright Knight</u> series will rip your little heart out and trod all over it and then patch it back up with sweetness and love and the undeniable allure of a fabulously wealthy hero.

Roza Rahilly. The only person who knew me by my real name first to have made it through all four books of The Angstiad. Also, author of hilarious, witty, touching, educational, sweet, feminist-minded stories, which she refuses to publish until they're polished, which is weird to me, but I support it.

Sarah, for tolerating my constant nattering about the cover, as well as my epic and lasting silences when a little more responsiveness on my end probably would have made both our jobs a lot easier. Oh, and for an excellent fucking job.

Social Grace. Passionate reader turned expert editor, and overall bad-ass bitch. I don't think there's a greater compliment a writer can receive than assurance that The Story is sufficiently entertaining to remove The Reader from Real Life Struggles. So here's to a good book (not this one, obviously) and the sound of rain and wind-chimes.

The Wattpad community at large. Honestly, I was a little worried I wouldn't be able to find a place for myself on a website with such a monumental breadth and depth of Harry Styles fanfiction (no hate, just not my cup o' tea). But over the last few years I've managed to accumulate a mass of friends, both readers and writers, with so much talent and passion and kindness it blows me away on a routine basis.

The reader, whoever you are. For those of you who have followed me here from Wattpad, *thank you* for your support and your encouragement. To everyone who sent me messages or left comments and reviews, *thank you* for making me believe this story was worth reading. To everyone who subscribed to my mailing list, *thank you* for riding along with me on this no-doubt disastrous adventure. To the ARC reviewers, *thank you* for the safety net, without which I wouldn't have dared publish these stupid things. And to the silent readers who are still lurking, *thank you*. Honestly, I'm bad about reviewing too. Whether you're lazy like me or just shy, it doesn't matter. I still love you.

Last but not least, Storm, who cannot read or even understand the spoken word, except for the important stuff like 'Sit' and 'C'mere' and 'Go to bed' and 'Do you want a treat?' But I do think I'd be remiss if I let a whole acknowledgments section pass by without once mentioning my most faithful writing buddy and the sweetest, quietest little bitch who ever did live.